Hearts on the Rocks

by

Terry Newman

Whimsical Hearts, Book Two

Dedication

To my critique partner, cheerleader, and good friend, Nicki Pascarella. Thank you.

Chapter 1

Cagney

Cagney Adler knew this blind date would be like all the others. Agonizingly long. And it would end just like every other one. Tragically.

She might have exaggerated slightly. It certainly wouldn't be a Pearl Harbor, or even a Watergate. But Mr. Rock Nerd to her left had all the charisma of, well, a box of rocks.

She wondered if the recent rash of blind dates had given her combat fatigue. Brian, no wait, Brad, was the fourth one in two months. Okay, maybe that didn't seem like a lot, but every man could have been a cardboard cutout of Brian, no that's not right, Bradley, it's Bradley Townsend.

She knew it would be a disaster the moment her friend, Molly Driscoll, began the conversation. Molly had talked her—no, cajoled her—into this. By the way, it appeared she had looked forward to this pitiful occasion. Molly had dressed for it. She wore her favorite grunge jeans, striped short-sleeved blouse, and a snappy short jacket. It hung perfectly on her five-foot-seven frame. Cagney had dressed in her best T-shirt—it was a dark pink—and her jeans. She dressed for utility, not show.

"Brad, I hear you're a geology major," Molly said.

Cagney should have run then.

"Yes, I'm working on my dissertation."

Bradley's body did not match his area of interest. Weren't scientists, especially those in geology, supposed to be less than attractive and more nerdlike? That's how television shows portrayed them. Every single one she had ever watched.

He was easily six feet, and the gray button-down shirt only highlighted his deep-blue eyes. His dark brown hair had a relaxed and attractive wave that she actually envied. He wore a tightly cropped beard that gave the man a hint of mystery. Dammit, even his glasses didn't detract from his good looks. And the body? It looked as if he worked out in a quarry. She might be watching the wrong television shows.

"Did you know Cagney's working on her dissertation, too?"

That was Logan Adams, Molly's boyfriend. She suspected he engineered this fiasco.

"Really?" He sat up a bit straighter and almost smiled. "What area of science are you in?"

Cagney shot Logan a quick glare before she answered. "I'm in the history department."

"Oh." The disappointment echoed in his voice. Then he smiled, as if he'd just thought of something. "Egyptian history? I love Egyptian history." For the first time, he turned his body toward her. The curl on his right side teasingly tugged his ear as if defying the comb.

She pursed her lips. "No, American history."

"Oh." His body slumped.

Silence.

Why did she agree to this? Again. Brian, no Brad, wasn't the bottom of the blind-date barrel. That position would always and forever be assigned to Morgan Belmont, zombie apocalypse prepper extraordinaire.

Surprisingly, this bizarre version of the end of the world didn't come from a movie or television show. Nope. It came straight from The Centers for Disease Control. The CDC gives instructions on how to survive such an event on its website. Apparently, he intended to follow them to a tee.

"Why don't we go up and order?" Logan pushed his chair back and stood. He nodded to Molly.

"That's a great idea." She got up too.

Her blind date rose and the three of them headed toward the counter. She forced herself to follow.

Molly hung back and waited for her. "Isn't he cute?"

She cocked her head and studied his cute butt for the first time, all tight and taut. He could have easily been mistaken for a model. And in that one moment he thought she studied Egyptian history, he smiled. And it looked good on him.

But, my God, they lived in different universes.

And in her universe, her thoughts revolved around Alonzo Reichard, the leading expert on Warren G. Harding, the subject of her dissertation, and when he would get around to answering her email. And the one paragraph she couldn't get to sound right for Dr. Bremner's nineteenth-century social history class. And she wondered when the hell that book would come in that she had reserved on interlibrary loan.

So she just nodded and agreed.

"I think you two are going to hit it off just fine."

"Really? He's into geology and already disappointed I'm not studying Egyptian history. How's that hitting it off *just fine?*"

"You're just a little nervous. Relax. Logan said he thought you two would make a great couple."

Cagney rolled her eyes. "You do remember I'm not looking to become a couple with anyone, let alone Brian the rock nerd?"

"His name is Bradley." Molly's voice spat out irritation. She pursed her lips. Hard. It looked as if she had just sucked a lemon. "You could at least do him the courtesy of getting his name right." Molly usually gave her an admonishing look when it came to Cagney's dating habits, or lack of them. But this look went beyond admonishing, crashing into new territory.

Apparently, she had crossed the line. It was one thing, she supposed, to be recalcitrant in accepting unsolicited help on the dating scene. It was completely another thing to get the name of your rock nerd and amateur Egyptologist date wrong. She should make a mental note of that so she didn't make the mistake again. But she really didn't care.

And yes, the evening certainly would be agonizingly long.

****

Brad

As he waited for her to arrive, he questioned his sanity. Why did he allow his roommate, Logan, to arrange a blind date for him…again? To be fair, saying no to Logan when he had made up his mind was like trying to stop a tornado in its tracks.

That's how Brad Townsend found himself out on yet another Friday evening waiting to meet a woman who would ultimately reject him. It was a foregone conclusion, regardless of what Logan thought. Oh, his roommate always thought that the next blind date would be the woman Brad would fall madly in love with. "You two will make a great couple," Logan blurted out every time he proposed a double date. Every damn time.

And every damn time, he and his date had decided they wouldn't make a great couple, mumbled a few apologies, and never saw each other again. It would all replay over again tonight with Casey Adler. The only thing he knew about her was she was a friend of Logan's girlfriend, Molly.

Logan's nudge in the ribs interrupted Brad's internal whining. "There they are now. They just walked in." You'd think by the excitement in his voice, he was the one meeting someone new.

Brad glanced toward the door, not eager to meet his date. He did a double-take, though, when he saw the woman next to Molly. Short and slim, she wore her dark blonde hair pulled back in a ponytail, accenting her high cheekbones. She carried a certain *je ne sais quoi* that gave her a natural elegance. Her simple T-shirt bore a striking resemblance to a dark pink quartz. While she didn't smile—she probably felt the same way he did about tonight—she looked beautiful.

He gulped. Logan greeted Molly with a kiss on the lips as Brad shuffled his feet awkwardly as he stared at Casey. Her eyes were the color of expertly cut emeralds.

"Hi." What a lame thing to say. "I'm Brad." He paused. "Brad Townsend."

He glanced over to Logan and Molly, already involved in the start of a conversation. They didn't even bother to introduce Casey to him.

"I'm Cagney." He barely heard her soft voice over the excited Friday-night buzz at the café. "Cagney Adler."

Did she say her name was Cagney? He thought it was Casey.

Molly must have remembered them because she finally acknowledged them. "Cagney, this is Brad."

She called her Cagney. Well, that's it. He furrowed his brow as he recalled Logan's announcement of the date. *He never asked if I were available, or even interested.* Anger and frustration gnawed at him, and he might have heard him say Casey.

He needed to remember her name was Cagney. He could do that. At least for the evening. He knew he'd never see her again. Guaranteed.

When Logan suggested they order, Brad had followed his lead. Keenly aware Casey—damn it, Cagney—lagged behind, he knew why. He had acted like a major ass, asking her the area of science she studied. Then he had to ask if she studied Egyptian history. Where the hell had that come from? He must have pulled it out of his middle school memory.

He had been anxious and awkward on the other blind dates, but this one rattled him in ways he couldn't understand.

Chapter 2

Cagney

Cagney stabbed at her Theoretical Grilled Chicken Salad, her go-to meal at the Physics Café. A favorite of University of Northern Ohio students and residents of Bell Wyck, the café elevated physics and other sciences to an epicurean adventure.

Every menu item had a science-related name and once the customers ordered, they carried back to their table the atomic number of an element of the periodic table to identify their order. Tonight, her element had been *1H*—hydrogen.

The café's décor didn't disappoint, either. Portraits of physicists hung on the walls as well as the equations that made them famous. Cagney had learned quite a bit about the branches of physics simply by studying the walls.

She glanced around the table. Molly had moved her chair closer to Logan so their elbows touched slightly. Brian, uh, Brad, seemed to be enjoying his Higgs-Boson Bison Burger. He ate as if no one else was around.

As if he read her mind, he turned to her. "Fun science fact. Do you know what a Higgs-Boson is?"

She put down her fork, as she thought about how to answer the question. Molly and Logan stared at her expectantly. She figured the question was addressed to her.

"I'm no scientist, but from what I understand"—she struggled to keep from sounding sarcastic—"it's the particle that carries the force of the Higgs field. And the Higgs field is what gives all other particles their mass."

She tried hard not to smile. Brad's mouth hung open, but she wanted to get in one more detail. "Some call it the God particle. But any true physicist would wince at that name, right?"

"Yes," Brian, uh, Brad, said. "Yes, they would." His voice was low, as if she had taken the wind out of his scientific sail.

Was that a test? Maybe he thought a woman in the humanities wouldn't know anything about physics?

Silence hung over the table. She glanced at Molly who had that lemon-sucking look on her face again. What? *She wanted me to feign ignorance to boost the male science ego? No way.*

"I find it very creative the way the Alvin and the guys named every menu item after a scientific concept." Molly's voice cracked. Alvin was one of the three owners of the café, all physics graduate students at one time.

"I mean, Fission Chips?" She pointed to her plate. "Isn't that clever?"

"Who said scientists aren't creative?" Brad laughed.

Cagney couldn't take much more of this nightmare.

Logan and Molly made small talk during the meal and occasionally her supposed date did too. She really couldn't add much to the conversation. Molly knew that she didn't talk much in groups. She felt comfortable talking with an individual and even when two others

8

were present. But she hit her limit in a conversation with four. Why? Who knew?

"Cag, didn't you just say—"

Logan nudged Molly. "Why don't we go get dessert? They have a great Newton's Apple Caramel Cheesecake."

"I really shouldn't eat any—"

"Let's. Go. Look. At. Desserts." His voice slow, his eyebrows raised. Molly finally caught on to his less-than-subtle excuse to leave Cagney alone with Mr. Rock Nerd.

"Yeah, that sounds good. Cagney, do you want anything?"

She shook her head. "I'm good."

As Molly rose, she shot Cagney a look that said she had better start interacting with Brad. She wanted to die. Right there. She started to protest but thought better of it. It would prove futile.

Molly and Logan left, holding hands.

"The only history I know anything about is Egyptian history." Brad played with one of the few fries left on his plate.

"That's cool." She didn't lie. She found the Pharaohs and the pyramids fascinating in middle school. But that was in middle school. "I'm just not that into it."

His large hand rubbed his beard. She couldn't read his expression.

"What kind of history are you studying?" His blue eyes penetrated her. He sounded surprised that any history other than Egyptian existed.

"American history. Specifically presidential history. My dissertation is a continuation of my thesis.

It's on the death of President Warren G. Harding."

Did his eyes just glaze over? Damn, she gave out too much information again.

"Didn't that happen in the"—he waved a hand—"nineteen sixties or something?"

"No, the nineteen twenties."

Brian, no Brad, scratched his beard. He looked as if he were thinking. He didn't look unattractive. "I guess I'm not good at history. Sorry."

"No need to apologize. Everyone has their strengths."

Silence.

"Uhm…what's your dissertation on?"

His eyes brightened. Obviously, the moment he had been waiting for. "I'm researching the effects of kinetic energy on the metamorphosis of rocks."

"Like erosion?" Could you really study that in detail in graduate school? She'd learned about it in Mrs. Higgs's fifth grade class. *Oh, shut up. I'm sure there's more to it than that.*

"Yes, but recently we've discovered the process includes gradual crystal reorientation and foliation in certain types of rocks."

She quirked an eyebrow, and he continued.

"Crystal reorientation is when…I'm sorry. I'm boring you." Before Cagney could protest, he continued. "I bore everyone with my dissertation." He laughed. Weakly. "I think I even bore my advisor."

The silence hung between them.

"Look," he said, "I'm not sure why Logan thinks we have anything in common. I'm sorry you had to come out here tonight."

"I'm sure you're a nice guy." Cagney shrugged.

"I'm not interested in dating." She stared him straight in his blue eyes—the most captivating blue eyes. "Anyone."

And especially you. Did she say she had nothing—at all—in common with him?

"Casey…"

"It's Cagney."

"Yeah, you're right. Logan told me your name. I'm sorry, Cagney." He emphasized the name like he was memorizing the latest addition to the periodic table. He glanced down at his coffee cup briefly. "Then what are you doing here?" He swept his hand around the café to indicate that it was the "here" to which he was referring.

"I'm here"—she mimicked his hand motion—"because of a friend who believes I need to get out more, date, and meet a nice guy." She raised a side of her lips in a smile.

He laughed. Admittedly, it was funny.

"Me too." He held up a hand, palm open as if he were taking a pledge. "My friends, Logan in particular, think it's high time I did more than just work on my PhD. They don't understand the pressure involved—and that's no pun on how metaphoric rock is formed."

Cagney laughed. "That's a good one. I don't know much about geology, but I did have a rock collection when I was in grade school. My mother found it in my closet and asked what the rocks were doing there."

Brad laughed. "Where else would you keep a rock collection?"

"Exactly."

"See, everyone loves rocks." His shy persona disappeared. He sat straighter in his chair. Enthusiasm filled his voice. "They just won't admit it. But I'm the one who looks like a nerd studying them."

"I never said you were a nerd."

"You didn't have to. Your eyes said it when you first walked in." When she'd first caught sight of him, his appearance surprised her because he didn't look like the typical nerd. If she'd met him on the street and knew nothing about him, she wouldn't immediately peg him as a nerd. Until he spoke.

But despite that, she couldn't imagine a person with whom she had less in common. How could anyone look at Brad and her and think they'd be a good couple?

Chapter 3

Cagney

Cagney collapsed on the couch, relieved the date had ended. After Molly and Logan had returned and shared the cheesecake, and she had exhausted topics for her conversation with Brad, the four of them sat in an awkward silence. Logan evidently had abandoned his experiment at socialization for two PhD students, realized it proved to be an utter failure, and called an end to the torture.

What had she done wrong in her life to warrant this type of punishment?

"I've tried to be a good person," she said as she counted the cracks in the ceiling in her rental apartment. "I haven't killed anyone. Yet. That's got to be a plus."

For a fleeting moment, she felt sympathy for Brad, because he was in the same position as she was: On a date with a total stranger who shared none of his interests. Was he staring at his ceiling wondering what kind of karma placed him with a humanities major?

She shot up off the couch. What? Why am I even thinking about Brad? Why should I care if he's staring at his ceiling? *I hope at least if he is, there aren't as many cracks as mine.*

She glanced up at the ceiling again. Darn, the landlord needed to fix this.

"I forgot how much energy these blind dates

sucked out of me." She trudged to the small bedroom and changed into her favorite pair of pajamas, the one with adorable images of cats.

She climbed into bed, cocooned herself in her covers, which also happened to have cats on them, and closed her eyes. But evidently her mind didn't get the memo to shut down. It raced with all sorts of thoughts, but mostly that she hadn't checked her email when she got home. What if Reichard had written back? His answer could be crucial to her research.

She jumped out of bed and hurried into the small dining room which she used as an office. She opened the laptop and waited for it to come to life. It was old and slow and she needed a new one, but on a graduate student's stipend, she'd have to use what she had. Finally, she got into her email app only to find he hadn't responded. Disappointment didn't adequately define her feelings.

"How am I ever going to finish and get out of grad school before I turn thirty if no one answers my questions?" She needed a travel grant so she could dig through the libraries in Washington, D.C., especially the Archives. But so far, all her applications had been rejected.

She closed the laptop. She rose to go back to bed when she noticed a book on her desk. "How did that get there?"

She hadn't seen it when she sat down a moment ago, and she didn't recall putting it there. It was the novel her advisor, Dr. J. Jordan St. Clair, had given her.

She remembered being surprised to find that Dr. St. Clair was also the best-selling romance author, JJ Spritely. And when she discovered that Cagney was a fan, she pulled a copy of her latest release, *Love's Surprise*, off her bookshelf, autographed it, and handed it to her.

Cagney clearly remembered putting it on her bookcase, right next to the other Spritely novel. She picked up the book to put it back but stopped. "I'm up. I can't sleep. Let's start it."

She traipsed back to her bedroom, arranged the pillows, and opened the book. She immediately loved the heroine, Alex Zurich. And her boyfriend, Blake Teesdale? Perhaps a bit goofy at times, but what a romantic hero. Handsome, too. What talent her advisor had.

****

Brad

"What the hell was that about?"

Brad had just stepped into the apartment. "What?"

He shrugged off his coat.

Logan had offered Brad a ride home after the date but he refused. He needed time alone. Logan had been setting these events up for him with a greater frequency and each one got a bit more difficult. How many times could a guy be rejected?

"You know what." Logan lifted his legs off the coffee table and set them on the floor. "She was a great girl. What was wrong with her? You do know Molly had to coax Cagney to come out tonight. And then you act like you're not even interested."

Brad turned his back to him, opened the closet door in the hallway, and hung his coat up. He walked into the small living room. "She wasn't interested in me."

"You didn't give her a chance."

He sat on the nearest chair. Okay, the only chair.

"Look, we talked when you and Molly left us for that little bit. She's focused on her dissertation about some dead president." Brad remembered the dead president's name. He remembered just about everything she had said. But saying the name of that dead president, Harding, here would only make his roommate think he was interested in her. Was he?

Of all the blind dates he had been on recently—and there were quite a few—Casey, no, Cagney, had not only been the most beautiful, but the most intelligent. *Heck, how many people know what Higgs-Boson is*?

He tried hard to hide the fact he was captivated by her blonde, bouncy ponytail, her green eyes, and well…just about every part of her short, little frame.

"She asked me about my dissertation topic and, well, let's just say I had the presence of mind to stop talking before I bored her to death."

"You don't know that. You really needed to give her more of a chance. That was your first meeting with Cagney. Maybe if you two went out for coffee sometime?"

Brad groaned, but Logan plodded on.

"You are uber-focused on your studies. I get it. But you really need—"

"Don't tell me I need to socialize more. You make me sound like a stray dog. I'm trying to get my doctoral degree. That's intense."

"Well, you do need to socialize more. You didn't like the last girl I found you either. What was wrong with her?"

"Nothing was 'wrong' "—he gestured air quotes—"I'm just not interested." He paused. "Your hobby lately seems to be planning blind dates for me. How many has this been since the term began?"

"Look, Brad, I'm only looking out for your best interests." Logan reached for the open beer can on the coffee table, evidently ignoring the question. "You don't want to end up alone and miserable like my Aunt Colleen, do you?"

"What?" Brad laughed. "I've never heard you talk about Aunt Colleen."

"Well, that's because she's boring. She lives alone in a two-bedroom apartment with three cats. What's there to talk about, really?"

"I'm not a spinster, if that's what you're getting at." He looked around his own two-bedroom apartment. "And I don't see any cats."

"Just wait." Logan stood and walked into the kitchen. "Wait till I leave." He threw the can into the trash. "There'll be cats everywhere."

"Don't be too sure." As Logan left the kitchen, Brad entered and retrieved the can from the trash and placed it in a small recycle receptacle he kept in the nearby closet.

He sighed. "I get it, Logan. You're trying to help me." He followed his roommate back into the living room. "But I don't think I'm cut out for dating. It doesn't come naturally to me like it does to you."

"That's because you're not giving it a chance. You didn't give Cagney a chance. You didn't give what's-her-face a chance either." Logan's tone sounded less harsh, almost as if he were trying to put himself in Brad's shoes.

"Who's what's-her-face?" Brad furrowed his brows.

"Georgette. Georgette, uhm…"

"Georgette Daniels."

"Yeah, that's it. You dismissed her out of hand. Wasn't she interested?"

She might have been. But Brad had lacked the courage to take the next step. Was it the same for Cagney? No, he immediately dismissed that. They couldn't be farther away in terms of interests. Still...

"There's so much pressure. What if it doesn't work out? What if she walks out on me on our very first date?"

"Why would any girl walk out on you?"

"Didn't we just have this conversation? I'm boring." He strung out the last word for emphasis.

"I don't find you boring. Actually, some of the best conversations have been with you. I can't imagine anyone finding you boring."

"That's different. We talk guy stuff. I don't know what to say to women." Brad ran a hand through his hair.

Logan rose. "I'm going to bed. I have a breakfast date with Molly tomorrow. I'm sure I'll get an earful from her about how this didn't work out." He strode toward his bedroom, opened the door, then turned. "I get it, Brad, I really do. You're a great guy. You'll find someone."

Considering the late hour, Brad should have gone to bed too. Instead, he walked out of the living room and through the dining room to the balcony. "What's wrong with me?"

At least here, he felt at home. He chose the apartment specifically for the balcony. While it was small, it had enough space for his telescope. The roommate came later. And right about now, he regretted allowing Logan to room with him.

Logan, several years younger and a senior at University of Northern Ohio, couldn't be called a great student, but that didn't matter, because when he graduated, he'd work for his dad. His roommate didn't understand the drive that pushed him.

He put his eye to the telescope. It was the perfect night for watching the stars. His close-up view of the celestial objects allowed him to see they were much more than merely twinkling objects.

He felt whole when he watched the stars, just like he felt when he studied geology. He reached into his pocket and touched the quartz rock he kept with him at all times. It would be okay. If only women could see he was more than just a rock nerd.

Chapter 4

Cagney

Cagney didn't know when it happened, but apparently, she had fallen asleep reading. She woke up Saturday morning to the birds chirping and the sun peeking through her bedroom window. The book lay at the bottom of the bed. "I suppose I put it there, but I sure don't remember."

She smiled as reached down and picked up the book. Her advisor, JJ Spritely, had written another great romance. She got out of bed, and as she walked through the apartment on her way to her first cup of coffee, dropped the volume on her desk.

If only she had the time during the weekend to finish it. Maybe I'll sneak a look later at it, she thought, as she watched the dark liquid fill her favorite mug. It read "Well-behaved women rarely make history." Molly had given it to her on her last birthday.

"Maybe Reichard emailed me back?" Which was a crazy thought. It had only been several hours since she last checked. Like he would wake up in the middle of the night to answer the question of a grad student he didn't know? But she had to try.

She sat at her laptop and turned it on. She sniffed the coffee while she waited, then took a sip. *Yes, this is exactly what I needed.* She checked her email. What did she expect? The busy scholar obviously had better things to do and more important people to email.

She took a deep breath and put it out of her mind. Instead, she took the notebook she kept by the computer and made her weekend to-do list. She had to go the library and check out a source and…darn…she had term papers to grade. She had stashed them on the floor on the other side of the room.

The library would have to wait. Her students were expecting their papers back Monday morning. What kind of teacher was she if she required her students to have their assignments on time when she couldn't get hers done on time? That would take up her entire Saturday and undoubtedly some of Sunday as well.

****

"I cannot read another essay until I eat something." She glanced at her phone. After one p.m. "No wonder I'm starved." She shoved herself from the table and headed for the kitchen. She set her turkey and cheese sandwich on the coffee table in the living room, then picked up a pile of essays in her office.

"If I have to read these, I could at least do it in comfort." She sat on the couch, swung her legs up, and leaned against the arm. She was ready. Two hours later, she had only made it through seven essays, her sandwich had been eaten an hour and a half before, and she was restless.

She brought her legs down and that's when she saw it. On the coffee table next to her empty plate. "That's eerie. How in the world did that get here?" She picked up *Love's Surprise* and examined the front and back. *Like that'll give me any clue of how it got here.* She had purposely put it on the desk, right? Or was she going crazy?

Regardless, she needed a break, and curiosity about Alex and Blake's relationship got the better of her. She had left them at the point where Blake thought it was better if they went their separate ways. What was he thinking? The pair was made for each other.

The empty plate that once held the sandwich had been replaced with a cup of hot tea and a piece, maybe two, of dark chocolate. Cagney sat on the couch, legs curled under her as she read.

After an hour and a half, she closed the book. "I have to finish grading. Be strong. Alex and Blake aren't going anywhere." She rose, full of determination to complete the task.

****

Brad

Brad woke the next morning after Logan had already left for his breakfast with Molly. He pulled on jeans and headed bare-chested to the kitchen. He never bothered overdressing for the first meal of the day.

He toasted a bagel, slathered peanut butter on it, and carried it back to his room. He wanted to get started early on his research. A new article had been published in one of the scientific journals that touched on the problem he faced in his dissertation. It could be useful.

He hadn't taken two bites of his breakfast when Logan burst into the room. "Look at this, Brad. Just look at her."

Logan brandished his phone. "Meet Emma. She's sits next to Molly in her…well, to be honest, I'm not sure what class." He pushed the phone under Brad's nose. Her photo blurred. "We're meeting her Friday. The Physics Café."

"W-w-what? W-w-we?" He glared at Logan. "No,

not again. I swear if I have to go on one more blind date—"

"You'll like Emma." Logan turned, walked out of the room, and shut the door behind him.

Brad wasn't sure what to do. "I don't want to go on another blind date." He sighed.

"There's so much pressure in dating. And I don't want to meet another woman. I just don't. I wish someone would invent a way to date without all that pressure." He chuckled as he went back to reading his article. "Yeah, right."

But he couldn't concentrate on geology. He needed Logan to stop setting him up on blind dates. That would never happen while he was single.

If only there were a way to date without the pressure of what the woman thought about me.

"Dating without pressure? What if…" An idea popped into his head. "It would make Logan think I was dating."

He shook his head. "No, it's a stupid idea." He couldn't face another woman. "Or not."

Then his mind flashed to Casey, no, Cagney. "Could I convince her?"

Chapter 5

Cagney

"Casey. Casey. Wait up."

Cagney heard hurried footsteps behind her; each one sounded closer. With her office hours done, she looked forward to her yoga class. A class she needed after the blind date disaster and the weekend of grading papers. And that damn book of her advisor's that seemed to pop up everywhere. She had spent too much time reading it.

"Casey, please stop."

Brian, no, Bradley Townsend, appeared at her side. She stopped and looked at him. His eyes were every bit as blue as they were Friday night. "What is your problem?"

"Why didn't you answer me? Didn't you hear me calling your name?" Brad's brow furrowed and he ran a hand through his curls.

"I heard someone call a Casey. My name is Cagney."

She met this man once. They mutually decided they had nothing in common. Why was he chasing after her? Was he stalking her? Was she in danger?

She took a step back and tightened her grip on the backpack hanging off her right shoulder. She'd use it if she had to. She'd swing it as hard as she could into his balls. That should be enough to give her a head start.

Then she'd scream as loud as she could. No way he'd touch her after that.

"I'm sorry. You're right. Your name is Cagney. I did it again, didn't I?" He looked at his shoes. "I'm not good with names."

He looked like a little boy. The threat of a stalker dissipated.

"I wanted to talk to you before your office hours ended."

"You knew when my office hours were?" She scanned Brad from head to toe. Suddenly, he did look dangerous. "What kind of stalker are you?"

"I'm not a stalker, I promise." He held up one hand. His blue eyes bore into her. "I asked Logan to ask Molly what your hours were, so I could talk to you. I have an idea about us."

That was it. That's all she had to hear. "There is no us. We both agreed to that Friday night." She walked. It shouldn't have surprised her that he followed along beside her. "We decided we have nothing in common. Nothing."

"I know. But I've got this idea."

"Yeah, you've said that before." She hurried her pace. Why? It's not like she could out-walk him. Now that she saw him standing in the bright light, she knew him to be at least six feet tall—to her meager five four. He probably slowed his pace so not to get ahead of her.

Luckily, Alexander Hall was close. She stood at the door to the building. "I'm going to do yoga to calm my nerves." She looked up at his blue eyes. That beard. "You claim not to be a stalker, but you're acting very much like one."

He gave her the hint of a smile. Her initial anxiety

he would try something had faded a while ago. She wasn't sure when. But she didn't want him to know that. Now he was just an annoyance. Granted, a good-looking annoyance.

"Goodbye, Brad. Maybe we'll see each other around the Physics Café."

She reached for the door, but he beat her by several seconds and opened it for her. Very stalker-like. She ignored it and entered the building and headed straight for the room. He followed her.

"You'll want to hear my idea," he said enthusiastically. What could he possibly be enthusiastic about?

She entered the classroom, dumped her backpack at the door, and tore off her jacket, revealing a loose T-shirt.

Brad watched her. She took her place in the middle of the floor and sat. He sat beside her. "I've got a foolproof way—"

"Sir, do you plan on taking the class today? This is not a university-sponsored class. You'll need to pay the twenty-dollar fee if you intend to participate."

She stifled a giggle. That should do it. That would get him out of the room. Out of her business. Out of her life, if she had any type of luck.

"Sure, I'll take it." He stood and pulled a wallet out of his jeans pocket. It appeared she had little to no luck.

The instructor, Harmony McKenzie, immediately started class once Brad sat next to her. "We'll begin, as usual, sitting legs crossed. Keep your back nice and tall." He had no chance to broach his idea, however absurd she was sure it would be.

Brad crossed his long legs and rested his hands on

his knees. His eyes focused on the instructor.

"Listen, you're tired of blind dates, right?"

"Now, we're going to slowly roll ourselves onto our backs."

Cagney leaned back and glanced toward Brad. He was already down and staring at her.

"I'm tired of blind dates, too."

"Draw your right knee toward your chest."

As she raised her leg, she watched Brad complete the task. Once he was done, he looked her way. "What if we hang out together in public, so people think we're dating?"

"Extend the leg toward the ceiling."

"What?" Cagney held on to her leg. "You mean you want me to pretend to date you?"

The instructor gave instructions to get back into the cross-legged position.

"Why would I want to do that?" The man had some nerve.

"So Molly won't try to set you up with another man."

Harmony gave commands for the downward facing dog pose. He raised his butt off the floor. Once again, she noticed how tight and cute it was.

He glanced at her from the full pose, not looking the least bit comfortable. "Look, Logan already has me scheduled to meet someone Friday. And I'm sure—"

"A week from Friday for me." Cagney watched his unsteady legs from her own downward facing dog pose. "But we don't have anything in common. I wouldn't know what to talk about."

"But that's the beauty of it. We don't have to talk. We're just two people together, working on our separate dissertations."

She noticed his legs quivered even more. And he sounded out of breath.

"There's no way we can develop any type of relat…friendship that would take time away from our studies." It looked as if his legs had had enough of the downward facing dog.

He sucked in a breath. She wasn't sure that was proper yoga form. "But the best part is that neither Logan nor Molly will try to set us up on blind dates again." He paused. She prayed he didn't faint.

"At least not for a long time." He turned his head in her direction and smiled. "It's a win-win."

"Relax, class."

Brad plopped full force on the floor. "Do you do this often?" He rolled over.

The man looked pitiful, lying on his back, his arms extended out, breathing heavily.

"Yup, three times a week." Cagney did a few leg stretches.

He shook his head. The small, dark curls moved ever so slightly. "Do you like this torture? This, by the way, is called upward facing dead dog."

Chapter 6

Brad

"Think about it, Casey. It'll get you out of those awkward blind dates."

Yoga class was over, thank God. He about died in there. How did that woman do it three times a week? They stood outside the building about to go their separate ways. He hadn't convinced her of the idea of pretending to date.

"It's Cagney." She sighed.

His body stiffened. What an ass he was. Of course, her name was Cagney. He needed to remember that.

"I kinda," he heard hesitation in her voice, "keep wanting to call you Brian. I'm sorry." She stared at the ground.

Brad laughed. "That's okay. Maybe if we pretend to date, we can learn each other's name."

An uncomfortable silence fell over them. She must not have thought it funny. He did have a weird sense of humor.

"I have a class to teach," he said. "Here, let me give you my number. Text me later and let me know what you think." She took it—albeit reluctantly.

Cagney nodded. "I've got a meeting with my advisor." And she turned and walked away.

Brian sighed. "I don't think she likes the idea." As he trudged off to class, he wondered what she thought

29

of him. He stopped. "Why do I care?" He tried to put Cagney—yeah, that's her name—out of his mind as he mentally prepared for class.

****

"Today we're discussing earthquakes. Have any of you ever experienced an earthquake?" Brad asked.

One student raised her hand. "I felt the earth move several years ago. I'm from Prague, Ohio and they said it was because of the fracking."

Brad nodded. "That's right. We'll learn about how fracking affects the environment later in the course. But that quake is nothing to what they experience in other parts of the country and the world."

He strode to the white board and wrote earthquake. "An earthquake is the abrupt releasing of energy in the earth's crust—"

"Dr. Townsend." A student interrupted him. "Have you ever been in an earthquake?"

"It's Mr. Townsend, Piper. I'm not a professor…yet."

Quiet laughter rippled through the room.

"And no, I've never been in an earthquake." At least her question brought the class to life. Most of these students had no interest in geology and were there only to claim the required science credits.

"Are there any other questions?" He waggled a brow and waited the customary three seconds of a seasoned professor.

"Then, let's continue." He rubbed his beard as he talked about fault lines. He didn't need to scan the room to know Piper watched his every move. Awkward. She didn't seem to be a student absorbed in the study of rocks, if her fashionably too-tight jeans and dangerously low-cut blouse were any indication.

"Seismic waves,"—he made every effort not to look at Piper—"are classified into two types." He held up two fingers. "Body waves—"

Did he hear Piper sigh? Over what? "Am I going over this material too fast, Piper?" After he said the words, he regretted them. He never liked being called out in class and here he had just done it to a student.

"No, no, Dr. Townsend. I just thought the term body waves was…" She waved a hand and the class laughed.

"I did that last summer in California, Mr. Townsend," George in the last row said. "I body waved that surf like nobody's business." The class laughed again.

Brad rolled his eyes. When did he lose control of the class? "While not quite the same, you get the idea. Body waves travel underground while the other surface waves travel along the earth's surface."

He glanced at his watch. The class was nearly over, but he wanted to get one more concept through to them.

"And surface waves," he continued, "are divided into two types. Rayleigh waves, which mimic the motion of an ocean wave. They move along the surface of the earth in a circle, first forward, and down, then back and up. The second type of wave is the Love wave. They shake the earth's surface from side to side."

"Love waves," gushed Piper. "Why are they called that?"

"Yeah," said the surfer guy in the back of the room, "seems like an oxymoron to call a seismic wave love."

The surfer guy knew the word oxymoron? "The

name has nothing to do with love, romantic or platonic," he heard himself saying. "It has everything to do with the British mathematician who discovered this seismic action, Augustus Love."

He could tell by the shoving of textbooks and notebooks into backpacks the class was over. Not a moment too soon. Every session seemed to bring its own set of awkward moments. *Then again, maybe it's just me.*

"See you all Wednesday." A few of the students waved at him. He turned to gather his own backpack.

"Dr. Townsend." He recognized the voice immediately. He looked up. "Yes, Piper."

"I'm having trouble understanding exactly what's going on in this section of the book. Do you think we could discuss it?"

She did not just wink at him. He closed his eyes for a moment. What was this young lady doing?

"But of course. My office hours are Thursdays and Fridays. Nine a.m. to ten a.m.

Yeah, it sounded like he was a prick choosing such early office hours. But he had discovered last year most students didn't make use of the time. And those that had come to see him at more sensible hours just wanted to waste his time. So yeah, he was a prick.

"Can't you meet me at the Physics Café later today? I really don't want to wait that long."

He took in a big breath. "No, I have several prior commitments this afternoon. If you'd like"—he knew he would regret this—"I have an hour between my lab and a seminar. From two to three tomorrow. I could see you then in my office."

"Oh, that's wonderful, Dr. Townsend. Thank you."

No, she did not just wink at me again, did she? And was she purposely leaning forward to show more cleavage? What was her problem?

He watched her leave. *Did all women sway their hips like that?* If Cagney agreed to pretend to date him, maybe he would ask her.

Chapter 7

Cagney

Cagney sat at a booth at the Physics Café. The unscripted yoga class with Bri—dammit, Brad—had flustered her. A forty-minute period designed to calm her had left her jittery and skittish. The man appeared sincere about his proposal of pretending to date, however insane it sounded.

It was absurd. Totally absurd. She couldn't imagine how that would possibly work. She couldn't even call him by his own name. She laughed. Apparently, he couldn't remember her name either. Great. The basis of every successful pretend relationship.

She took a deep breath. Get your act together, she admonished herself. Dr. St. Clair would be here in about an hour and a half for a progress report.

Alvin called her element, 80Hg, and she strode across the café to get it. A Philadelphia Experiment Cheesesteak Sandwich and a side of Feynman Fries. She remembered the first time she asked about the sandwich. Alvin smiled. "One of our best sellers. It's named after the movie. You know the one. How the government tried to de-particlize an aircraft carrier to make it invisible. The attempt was less than stellar. One minute it was there, the next it was gone."

Cagney had remembered the movie—one of her dad's favorites.

"Well, Ted made this de-particlizer gun. Obviously, it's not strong enough to make an aircraft carrier disappear. But we turn it on the sandwich to make the onions disappear. It just doesn't always work when we want it to. Sometimes there's a delayed effect. If you get a sandwich with onions and they disappear while you're eating it, you get a free cappuccino."

Well, that was all Cagney had to hear. It was one of her standard meals at the café. And no, she never received a free cappuccino.

Once she had eaten, she reached into the backpack to retrieve her notebook to review the items she and Dr. St. Clair were to talk about. In addition to her dissertation, she wanted to ask…

…*wait, how did that get in there?* She pulled it out. *Love's Surprise?* "I did not put this in here. I'm positive of that." It was as if the book had followed her all weekend—and now into Monday. But that's ridiculous.

Despite the eeriness of it, she wanted to pick it up and read it. She had just reached the point where Alex sat alone at a restaurant waiting for Blake. She feared he broke up with her but forgot to tell her. She could feel the anxiety and despair in the words her advisor had written.

Cagney looked at her watch. She had nearly an hour before her meeting. While she had planned to review her progress and perhaps do a bit more writing, she knew she was still too unnerved from Bri—no, Brad's—stalking to do that.

She put her backpack on the table and scooted herself toward the wall. She flung her legs up on the bench. Why not? Only one chapter, she told herself. It would take her mind off Brad—hey, she got his name right—and calm her for the meeting.

"Alex, I'm not good at this," Blake said as he looked into her eyes. She sighed. This had been the moment she had waited for since their first encounter. She knew he was the man of her dreams. It took him long enough, she thought.

The scene sucked her in. As she read the words, she clearly heard their voices. Blake's voice had a deep tone, not quite a baritone, but sexy as hell with his British accent. Alex was soft-spoken, her words barely uttered above a whisper. She felt she had to lean in to hear her. But she spoke with a confidence that Cagney envied. It felt as if they were sitting across from her.

"You did hear my voice. Well, our voices."

Cagney smiled. *I know JJ's a great writer, but now I'm imagining they're talking to me.*

"Are you just going to sit there and pretend we're not here?" That British accent sounded like it should belong to Blake. She shook her head.

"Yoohoo! We're over here." A large hand thrust itself between her face and the book and waved.

"What the—?" She followed the arm and...

...found a couple sitting across from her. She quickly swung her legs to the ground and stared at them. Chills ran up her spine.

When did they get there? Who were they?

"That's better." The man massaged his hand and then shook it. "I wondered how long it was going to take you to see us."

"W-w-what..."

Cagney had intended to ask a question, but her shock at seeing them—whoever "them" were— rendered her speechless.

"We tend to have that effect on people." The woman had spoken to the man. She patted his arm. "Let's not scare the poor woman any more than she is."

The man nodded. "You're right. We don't want her fainting away like JJ did when we popped in on her."

"JJ? You know JJ Spritely?" Cagney shivered at the sound of her advisor's pen name.

The woman laughed softly. "Of course, we do. She created us."

"I'm Blake Teesdale and this lovely lady to my left is Alex Zurich."

Cagney surveyed the two. Then slowly shook her head. "You're trying to pass yourselves off as the characters in this book?" It had dropped to the table when she bolted upright.

She picked it up and studied the cover. The images did look like the strangers. Wait. *What am I even thinking?* Those vague pictures could resemble any number of people. Probably more than a million.

"We're not trying to do anything. We are those characters, Cagney." The woman's voice was calming, if a bit condescending. She nodded toward the book.

"Wait. How did you know my name?" She narrowed her eyes.

"Yeah, how do you know my name? Who put you up to this? It's got to be Dr. St. Clair. Is this her idea of a joke?"

The man shook his head. His black wavy hair flew from side to side. Just like in the book. A gigantic coincidence. "You did."

Cagney opened her mouth, but no words came out.

"You've been reading about us all weekend. Even today. You can't deny it, because we caught you with the book in your hand." He looked rather proud of this observation.

"And you even fell asleep the other night reading about our love story." The woman, whose nearly black hair hung down to her shoulders, sighed as she said the words slowly. She also fit the description of Alex in *Love's Surprise*.

Cagney shook her head. The woman spoke the truth—somehow. She'd neglected her dissertation and immersed herself in a wonderful world where she knew there'd be a happily ever after. "I did. I just was…How would that even work?" She figured she knew enough about the laws of physics that fictional people just didn't pop up into the real world.

"It's difficult to explain how we get here. Heck, we really don't know, exactly—"

The man's hair bounced as he apparently weighed his words. Just like Blake's hair did in the book. *Oh, stop that.*

"The last time we were here"—he waved a hand toward the woman sitting next to him—"I had discovered the concept, articulated by quite a few different writers, that the universe doesn't know the difference between action based on thought alone, or what we call imagination, and action that's based on facts."

Cagney nodded. "Okay, so." She strung out the last word.

This entire situation was no longer weird. It had taken a giant leap into the realm of the bizarre.

"Because as you fell asleep you were thinking about us. And the universe can't tell the difference from—"

"Action based on our imaginations or on fact. Yeah, yeah. I caught that part." She took a deep breath. "What you're saying is that because I was involved in the book I was reading, your book, that is, and I fell asleep thinking about it, you popped into my life."

"Exactly." The man who claimed to be Blake nodded his head, his hair moving enthusiastically.

"I've fallen asleep before reading. I've fallen asleep reading about Warren G. Harding. And he didn't pop into my life."

"Of course not." The alleged Alex laughed. "He's dead."

"True. But you two are fictional."

The man who—What the hell, Cagney? Just call them by those names already. Blake nodded slowly as if he were in thought.

"That's because we're originally a creation of thought." He glanced at Alex for confirmation.

"That's brilliant. Of course, that makes sense." Alex sighed.

It appeared the fictional couple had rested their case. However shaky that might have been.

"I'm still not buying it." She sighed. She didn't need this distraction. "Just leave, please. Now."

She opened her laptop.

"That's it." Blake leaped out of his seat. "That's what we'll do. We'll leave."

"Honey, that doesn't help Cagney at all. We're here on a mission, remember?"

"No," he said, his hair bouncing. "We're taking Cagney with us."

She slammed the laptop closed. "You've gone too far. That's called kidnapping, and as I recall it's a federal offense."

"You're right, because of the Lindberg kidnapping." Blake pointed at her. "Which is a sad situation. Charles and his wife left the country for several years, settling in the English countryside and then—"

"Blake." Alex shook his shoulder.

"Oh, righto. Sorry about that."

"We have no intention of kidnapping you. The three of us are going to visit JJ."

"Let's go." Alex scooted toward Blake, fully prepared to leave.

"You don't have to kidnap me. Dr. St. Clair—"

Just at that moment her advisor walked up to the booth. "I know I'm early—"

"JJ!" The two strangers screamed her name in unison. The woman pushed the man out of the booth in an effort to get to her. He fell flat on his butt and his unruly hair bounced around.

"Honey, I'm so sorry. I was just so happy to see JJ again." Still on the bench, she pushed his hair down on the left side only to have it jut back up. She cocked her head and tried the same tactic in the back. Still nothing. She shrugged. "Are you okay?"

He looked up at the woman with his chocolate-brown eyes—just like in the book—and smiled. "No worries." He pulled himself up off the floor. "No injuries."

The woman scooted out of the booth and wrapped her arms around Dr. St. Clair. Was that a flicker of fear—or horror?—before a welcoming smile formed?

After the woman let go of her, the man approached and pumped her hand, his hair dancing with the movement of the handshake. It lasted longer than was socially acceptable.

"Jolly good to see you." He finally pulled his hand away.

"Cagney…"

"They just appeared out of nowhere." She shrugged.

"She doesn't believe us." She was about the right height to be Alex Zurich. Wait. *There's no way.*

"But she didn't faint dead away like you did on us. We count that as a plus." The man nodded. Yeah, that hair moved with the nod. Just like in the damned book.

"Would you please tell her who we are?" Alex crossed her arms.

Now, she was being talked about like she wasn't present.

"Let's all sit down, for starters." Dr. St. Clair lowered herself to Cagney's side. The couple returned to their seats.

Cagney turned toward her advisor. "Is this some kind of prank? Did you pay these two to do this to me?"

The man harrumphed and pointed at Cagney. "Tell her who we are, JJ. She'll believe you."

"Who are they?" She worried her tone appeared sharper than she had intended. Under normal conditions she would never raise her voice to her advisor. But when two individuals burst out of nowhere without even a puff of blue smoke, well, that unnerved her. To the core.

Dr. St. Clair sighed. "Meet Alex Zurich and Blake Teesdale." She waved a hand in their direction. "They're the characters you've been reading about." She inclined her chin toward the book on the table.

"Okay, you can stop the charade. Just tell me who they are. Please. I've had a strange day to begin with."

"That's why we're here," the woman said.

Just as her advisor opened her mouth, Alvin walked up to the table. "Blake. Alex. So good to see you."

The man leapt out of the seat and shook Alvin's hand. Even though it was once again a longer-than-socially-acceptable handshake, Alvin didn't appear concerned.

Once that ended, the woman scooted out of the booth and hugged Alvin.

"Don't tell me you're in on this joke, too?"

"What joke?" Alvin's blank stare told Cagney he had no idea what she was talking about. Another set of shivers wriggled down her spine.

"You can't expect me to believe these are characters—"

"My cousin and her fiancé," Dr. St. Clair said, "certainly are characters, aren't they?"

"Everyone, stop it. My brain is on overload."

The man who everyone called Blake dropped down onto the bench again and gazed into her eyes. The brownest eyes she had ever seen. "It's difficult to comprehend, love, I know. It's bizarre even for us."

Alvin shook his head. "I don't know what's going on, but I do know I'm glad to have you guys back. Do you want your usual? It's on the house."

What the heck? The usual? Cagney was sure she was having a breakdown of some sort.

"Yes, please. I haven't had Fission Chips in ages." Blake nudged Alex.

"If you still have your delicious Onion String

Theory, I'll take a side with my Time Warp Chicken Wrap."

"Anything for you two. Coming right up." Alvin turned on a heel and left.

"Blake, Alex, why don't you two go find Ted and Simon. I need a few minutes alone with Cagney."

The woman readily agreed, but the man protested. "I'm sure they're busy right now—"

"Blake, let's go and leave JJ alone with Cagney." Alex raised her eyebrows and glared at him. She grabbed his elbow and pulled him along. He stepped over his own feet to keep up with her.

Cagney watched them for a while, then turned to her advisor. "What in the world is happening?"

Chapter 8

Brad

"So, what did she say?" Logan stepped into Brad's view. "Did she say yes?"

Normally, after class, Brad would be either in the library or his bedroom, not sitting out on the balcony in the middle of the afternoon. Yet, here he was.

"What? Did who say yes?"

"Cagney. Didn't you ask her on a date?"

Brad recognized the irritation in his tone. He had nearly forgotten that he had to get Logan and Molly involved in his scheme. And now the consequences of his lying just sat down next to him.

He took a deep breath. "She said she'd think about it. She may text me later."

"What a bummer. Molly and I were rooting for you. We were hoping she'd say yes."

"She still might."

Brad sighed. "I screwed up, man. I did stupid things. There's no way in hell she'd want to pre...uhm, date me."

"How could you screw up?" Logan's seemed genuinely concerned.

"Remember how you gave me her office hours?"

"Yeah..."

"Well, I was running late. I caught her right outside the history building. So I called to her." He sighed. "I called her Casey. Casey. I couldn't even get her name right."

Logan groaned. "Man, that's not good."

"You're telling me. Then I followed her into her yoga class. I proposed the idea of…well, I asked her on a date while we were doing the downward facing dog."

"The what?"

"It's a yoga pose." He ran a hand over his beard. "A very difficult yoga pose. Yoga's tough. Cagney makes it look so simple."

"You took a yoga class just to talk to her?"

Brad nodded. It was the only way.

"Boy, you do have it bad. I've never taken a yoga class for Molly." He pursed his lips.

"Listen, Brad. I'm sorry. I know you have a difficult time around women. I know it had to be tough to get the courage up to ask her. But there are other women. You're good looking. You're bright. And you have a great sense of humor. Any woman on the campus of the University of Northern Ohio would be thrilled to date you."

Brad nearly said it out loud. *And you're determined that I meet every one of them on those blind dates you set up for me all the time.*

There. That was the entire reason he had asked Cagney. Those idiotic, demeaning blind dates. Getting set up like he was a piece of meat.

Had he even blown a fake relationship…before it started? *Don't answer that, Brad. Don't answer that.*

"You said she'd text, right?"

Brad shifted his weight in the chair. "Yeah."

"Then she may still want to go out."

Logan rose. "I've got some studying to do."

"Logan, can I ask you a question? I promise it doesn't involve Cagney." This was the other thing nagging at him. He needed to know what was going on. Could it be what he thought? No. No, it couldn't.

"Sure, shoot."

"There's this girl in the class I teach. I think"—he scrubbed the back of his neck as he decided on the right words—"she's hitting on me?"

Logan ran a hand through his hair. Sitting back down, he turned his body toward Brad.

"Whoa. Really? Give me the details."

He explained Piper's choice of clothing and her actions.

"She's coming to my office tomorrow to get a little tutoring. But I'm not sure how interested she is in earthquakes."

He sighed. While he felt relieved to get it off his chest, he also felt dumb. This should have been something he could have figured out for himself. He shouldn't need to ask Logan about it.

"Sounds like she is hitting on you. What are you going to do about it?"

Brad shook his head. "Really? Why? There are any number of good-looking men wandering around campus. Why me?"

His roommate shook his head. "You just don't get it. You're attractive. Women are attracted to you."

Cagney isn't. "But I'm her instructor."

"Yeah, that's an issue."

"And I'm not interested in her."

I may be interested in Cagney. The more I think about her, the more I remember her smile, her voice, and those eyes. Stop it. We have nothing in common.

"You'll need to make it clear to this girl you two can't do anything."

Logan rose, again. "Until the end of the term and you're no longer her instructor."

He closed his eyes. "I. Am. Not. Interested. In. Her."

Before Logan left, he said, "Pizza tonight? I don't feel like making anything. Do you?"

Brad laughed. "No, pizza sounds good." Then, he leaned back in the chair and watched the clouds. He had two women on his mind.

Chapter 9

Cagney

Cagney watched as the mysterious couple followed Alvin to the front of the café. Her head hurt. Badly. Had she fallen into some time-warp continuum? She didn't even know what she was talking about. She just knew those two couldn't be the characters from the book. There was no way in hell. The only alternative was that everyone was playing a gigantic prank on her.

She turned her gaze to Dr. St. Clair. "Well?"

The professor rubbed her temples. Why did she need to do that? *I'm the one having the hallucinations. No, they're actors. No hallucinations involved.*

"Cagney," Dr. St. Clair placed a knee on the bench so she could look her in the eye. "As strange as this sounds, those two individuals are from my novel. The novel you're reading, *Love's Surprise.*"

"Cut it out. You and I both know that's impossible."

"Yeah, that's what I thought until about a year and a half ago." Dr. St. Clair ran a hand through her hair. "It's not something I've told anyone." She looked around the café as if to check if anyone was watching them.

"I haven't even told Kenn this."

Cagney leaned back. Dr. Kennedy King Cooper and Dr. St. Clair were an item in the history department. She had heard the story of how the two of them were caught kissing rather passionately on the Jumbotron at a home football game a year or so ago. And he didn't know this? Wait, maybe because it was just her imagination?

"When I was writing their story, I was, well, let's say rather stressed. They jumped out of their pages and onto my loveseat in my home office. I wasn't teaching then."

Already this story sounded implausible.

"They said they were on a mission to find me the man of my dreams." She played with her heart necklace. "And they believed Dr. Cooper was that man." She held up her hand as if to stop Cagney from asking a question.

"At that time, I had just met him and he came off as a pompous ass." She chuckled as if she were recalling the meeting.

"The entire department believes you two were made for each other."

"Let's just say our relationship started out bumpy. But because in large part due to Alex and Blake—who I said were my cousin and her fiancé—we're happy together."

It sounded like a wonderfully romantic story, but not one thing her advisor said convinced her the couple was nothing more than character actors. How appropriate. The two were playing characters from a book.

"How could they be actors, Cagney? How could anyone know you were reading the book?"

She sighed. She had her there. "I didn't even know I would read that book over the weekend. But I needed to destress after the blind date I had Friday."

"A blind date?" The professor's lip quirked up as if she found the idea cute. "That explains a lot of things."

Just then the people who claimed to be Alex and Blake returned with their food. "Did we give you enough time, JJ?" The woman placed her meal on the table, then slid in.

"I haven't had Fission Chips in a million years," the man announced, his hair bouncing from the trip across the café. He sat next to her.

"Cagney tells me she had a blind date last weekend." Dr. St. Clair looked from the man to the woman.

The man had just taken a bite of his meal. Damn, he resembled the character in the book. He held up a finger as he finished chewing. "Yes, she did."

"How do you know that?" Chills ran up Cagney's spine. Again. Her head pounded.

"Easy." The woman inspected her onion string. "You were reading about us. We could sense it."

She was not an iota closer to understanding the situation than before her advisor appeared. Yet, everyone was so adamant about it.

"And what difference does that make?" Cagney pounded a fist on the table.

Dr. St. Clair shook her head. "They're here to help you find your true love." The words came out softly, but with a conviction behind them.

"We are." The woman sipped her proton shake.

"I think we're able to do this," the man began, "because we've made the leap once before with Dr. JJ. And since you're her protégé, so to speak, we're able to help you."

"What if you two could do this with everyone who reads your story?" Dr. St. Clair cocked her head.

"What kind of question is that?" This conversation had deteriorated fast.

Cagney reached for *Love's Surprise*, still on the table. Everyone's eyes were on her. "This is the spot where I was reading when you interrupted me. It says Alex was wearing a pink short-sleeved blouse with a small, flowered print." She raised her head to check. That's exactly what she was wearing. Alex raised her brows and a slow, knowing smile spread over her face.

"Okay, a coincidence." She studied what the man who claimed to be Blake had on. "It says here"—she searched the page—"he wore a cream-colored pullover accented with three snaps at the collar."

She took a deep breath before she closed the book. "That's it, love."

Cagney's lunch came perilously close to making a repeat appearance.

"Okay, let's say that perhaps through some strange break in the laws of reality, you two really are Alex Zurich"—she pointed a finger at the woman—"and Blake Teesdale"—she nodded to the man. "Why, then, are you here? Why are you visiting me? It would be more logical"—she couldn't believe she was even using that word in this bizarre situation—"to visit Dr. St. Clair." She couldn't bring herself to call her advisor JJ.

"No." The man's answer was unexpectedly forceful. *God, I should just call him Blake to make my life easier.*

"Because JJ isn't the one needing help this time. We helped her last time."

The woman who claimed to be Alex sighed. "And

look how well that worked out. She and Kenn are still going strong." She knitted her brow. "You are, aren't you, JJ?"

JJ, no, Dr. St. Clair, laughed. "Yes, we are. But what about Cagney?"

"What about Cagney? I'm fine. No problems. Nothing to see here, folks. You can move along."

"No, we can't." Alex said. Yeah, it was just easier calling these two characters by the names they thought they had.

"We know for a fact Brad asked you to pretend to date him."

Cagney leaned forward in the booth. "How in the world do you know that?"

"It's easy." Blake shook his head, his hair swayed with the timing of a metronome. His face fell. "It's not quite that easy, but the gist is when you think about something hard enough and long enough, the Universe gives it to you."

"But I—"

"You were reading about us." Alex tilted her head. "And you thought our romance sounded...I don't mean to be rude, but better than your love life at the moment."

"I don't have a love life." Cagney rubbed her forehead.

"Exactly. But the Universe is presenting you with an opportunity." Blake glanced at Alex as if to confirm the statement.

"It is." Alex nodded. Her green eyes flashed. "In the form of Brad, who only wants you to pretend you're dating him." She held her palms upward. "How harmless is that?"

"So that's what this is all about?" Dr. St. Clair laughed. "Now I get it. These two really are here to help with your love life."

"I just said I have—"

"Have you given Brad an answer?"

Was that a glint of amusement in Dr. St. Clair's eyes?

"No, Dr. St. Clair." Cagney emphasized her advisor's title. "I have not."

"I'm not advising you on this." She raised both hands, palms up. "That's a choice clearly up to you. I don't even know the man."

"He's cute," Alex said. "And seems like a sincere person."

"How do you…" Cagney gave up. It was probably that damned universe again. For a conversation taking place in the Physics Café, it sure appeared that every law of that science had just been broken. Several times over.

"What I was going to say…" Dr. St. Clair shot an admonishing look at Alex. "…was that Alex and Blake are probably going to hang around until you start taking their advice. That's how it worked for me. So if you want to get rid of them—"

"Not fair." Blake shook his head. "You mean you didn't like our company? You don't like our company?"

"No, that's not what I mean." The professor looked as if she were figuring a way to get her foot out of her mouth.

"Wait." Cagney held up a hand. "Let me see if I understand the situation." She took a deep breath. "Alex and Blake"—she pointed at the two—"visited you to help you with Dr. Cooper?"

All three nodded. "And left when you were securely in your relationship?"

Again, they all nodded. "So all I have to do is pretend to date Brad Townsend and their mission will be complete and they'll disappear?"

Dr. St. Clair looked thoughtful. "Basically, yes."

They were pushing her over the edge. Should she do it? Fake date Brad?

"Will you?" Alex asked.

The pair smiled at her. They appeared eager to, well, she didn't know what. "Will you leave if I agree to pretend to be Brad's girlfriend?" *Please say you'll leave.*

"I'm not sure we're the ones in control of that." Alex ran a hand through her hair, making her look all too casual for this potentially life-changing decision. "But it should work that way."

"Okay, I'll do it." God, she didn't want to. But if it got Alex and Blake out of her life it might be worth it. And it would stop Molly from finding her random men to go out with. She'd almost forgotten about Molly Matchmaker, she was so preoccupied with whatever this was.

"Yay!" Alex bounced in her seat. "Text him now. I want to see what he says."

Rather pushy, wasn't she? But the sooner she texted him, the sooner he said yes. And that meant the sooner these two characters would be out of her life.

She pulled out her phone. As she hit the keys, she heard Blake say, "We may need a place to stay tonight, JJ. Is our room still available?"

They had a room in her house? Why, of course

they did. Thank God they weren't asking to stay with her.

"Okay. It's sent. We'll see what he says." He'll say great. That's what he'll say. *And I'm sure I'll come to rue this very moment.*

"You're always welcome at my home. Kenn will be so happy to see you."

Cagney's phone chirped. It was Brad. Wow. That didn't take any time at all. "He says great. Asks when I can meet."

Alex bounced in her seat. "Tomorrow, of course. You can't put fate off. This is destiny. Right, JJ? Cagney has started her grand journey of love."

She clasped her hands and sighed.

"Yeah, right. It's a prearranged meeting with some guy to avoid going out with anyone else." Cagney glared at the lovestruck woman across from her. "Nothing more."

She stared at her phone. She just knew Brad had his in his hand. "Why not tomorrow?"

She punched it in.

—*Tomorrow? 3 pm? Physics Café?*—

She hit the send button. The answer came instantaneously.

"It's a go." She studied the phone. "Hopefully, you two will go, too."

Chapter 10

Brad

Brad glanced at his watch. Two forty-five. Piper had been in his office for forty-five minutes. It had been evident after the first fifteen minutes she was more interested in attention than in geology.

When he had made the date, the fake one that is, with Cagney, he had completely forgotten about his promise to help Piper with her studies. As he recalled, he had forgotten about nearly everything. He was that happy to be seeing her again. On a fake date, that is. A fake date.

Piper had arrived five minutes early and startled him. "Oh, that's right," he said, trying hard not to be completely shocked by her presence, "we did have a meeting."

"How could you forget that, Dr. Townsend?"

He had given up explaining he didn't hold a doctorate. "What aren't you understanding, Piper?"

"Hello to you too." Piper's voice filled with indignation.

"Piper," he emphasized her name, "you asked for this meeting, outside of my normal office hours, because you said you weren't understanding the material." He quirked a brow.

"Fine. If you want to be that way." She shook her head. "If you want to know the truth, I don't understand a thing about geology. I think I need a tutor."

"The university has a tutoring program. I know several of the geology tutors personally. They're smart and are excellent at explaining the material so you can understand it."

Piper crossed her legs at the knee. That's when he noticed her short skirt. He tried not to look. "But I don't want one of those tutors, Dr. Townsend. I want you."

He also just realized how low the cut of her blouse was. He rubbed his temple. "I can certainly help you with some material right now. But you know my office hours—"

"Are at a ridiculously early hour that I can't make." She sighed. Loudly. "I'd be willing to come at this time a couple times a week." She tilted her head and looked him in the eyes.

"This isn't a good time for me, Piper. And if you need as much help as you indicate, then it would be more profitable for you to enroll yourself in the tutoring program and go that route."

She grumbled and noisily pulled a notebook from her backpack. "I don't understand the different waves of an earthquake. Can you go over them again for me?"

"Every wave we've studied is in the textbook." He shook his head and resigned himself to going over the material for her.

Normally, he loved tutoring students, helping them to learn to love the subject that he loved. With Piper it was different. He didn't think she had an interest in the subject. Maybe Logan was right. *Maybe she is hitting on me.*

"Seismic waves are classified into two overarching types: body and surface waves." He waited while she scribbled something in her notebook.

"Body waves are further classified into P-waves and S-waves. P-waves are waves that can travel through all three states of matter." He probably needed to make sure she knew them. "Solids, liquids, and gases." She scribbled in her notebook. Perhaps she had a sincere interest in learning. "S-waves, on the other hand, can only travel through solids."

He continued describing waves and she continued to take notes—or so it looked like—until he glanced at his watch. Time to pack up and leave. Throughout the rerun of his lecture from the other day, he thought about his fake date. He thought about Cagney. Would she wear the same T-shirt she had worn for the blind date. The pink quartz one.

"Our time is just about up," he said at two forty-five.

"But you said you'd meet with me from two to three?" Brad's spine shivered as she whined.

"I did. But we covered a lot of ground, and you should have a better grip on seismic waves." He rubbed his beard. "And I do have an appointment across campus." It wasn't quite across campus, but it was a good ten-minute walk.

"But you promised." Her eyes locked on to his again.

"We've covered enough for one session. Again, if you can't make my office hours and you require continuing help, you should stop by the tutoring program."

She didn't make a move to leave, so Brad closed his laptop and put it in his backpack. She slowly put her notebook in her backpack and zipped it.

"Thank you, Dr. Townsend. That helped a lot. Maybe I can fit your office hours into my schedule. I'll give it a try."

****

He felt as if he were running behind even though he arrived at the Physics Café exactly at three. He scanned the tables and booths and discovered she wasn't there yet. He wasn't sure why, but he wanted to be there before Cagney. Weird.

He picked a booth and set up his laptop. He did say it would be a working fake date, didn't he? Real researching and writing. Fake dating. He went through his emails.

He looked up and saw her. She wore the dark-pink T-shirt. Was that the same one she wore on the blind date? And she had a light lavender-colored jacket thrown over that. It looked good on her. And she had that ponytail.

He rose when she approached the booth and took a step forward. What does a boyfriend do when they meet their girlfriend? He leaned in. They kiss her on the lips. Right? He'd seen it a hundred times in the movies. But it didn't feel right. This was only their first fake date.

He moved slightly to the right. Kiss her on the cheek? That didn't feel right either. Shit. At the last minute he knew that was totally inappropriate, put space between them, and extended his hand.

It took a moment, but she shook it. He couldn't read the expression on her face. It could have been anger, annoyance, or even amusement. God, he hoped he didn't tee her off on their first fake date.

She slid into the booth. "Thank you for agreeing to this arrangement." He closed his laptop. "I wasn't sure you'd think this was a good idea."

"I'm not convinced it is a good idea, but I felt, well, I thought I'd give it a try. Like you said, no one will be trying to set us up on blind dates anymore."

"Are you hungry? Do you want something to eat? I'm going to eat something." He ran a hand over his beard. "I'm not good at this. Please bear with me."

She laughed. He realized he liked her laugh. "I couldn't tell by the way you greeted me."

"I've never"—he struggled to how to phrase it—"actually been on a real date before." He closed an eye and shook his head. "Not one that wasn't set up with some poor unsuspecting woman."

She scrunched her nose.

"I want this to look like we're really dating, and I just didn't know how to greet you. Would kissing you on the lips be appropriate? I've seen Logan and Molly do that. But I'm not sure I should do it on the first date."

She laughed. Was she laughing at him?

"No, kissing me full on the lips on our first date, our first fake date, isn't a good idea. We're not that far enough into our fake relationship for that."

"Okay, then how far are we?"

She leaned back on the bench as if she were giving it serious thought. "Having never fake dated before, I'm not sure. But I'm sure we're beyond the handshaking stage."

His cheeks burned. "That was awkward, wasn't it? Sorry." His brain nagged at him to say something, but his mouth wouldn't cooperate. He took a deep breath. "Maybe a kiss on the cheek?" He ran a hand over his beard.

Cagney took what seemed like forever to answer, then slowly nodded. "Yes, I think that would be appropriate for future fake dates." Her smile disarmed him.

"And, uhm, you'll let me know when our fake dating gets to the, well, the lips-kissing level."

Again, she laughed. She looked as if she were studying him. Did he have something on his beard?

"Yes, Brad, I will. No worries. And yes, I am hungry. Let's go up and get some food."

Chapter 11

Cagney

Cagney stood next to Brad at the counter. She had been here before. She practically lived at the Physics Café. She did her best writing here. She graded term papers here.

This time it felt a bit weird, though. She felt self-conscious. And when Alvin looked at the two, it felt even weirder. But this is what they agreed on. To be seen in public as a couple. She didn't know when she agreed to this how the deception would make her feel. Uneasy. When Brad first suggested it, she didn't think farther than making Logan and Molly believe they were dating. As it turned out, everyone else would have to think that, too, for this to work.

Thankfully, it looked as if Alvin did his best to take their presence together in stride.

"Brad, why can't you trust atoms?"

She furrowed her brows. What?

"I don't know," Brad said. "Why can't I trust atoms?" He quirked a lip in a smile.

"Because they make up everything."

They laughed. Probably too much for how funny the joke was. Or wasn't. A short silence followed. She stared at the desserts next to the cash register, trying hard to look interested in them. Her cheeks burned. It was bad enough that this was their first time ordering as a couple, fake couple, but…

"Why did the rock take a shower every morning?" Apparently, it was Brad's turn to tell a bad joke. She turned her attention back to her fake boyfriend. *What have I gotten myself into?*

"I don't know. Why?" Alvin waited expectantly.

"Because he wanted to start with a clean slate."

Alvin laughed. So did Brad. Cagney was definitely out of the loop.

Then just like that they stopped laughing. She scanned the café quickly to see if anyone witnessed this display of juvenile humor. Really, is this the universe scientists lived in?

"What can I get you two?" And just like that, they were out of the joke mode. Go figure.

"Oh, we're separate." She paused, nearly panicked. Why? "I mean I'll pay for my own."

That brought a scowl from Brian, no, Brad. "No, I searched online last night what humanities PhD students make. It's pitiful."

"What? Wait?" She touched his shoulder. It was muscled. "You mean you make more than—" The fact that he had a higher stipend than she out-horrored her more than the fact that he had been looking up her salary last night.

"Apparently, I do. I'll pay." He handed his card to Alvin, who looked bemused.

"All right," he said slowly, almost as if he were afraid to ask the question, "what are you two having?"

They ordered and Cagney and Brad walked back to the booth in silence. As they slid in, Cagney asked, "What do you think Alvin thought?"

"About the jokes?" Brad smiled as he opened his

laptop. "I know they're bad, but he loves them. It's our thing."

"No, about our ordering together." She watched as he concentrated on the computer. "And you paying."

He raised his head to look at her. "I hope he thought we were dating. That's the point of this, right?"

She sighed. "Yes. Yes, it is."

Why didn't she realize how much deception would be involved?

****

She and Brad had just begun to eat, when Cagney heard Alvin say, "So good to have you guys around again." And then she heard that British accent. No. No. *No*. They were supposed to be gone. *I agreed to fake date. They agreed to leave.* She pursed her lips.

"Something wrong, Cagney?" Brad looked at her with concern in his blue eyes.

"No, nothing."

"Are you—"

"Cagney, I was hoping to find you here." That was the woman...Alex, let's just keep calling her Alex.

"Blake's ordering. Do you mind if we sit with you?"

She introduced Alex to Brad. "She's my advisor's cousin. And Blake, whom you'll meet soon, is her fiancé." The Theoretical Grilled Chicken Salad she had may come up. That'd be pretty gross for a first fake date.

"Nice to meet you. Please, sit down," he said, extending a hand. If Brad were irritated with the intrusion, he didn't show it.

"I love this café." Alex sat next to Cagney. She sighed as she gazed at the décor. You'd think the walls were decorated with classic paintings and not pictures of dead scientists and undecipherable equations the way she stared at them. Cagney wanted to ask her who her favorite scientist was but bit her tongue.

The woman seemed oblivious she was interrupting them. Why did Alex's presence upset her? It's not like she and Brad were on a real date. *Maybe just her presence masquerading as a fictional character irks me.* Oh, no. What if Alex or Blake told Brad they had popped out of a romance book?

She didn't know which would embarrass her more—the fact that they would tell Brad they were fictional or that he would discover she read romance novels.

She was so lost in her thoughts that she didn't see Blake had joined them and slid in next to Brad. She smiled. Brad held his own in the way of looks next to Blake. And Blake was handsome.

"Are you two students?" Brad turned to face Blake.

"Not yet." His hair danced with enthusiasm. "But JJ is talking to Dr. Chare to see if we can enroll late."

"Who's JJ?" Brad glanced at Cagney.

"She's my advisor. Dr. St. Clair. J. Jordan St. Clair. JJ." Crap. Dry throat. She needed a drink. "And Dr. Chare is the history department chair."

"It's her pen name." Alex waved a fry. "JJ Spritely. She writes romance novels." She sighed. "And she's so very good at it." She nudged Cagney. "Isn't she?"

Cagney tried hard to retain some shred of dignity. She didn't want this man to know she read romance novels. "Yes. Her books are on the bestsellers list." Were her cheeks red? They sure felt hot.

"She's an author?" Brad's lips rose slightly, as if

he found it amusing.

"The best romance author ever." Alex bounced in her seat.

"Not quite, love." Blake shook his head. "Many literary experts believe that Jane—"

"You know what I mean." Alex reached across the table for his hand and gazed into his eyes. "Because she created…" She tapped her index finger to her chest, then pointed it at him.

It was if a light bulb went off in his head. "Yes, yes, love, you're right." He nodded. "JJ Spritely is the best romance author ever. Hands down."

Whew. That was close. Those two lunatics almost let out that they were…oh, my God. *Who's the lunatic, Cagney?*

Chapter 12

Brad

"Sir, your name?" the instructor asked as Brad handed her the money for the yoga class.

"Brad. Brad Townsend."

"If you intend to take this class regularly,"—it was no exaggeration to say she scrutinized him from head to toe—"you may want to invest in a pair of pants that are more comfortable."

Soft laughter rippled through the room. Was Cagney laughing?

"Let's just say those jeans, as you probably know from our last session, can be slightly constrictive."

Brad nodded. He wanted to ask what kind of pants that would be, but he felt foolish as it was. He was determined the world saw him as Cagney's boyfriend. Surely, a boyfriend would share interests with his girlfriend. And if this was what Cagney liked, then here he was, too, right next to her.

Cagney leaned toward him. "Why are you even here?"

"Because this is what boyfriends do?"

She rolled her eyes, but smiled, so maybe this was what a real boyfriend would do.

He sat cross-legged next to her. And the stretching began. First with the left palm on the floor and moving the right arm overhead. He winced. He didn't remember being quite so stiff the last time.

"You okay over there?" As she changed sides, Cagney glanced at him, a mischievous look in her eye.

He nodded as they prepared for the next move. This one had him twisting his body like a pretzel and holding the pose for an unimaginably long time.

"If you like"—his eyes moved to the front of the room to the instructor speaking—"you can twist a bit deeper. Your body will thank you."

He let out a chuckle. "It will, you know," Cagney teased as she extended her twist. How did she do that and not break?

"My body says it's fine the way it is. Thank you very much."

A few beads of sweat formed on his forehead. He couldn't look as inept as he felt. Could he?

He struggled with many of the moves. Just like the last time. But this time he thought he did the whatever-dog pose a little better. He collapsed on the floor, rolled on his back, and closed his eyes. Thank God that was the end of it. He wasn't sure he was ready to face Cagney. *I don't know how she does this.* When he opened his eyes, she was looking down at him, smiling.

"Are you okay?" She offered him a hand. He took it and stood. "I'm fine. I'll get the hang of this…I think."

Every student in the class appeared to be watching him. He bent at the waist and whispered into Cagney's ear. "Did I make a scene? Did I embarrass you?"

He scanned the room again and realized he was the only male in the room.

"Mr. Townsend." He looked toward the instructor. "You did much better this week than last week. I hope you consider becoming a regular member. You have potential."

"Uhm…thank you? I think I'd like that. To attend regularly, I mean. Yes. Thanks."

He turned to Cagney. "Can we walk out together?"

"Of course. I'm just going to the café. I'll walk you to your building. Sound like something a girlfriend would do?" Was she fluttering her eyelashes, because her eyes were twinkling.

"Yeah. It does."

They exited the building. "There's something I've been meaning to ask you about but I couldn't think of how to bring it up during yoga."

She tilted her head. "What?"

He took in a deep breath. "Logan and Molly are going to the movies Friday and they want to know if we want to double date…fake double-date." He scrubbed his beard. "They want us to go with them."

She laughed. Well, that wasn't the reaction he expected.

"She mentioned you might be asking me." She studied her shoes. "I guess we don't have much choice. After all we're dating now…pretend dating. Which they don't know."

Brad rubbed his beard. "I didn't expect something like this to happen. Being invited on a double date." He spoke slowly because he truly was sorry. On several levels. While they wouldn't have to talk during the movie, he'd—they'd, really—be put on the spot to make conversation afterward. And he didn't mean to drag Cagney into this.

"I'm sorry," he said. "Hopefully, this is an anomaly."

"We'll see." They continued past the Quad lined with cherry trees bursting with blossoms.

"And one more thing." *I better tell her this too.* "Logan said it was his turn to pick the film. He naturally picked an action, superhero one. I guess from what he says Molly doesn't particularly care for them. Are you okay with it?"

He turned his head to check her reaction. She wasn't by his side. He'd lost Cagney? Before their first fake date? His heartbeat raced as he turned. She stood, motionless, several steps behind him, head tilted. Her dark blonde hair sparkled in the sun.

"What? I'm so sorry I didn't know—"

"No, it's okay. I'm just surprised you care if I like the movie or not. It's a guy's flick, I know."

"Yeah, but I don't want you to be bored. Like Molly says she'll be. I guess she can—"

She grazed her fingers over his arm. "I'm not Molly and we're just fake dating. I'll have popcorn and maybe nachos, and something to drink and it'll be fine. I may even like the movie."

He smiled. He had been worried for nothing.

They reached the MacDaniels building that housed the geology department. He bent down and kissed her on the cheek. "I hope that was appropriate."

"I think so, considering our stage of fake dating."

"At least it was less awkward than whatever it was I tried to do the last time. Sorry about that, again." He shrugged.

"No worries. I'll see you Friday night."

Her hips swayed ever so slightly as she walked away.

****

He began class by introducing his students to the concept of plate tectonics. As he turned to write the topic on the board, his muscles screamed in agony. Darn yoga. He'd blame Cagney, except it was his idea to pretend to be a couple. And his idea to join her in class.

"This theory,"—he faced the class and pushed his muscles to the back of his mind—"explains the major landforms are a result of the earth's subterranean, or underground, movements.

"It gained popularity in the 1960s and proved to be groundbreaking. No pun intended." He paused, waiting—more like hoping—for some laughter. A groan even.

"What this did—"

A knock at the classroom door interrupted him. The door creaked open and a mop of unruly hair popped in. The class laughed. *Sure, you laugh at that but not my pun.*

"Excuse me." The man looked familiar and Brad knew he had seen him before.

"I just signed up for this course. Sorry I'm late."

That's it. The English accent. The hair. He was—

"I'm Blake Teesdale. We met at the Physics Café the other day."

Brad smiled. While they hadn't spent a lot of time together, Brad had taken to this man instantly.

"Of course, I remember you."

Blake handed him the paperwork. "It's old-fashioned to still carry paperwork."

"It is. But remember where you are. Just have a seat, Blake. We were just talking about plate tectonics."

Blake slid into the nearest chair, which happened to

be next to Piper. Blake's height made it a bit hard for him to sit comfortably and the struggle played out as his hair flounced.

Piper studied Blake's every move.

****

Blake

The students chatted as they filed out of the classroom. All but the woman whom he'd sat next to. Did Brad call her Piper? Yes, Piper. She was standing a little too close to Brad asking some question about the class.

He assessed her attire and decided she tried too hard to be attractive. The jeans skirt a bit too short, the blue T-shirt a bit too tight. He heard Alex's voice in his head about other women who dressed similarly. "She has her eyes set on him, Blake. She's only after one thing. She doesn't care about the man's feelings." Alex was right about this, of course. On their last visit to JJ's world, more than one cheerleader had come up to him dressed like that. Alex had put each in her place.

"Dr. Townsend, all I'm asking is for us to go to the Physics Café tonight so you can explain a few of these ideas to me."

She inched closer to him. Her hand was perilously close to his. Blake's heart pounded. And he was only an observer. An observer who had to do something.

"It would be inappropriate for us to go out together. I'm your instructor. What would it look like?"

Blake knew. It would look like Piper was hitting on Brad.

"Piper, we've talked about this before. The tutoring program will help you the most."

"Yes, Dr. Townsend."

The words came out as a whine, which only confirmed Blake's thoughts.

So that's what Piper wanted. If Brad and she dated, what would happen to Cagney? He and Alex had a mission: to make sure Brad and Cagney fell in love. That certainly wouldn't happen if Piper persuaded Brad to…well, Blake wasn't sure what.

He needed to be the man Alex thought he was. He needed to intervene. He leaned forward in the small seat. "Brad."

That was all it took.

"Blake, I'm glad you're still here."

I bet you are.

Brad ran a quick hand through his hair.

"I've got some materials to get you caught up with the rest of the class."

"I guess I'll go now, Dr. Townsend. Maybe we can meet another time at the Physics Café." She took a tentative step toward the door.

"I don't think so, Piper. The tutoring program is your best bet."

She stomped to the door and slammed it as she left.

"Thanks, Blake. I'm glad you stayed." Brad shook his head as he riffled through papers in his backpack. "Piper seems obsessed with me tutoring her. She wants more time than I'm able to give her."

"She obsessed, but not with tutoring."

"What?" Brad looked up from his search. "What do you mean?"

Just as Blake suspected. Brad hadn't a clue what was going on. Thank God, Alex had taught him.

"She's obsessed with you."

Brad dropped the stack of papers and they scattered

to the floor.

Blake rose from his seat trying to be the enlightened man on campus. He took several steps to the front of the room and helped Brad pick up the papers.

"I told my roommate about her. He said she might be interested in me. But I didn't believe him. And I don't believe she's obsessed with me. Just maybe…"

"You're good looking, you're her teacher, and you're smart. She's definitely attracted to you."

Brad sighed as he straightened the papers and handed them to Blake. "By the way, these are some of the resources I've used."

Brad didn't say anything for a moment. "And no. I'm not that good looking." He paused as if he were evaluating the situation.

"Anyway, I'm on my way to the café." Blake thought it best to change the subject. "You want to come with? Maybe Alex and Cagney are there."

"Yeah, sure. That sounds great. Let me get my backpack together."

****

Brad

"Dr. Townsend." He'd recognized that voice anywhere.

Brad looked up from his Higgs-Boson Bison Burger. Piper. What was her problem now?

"I thought you said it was inappropriate to be out with a student."

"It is." Brad knitted his brows, wondering what she was talking about.

"You're out with Blake now, aren't you?" She placed a hand on her hip as she glared at him. "And he's your student."

Now she tapped her toe.

He shook his head. "That's different."

"No difference. We're both your students. Are you saying there's a double standard for male and female students?" She tilted her head as she evidently waited for a response.

Blake put down the Feynman Fry and cleared his throat. Piper shot him a dirty look. "It's different because Brad and I have been friends for eons. I'm just auditing the course, anyway. He's not giving me a grade."

Brad marveled at the man's ability to jump in and make some bull up. On. The. Spot.

"H-h-he's right. Way back." Brad's body tensed. "He surprised me today. We're just getting caught up."

Piper huffed. Brad wanted to laugh. Other than in novels, he never knew a person to actually huff.

"Whatever." She turned on a heel and returned to her table.

"Nice work, Blake. She bought it. How did you come up with that on the spot?"

Blake shook his head, his hair dancing. "I've had a bit of a history in that regard."

Brad thought better than to ask how, so he changed the subject. "What other classes are you taking? Do you have a major?"

"I'm taking an art history class that's fascinating." Blake's hair testified to his enthusiasm. "I was always interested in art, of course, but this class sheds so much light on so many artists."

"That sounds, uhm, interesting." It wasn't Brad's idea of fun, but he could see how Blake would like it.

He had only met him a day or so ago, but he felt like had had known the man for years.

"It is. Did you know that before Claude Monet starting painting, he worked as a caricaturist?"

"No, I never knew that." Brad wasn't quite sure who Monet was.

"He started when he was just fifteen, and he'd sell his work."

Blake slapped the table and leaned back on the bench seat. "Can you imagine owning one of those caricatures today?"

Before Brad could even shake his head, Blake continued. "People always confuse him Manet"—Blake emphasized the "a" sound in the name—"and they actually knew each other. Bloody amazing, if you ask me."

Brad nodded as he watched Blake's hair. "I guess I never really thought about it."

"You know, that's okay. Until I met you, I didn't think about rocks all that much. And when I did, well, I'm not sure what I thought. But I've got to tell you, there are also so very fine artists in their own right in that class."

"Really?" Brad didn't have an artistic bone in his body and sometimes felt a pang of envy at those who did. Like right at this moment.

"Do you draw or paint, Blake? Are you artistic?"

"No, I'm not. Always wished I were though." He looked wistful. "There's one woman with an immense amount of talent. I'm in awe of her."

Chapter 13

Cagney

"I've applied for another travel grant." Cagney pulled the paperwork from her backpack. "Is it possible you can write a reference for me?"

Dr. St. Clair leaned back in her chair and laughed. "Of course, I would love to. You should have been awarded the last one. I can't believe it went to Emily Wilson."

"Neither could I. And she flaunted it for so long. I just wanted to scream."

"Kenn, I mean, Dr. Cooper, feels the same way. He says she's into grand ideas, but her execution is lacking. She's driving him crazy. He's doing everything in his power to help her get that PhD, but—"

Dr. St. Clair covered her mouth with her hand. "You heard none of that. That's what our dates have been like lately. Kenn talking about Emily. It's a strange love triangle. Certainly, one I could never have invented in any of my books."

Cagney tried to imagine Kenn and her advisor on a date. It shouldn't have been difficult, except for the fact they were both professors. But to think that Dr. Cooper would spend the night talking about students.

Wait…

"Do you talk about your students often when you're out with Dr. Cooper, and does my name ever come up?" She spit the words out quickly before she lost her nerve to ask.

"We only talk about our troublemakers, Cag, never our outstanding students, like you."

Well, of course, she didn't believe it. And now in addition to applying for a travel grant, and fake dating, she worried about what her advisor said about her on dates. When did life get so complicated?

"I'll write the reference—"

"There you are."

Alex stood at the door, a hand on her hip. Yes, this was just what she needed at the moment. One more complication in her already over-complicated life. She glanced at Dr. St. Clair but couldn't read her expression. How many times did Alex and Blake pop in and out of this office throughout the day? She envisioned them stopping by and just plopping down in a chair ready to chat about their day—or in Blake's case, any abstract thing that might be on his mind. The conversations had to be fascinating.

"I've looked all over for you. I came here to ask JJ if she's seen you." Alex strode in and took the seat next to her.

"I thought you were supposed to go back to your fictional world. I took your advice. We've just had our first yoga class as a couple because"—she gestured air quotes—"that's what boyfriends do." She spoke the last words to Dr. St. Clair. When did she start confiding in her advisor about her fake love life?

Alex shook her head ever so slightly. "The fact that we're still here tells me our mission isn't finished."

Maybe if she tried to reason with Dr. St. Clair, she would have some influence over Alex's actions. "If her mission is to get me to fall in love with Brad Townsend, then she and Blake should start looking for houses to buy."

She slapped her hand on the desk. "Because it's not about to happen."

Dr. St. Clair leaned back in her chair, eyes wide. *Great, now I'm at the top of the discussion list when she and Dr. Cooper have their next date. Well done, Cag.*

"You know," Alex said, "Blake's taking Brad's introduction to geology. He likes Brad. A lot. And you know, JJ, what a good judge of character he is." Alex looked JJ in the eye.

Cagney didn't let her advisor answer. "Are you using peer pressure here? I'm a big girl and I make my own decisions."

"No, it's not that…It's just we were lying in bed last night trying to figure out what you don't like about him."

"Excuse me? Dr. St. Clair, can't you control these two?"

Her advisor opened her mouth, but Alex stood, fists balled. "How do you know you want nothing to do with him if you won't get to know him?"

"Dr. St. Clair, tell this person that she found the love of her life with your help." Cagney rose as well and pointed at Alex. "You made sure she and Blake would end up with each other and have a happily ever after."

She sighed. *No, not tears. Not in my advisor's office. Not in front of this fictional personage.*

"Alex, you do know—" Dr. St. Clair began.

"Tell this fictional woman that my happily ever after isn't guaranteed."

Dr. St. Clair nodded. "It's true, Alex."

"How can I have a happily ever after with someone I don't even know how to talk to, Dr. St. Clair? Would you explain that to her?"

"I'm trying." Her advisor sighed.

"He's into rocks and earthquakes and who knows what and I'm"—Cagney patted her chest—"I'm interested in American history and presidents. Tell this woman I can't see any middle ground."

"There is Mount Rushmore," Alex suggested. "That combines the two quite nicely."

Cagney groaned.

"Mount Rushmore aside, Alex," Dr. St. Clair began, "Cagney does have a point."

"But, JJ, the man's taking yoga with her."

"Is this true?" JJ placed her elbows on her desk.

"Only because he believes that's what boyfriends do." She plopped down into the seat. This argument was exhausting.

"But that's now something you have in common. It's something you can talk about." Alex smiled as if she'd just won the argument.

"Dr. St. Clair, tell romance woman over there, she's got her head in the stars. The man doesn't give a flying fig about yoga. I'm not about to talk to him about the downward facing dog or the warrior pose over a cup of coffee."

She threw a hand up in frustration. "Brad can barely get through class without killing himself."

"Sounds brutal, actually. You probably don't want to remind him of it."

"JJ, how can you say that? You of all people. A romance author? The man is trying. Cagney needs to give him a chance."

Her advisor nodded thoughtfully. "Alex, I think that it's too early in their relationship—"

"Relationship? What relationship?" Cagney shot to her feet. "We don't have a relationship. He's trying to make it look real. And he's trying too hard. We fulfill the requirement just by sitting at the same table at the Physics Café. I'm on one side researching and writing and he's on the other side doing, well, whatever geology doctoral students do. That's enough for me. I'd be happy if I could just phone this fake relationship in."

She closed her eyes and sighed. "I'm not looking forward to going to the movies with him Friday night." She opened her eyes and stared at her advisor who looked like she enjoyed hearing her bare her soul.

Alex jumped up and took her by the shoulders. "The movies? Really?" She let go of her and turned to Dr. St. Clair. "That's an interesting development. It occurred a lot faster than I thought it would. I thought she'd have to wait at least two weeks before they saw a movie together. What do you think, JJ?"

"It may be a plot twist." Dr. St. Clair raised a finger. "In the book I'm working—"

"Everyone stop." The words came out louder and sterner than Cagney had intended. "Look, it's nothing to get excited about. It's just a double date with Molly and Logan."

"Really?" Alex sat down slowly. Her voice now barely audible. She leaned closer to Cagney. "What movie are you seeing?"

"*Sawdust Man: Beyond the Forest.*"

"That's a superhero flick," Dr. St. Clair said. "Kenn's been dying to see that one."

81

"Maybe Dr. Cooper can go in my place. You should ask him."

"You don't mean that." Alex's voice was annoyingly soothing. "You'll enjoy yourself."

"At least during the movie, I don't have to make conversation." She shook her head. "I honestly don't know where to begin with that man."

Alex beamed. The frustration she showed earlier had apparently evaporated. "It won't feel like that forever. And, JJ, you know why? Tell her why?"

Dr. St. Clair raised her hands, palms outward. It appeared she didn't want any part of this.

"Okay, I'll tell her. It won't be like this forever because in all novels, and I do mean all,"—she winked at Dr. St. Clair liked they shared a secret—"fake dating situations end up with the participants falling in love for real."

Cagney groaned. Dr. St. Clair laughed. The nerve of her.

"Alex Zurich, I am not in a romance novel; you are." Cagney held her head. "I can't believe I'm saying this out loud. In my advisor's office." Had she come to accept this bizarre fact that seemed to defy all laws of physics? Not that she was the scientist in the pretend relationship.

"I'm going out on a limb here and I think Dr. St. Clair would agree with me"—she looked at her advisor—"that in real life, people who pursue a stupid idea like pretending to date are more likely to hate each other by the end of the agreement, not fall madly and hopelessly in love."

"Cagney, where is your romantic side?" Alex demanded.

"My romantic side? Not sure I have one." She rose. "As much as I enjoyed chatting with you, Alex, I've got to go. And it's not to run off into the sunset with some leading man. Goodbye."

"I'll write that reference for you," Dr. St. Clair said as Cagney left the room.

Chapter 14

Alex

"Come on, Blake, we're going to be late."

Alex tugged at his arm, but he wouldn't move. Make that couldn't move. The man was in the middle of ordering his snacks for the movie.

Blake had made a beeline for the concession stand the moment they entered the movie theater. "What options. What snacks. Why, I do believe I'm hungry. How about you, love? Don't those nachos sound good?"

"We've got to get in there, find where Cagney is sitting, then sit as close as possible without being obvious." She crossed her arms. She loved this man, but times like these strained her patience. Perhaps she needed to discuss this with JJ. Ah, but their love story had been cast. She wasn't sure what JJ could do now.

When Cagney said she and Brad were going to the movies, Alex knew she had to be there. It was major. They had just started to fake date. And to be in a dark movie theater on their first real fake date, well, who knew what would happen?

Besides, if the date somehow went off the rails, then she and Blake would be nearby to bail them out.

Blake had been staring at the vast selection behind the counter for what seemed like forever. If the menu choices were any indication, they may be standing there until the movie ended.

"I'll take the mac and cheese bites." The young man behind the counter rang it up. "And I'll take the loaded fries." He nodded, his hair bouncing along with each movement. "I did order the nachos already, didn't I?"

He eyed the man. "Yes, sir, you did." He slid his index finger along the computer screen. "And you ordered the chocolate-covered raisins, the chocolate-covered mints, two large sodas, and two large buttered popcorns, one with extra butter."

"Blake Teesdale, JJ is going to be furious when she sees how much money you wasted on her card for this junk food."

"Junk food? Junk food?" He pointed his hand toward the counter. "This isn't junk food. This is movie sustenance. It's a must-have for any movie. You don't expect me to go into that theater unarmed, do you?"

"Besides," he didn't give Alex time to respond, "JJ knows how I am. She knows I would do something like this. She created me, remember? I'm sure this is one of those flaws all authors write into their characters." He scratched his head. "Not that I think this is a flaw. Absolutely not."

"Blake. Don't you think you're going a bit crazy? There's no way you'll be able to eat this all. Besides, we're here to keep an eye on Cagney and Brad. Make sure their date goes smoothly."

Blake turned to her, and a nanosecond later his hair bounced. "And you are well aware that it's just a fake date, love? Cagney has no interest in Brad, other than a cover for no more future blind dates."

Alex stomped her foot. She hated it when he was

right. "That may be so. But we're here for a reason. And I'm sure that reason is for Cagney to find her happily-ever-after. That's what we do best. We were able to get JJ and Dr. Cooper together. And look, they're still a couple."

Blake sighed. "I'm not sure this is the same thing, love."

"Sir, are you done ordering? Should I ring this up now?"

"Oh, yes, wait…Did you want anything else?"

"No, I want to go into that movie and keep an eye on Cagney—"

"I know. I know. We'll get there."

He pivoted and handed the clerk the card. "Thank you. You've been a good sport."

"It'll take a few moments to get your food ready, sir."

Alex glared at him while his food, one item after another, showed up on the counter. "How are you carrying this all?"

He stared at her, then at the food. "That's a good question, love."

He placed his index finger to his lips, as if he were assessing his options. "My dear chap, would you mind if I left some of this here and come back for it in a bit? It seems I may have overcommitted myself."

"Overcommitted?" Alex burst out laughing. "Let's get moving."

Chapter 15

Cagney

Cagney reached for another handful of popcorn while keeping her eyes trained on the movie screen. The superhero action flick exceeded her expectations. What had she been missing by refusing to see these testosterone-filled movies before? She shoved another handful of popcorn in her mouth. Maybe Brad would take her to see more of these?

She gagged. *What did I just say?* Wishing for more time with Mr. Rock Nerd.

Brad leaned over offering a large glass of soda. "Need this?" He sounded concerned.

She took the soda and sucked through the straw. "Thank you. I'm a pig when it comes to popcorn," she whispered. "I'm sure I'll die eating the food."

He chuckled and returned to the movie.

Molly, sitting on the other side of her, nudged her in the arm. "Isn't this the worst thing to have to sit through?"

"Shh!" someone from behind admonished her.

"I like it. I didn't think it would have a plot." Cagney nodded ever so slightly. Then turned her attention back to the movie.

"Bloody good movie, love."

Cagney winced. That voice. That damn British accent. She closed her eyes and sucked in a breath.

That's why Alex had been so inquisitive about the movie details.

"Shh!"

That was definitely Alex. She didn't need to hear any more. Yet, she did hear so much more.

"We're not supposed to be here, remember?"

"Sorry. But this movie is so good. By the way, more nachos, love?"

"No thanks, I'm still working on the chocolate mints."

Cagney shrank down into her seat. Brad nudged her elbow. "Did I hear Blake back there?"

She nodded ever so slightly. If she could only disappear. That would be a great alternative to the cluster this night suddenly became.

"I didn't know they were coming. Did you? We should have invited them."

Obviously, we didn't have to. They showed up anyway. Again, she nodded.

When the movie finally ended, Logan and Molly, and Cagney and Brad stood in the lobby deciding what to do next. "Anyone want to go eat? I'm hungry."

"Logan, you're always hungry." Molly slapped him lightly on the arm.

That's when she saw them. Alex and Blake. The pair headed their way. Oh, my God. It was too late to try to pretend they were leaving.

"Brad, fancy meeting you here." Blake extended his hand and the two shook.

"Hi, Cagney," Alex said. "What a surprise to see you here."

"Is it really now?" Cagney said through clenched teeth.

Molly stepped closer and raised her eyebrows. There was no way around it. She'd have to introduce them.

"Molly"—Cagney took a deep breath—"I'd like you to meet someone."

She made the introductions and then Brad introduced Blake to Logan.

"We were just going to get something to eat. Would you two like to come with us?"

Cagney winced at Logan's invitation. Again. How many winces can one person do in one night? She must have broken the world record.

"How kind of you," Blake said.

Alex looked at Cagney, her green eyes pleading.

Cagney knew she was asking for permission. Cagney had no choice but to accept her fate. She nodded slightly.

Immediately Alex smiled. "I'd love to go. Thank you for asking."

"How about pizza?" Logan checked the faces of all, apparently to search for unity. Everyone seemed to be in agreement.

Molly took Logan by the hand and dragged him as she walked toward the exit. "Then let's go eat and discuss this poor excuse of a movie."

Cagney and Brad followed. "Cagney." She stopped and looked up at him. She knew he was tall, but just now realized how tall he was. "Would it be appropriate to hold hands, like they are?"

She wanted to say no. After all, she barely knew him. But she needed to ensure Molly bought their bogus relationship, so she relented. "Yeah, I think it would be."

He raised his eyebrows as if questioning her reply. She nodded and reached for his hand. She had never imagined it being quite so large, not that she thought about his hands at all. Never. Her own hand seemed to disappear in it. He held it tentatively, at first, then a bit firmer. Maybe he thought he'd break it? It had been a long time since she held hands with a man.

"Come on, you two," Logan called from the entrance. "My taxi isn't going to wait forever."

****

They entered the pizza place, and, of course, Alex and Blake had arrived before them, and claimed a table. Blake waved them over, his hair bouncing every which way.

"Over here, Cagney. We've saved you seats." Alex appeared to be in her element. And that would make sense if she really were the creation of a romance novel. What heroine wouldn't love a movie and dinner? Cagney couldn't help but smile at her enthusiasm.

Blake stood when they approached and didn't sit until Molly and herself had sat.

"Anyone up for pineapple pizza?" He raised a brow.

"Are you crazy?" Logan made a gagging sound.

Blake shrugged. "Couldn't blame a bloke for trying."

They ordered a pizza—hold the pineapple—and drinks.

Logan brought a pitcher of beer back to the table.

"None for me," Cagney said as Logan poured Molly a glass.

"Me neither," Brad said.

"Yeah, Brad, I know. You don't drink. And

apparently your girlfriend doesn't either."

"But…"

Cagney shut her mouth. She was Brad's girlfriend in the eyes of the world. They even held hands tonight. Because that's what girlfriends do. What had she gotten herself into?

"There's no way you liked that movie." Molly shook a slice at her.

Thank you, Molly, for changing the subject.

"I'm as surprised as anyone," she said, "but it was good. It was solid entertainment."

"Personally, I didn't understand a bit of it." Alex took a bite of her pizza and looked thoughtful while she chewed.

"Love, it's a metaphor for our times."

Cagney looked over at Blake. "Really? Tell me more."

"It's obvious, the superheroes represent everyman."

"Everyman?" Logan put his beer down and leaned in. "What's an everyman?"

"And shouldn't that be everyperson?" Molly asked. "Let's not be sexist."

"The term is from a fifteenth century morality play but wasn't used generally until the start of the twentieth century." Blake's hair flounced as he spoke. Alex hung on his every word. And really, Cagney thought, what he said interested her.

"The term refers to the average, ordinary person. Everyman." He paused. "I suppose in today's parlance you could say everyperson, but it doesn't have the same ring."

"Blake." Alex tapped his arm. "Would you please

focus and get to the point."

"Bloody well. The point is superheroes perform these magnificent feats every one of us wishes we could. And by doing so, they don't just change the world, but save it."

Logan didn't take his eyes off the man during the entire recitation. Cagney couldn't tell if Blake's words or hair interested him more.

He paused and glanced around the table. "Who among us wouldn't want to save the world?"

"Oh, Blake. That's a great interpretation." Alex embraced him and kissed him on the cheek.

Molly nudged Cagney and whispered, "Where did you meet these two?"

"She's my advisor's cousin and her fiancé."

"They're different, aren't they?"

She nodded. *If you only knew how different.*

Chapter 16

Brad

Brad took Cagney's hand as they left the pizza shop and crossed the parking lot to his truck, mimicking the actions of both the other couples. Unlike the first time, he didn't ask her permission. It felt every bit as soft as he remembered and it sent an unfamiliar, but pleasing buzz of electricity through him. *Did that happen the first time? Is this normal?*

When they reached the truck, he contemplated opening the door for her. As if reading his mind Cagney said, "I'll get in on my own. It's not a big deal." When she pulled her hand from his, he sighed. "Besides, Molly believes that behavior is some antiquated vestige of male chauvinism."

"Okay. Good to know." He scratched his head. "I don't think I want to dwell on that too long."

Thank God, she laughed.

By the time he climbed into the truck, she was in the passenger seat. He closed the door, started the engine, then reached for the seat belt.

"That sure escalated fast." He fastened the belt.

"What escalated?" Cagney pulled her belt around her.

"The fake dating idea. I misjudged my roommate's enthusiasm at seeing me go out with a gir…uhm, woman."

He turned to her and raised a palm up. "Honestly, I only envisioned our pretend dating as a couple-days-a-week commitment, sitting across from each other working on our own stuff. Friday nights weren't in the equation. Nor weekends. Please believe me."

Cagney's seatbelt clicked and she laughed. Laughed? He'd been worried that at the end of the evening she'd call off the agreement. And she laughed?

"No worries. It's not your fault. Molly's ecstatic thinking I'm dating." She cocked her head and eyed him. "I'm not sure why she feels she needs to be my matchmaker."

"Don't look to me for an answer. I've got a matchmaker of my own."

He backed the truck out of the spot and exited the parking lot. He waited a few moments, hoping she'd say something else. She didn't. Excruciatingly painful silence filled the cab. His fake-dating scheme should have prevented this awkwardness. He racked his brain for a conversation starter.

"Blake and Alex are a curious couple. I mean, don't get me wrong, they're nice. Blake's a great guy. He just is almost too great." He stopped the truck for a red light. "It's almost as if he's some character out of a novel."

Cagney coughed.

"Are you okay? Do you want me to stop and find you some water?"

The light turned green, and he pressed the gas pedal.

She shook her head before she spoke. "No, I'm fine. I think I just swallowed air. I must be getting old or something."

"I didn't hurt your feelings by saying that, did I? I know they're your friends."

When he heard her laugh in response, his body relaxed. "No, technically, they're my advisor's cousin and fiancé. You're not hurting my feelings. They are different, yeah."

Silence. Again. Damn it.

"Brad?" Her tone sounded serious.

"What? Do you need that water, because I can pull over now and—"

"No, but I wanted to tell you something about Alex and Blake."

"Oh." Well, he just might have made a fool of himself. He sounded urgent there, even to himself. "What about them?"

She took a deep breath and took far too long to answer, in his opinion. What could she possibly have difficulty talking about?

"Alex and Blake were there when I texted you about accepting our fake-dating agreement."

He nodded. "And…?"

"They know our dating isn't real. They encouraged me to agree to it."

Out of the corner of his eye, he saw her looking his way.

Before he could comment, she continued.

"But they won't tell Molly or Logan. They'll keep it a secret."

"Well, I guess that will work." Their discrete arrangement was less discrete than he had thought.

"Brad? Are you mad? You're not saying anything."

"No, it's okay." He sighed. What else could he be? It's not like they could unknow it. "If it's only them, I think we'll be okay."

"Well, now that you mention it."

Brad glanced her way. "Does somebody else know? Who else knows?" He focused on the road again. Holy moley. Can this woman not keep a secret?

"My advisor, Dr. St. Clair. She knows."

He could barely hear her. He felt badly about his inward scolding of her. "She was there as well when I texted. But, of course, as my advisor, she couldn't encourage me to accept." She shrugged.

"Good to know she stayed neutral in all of this." He didn't mean for the words to come out as sarcastically as they did. But…

"Okay, I hate to ask this. Anyone else?" He ran a hand through his hair.

"Well, Dr. St. Clair dates Dr. Cooper so…"

"Who the hell is Dr. Cooper?"

"Another history professor? And my advisor's boyfriend?"

The words came out timidly. *My God, do I sound intimidating?* Thankfully, they were at her apartment complex. He turned into a parking spot, cut the engine, and turned to her. "I'm sorry. I didn't mean to come across as so angry about it. Forgive me."

Her eyes met his and she smiled. "It's so complicated. I'm sorry. But none of those people will let it leak to Molly and Logan. I can promise you that."

"I'm sure they won't."

She opened the passenger-side door. "Thanks for being my fake date tonight. I really did enjoy the movie." She smiled at him. Again. And something in his heart went fuzzy. What the hell?

"Oh, by the way,"—she opened her small purse—

"let me pay you for my portion of the bill. I don't want you to—"

He touched her hand. His heart beat louder. "No, I wanted to pay. Tonight was on me." He opened his door. "Let me walk you to your door, too."

"No, you don't need to do that."

Oh, yes, I do need to. "I just want to make sure you get in safely, that's all. I think that's what a boyfriend would do. Right?"

She nodded. "Okay. I guess so. But nobody's watching. There's no one to act like a boyfriend for."

Hmm, she had a point. What possessed him to insist?

They stood at her door. She had her key in her hand. Unsure of how to say goodbye, he shrugged. "I'll see you at the café next week?" His words came out as a question. Truly after tonight, he wouldn't be surprised if she did call the fake dating off.

"Of course."

"Well, goodbye." He took a step, then pivoted. Impulsively, he leaned forward and kissed her on the cheek. His lips tingled. "Uhm…see you Monday."

She opened the door as he stepped away. He heard the door close and lock. She was safe.

He climbed back into the truck. "What the hell happened when I kissed her? It felt like an electric current ran through my body. What is happening to me?"

Chapter 17

Cagney

The following Monday, Cagney was making herself a cup of coffee in the graduate student lounge.

"Your friends are amazing."

"Good morning to you, too, Molly." Cagney retrieved her cup from the coffeemaker. She took the few steps to one of the card tables and sat.

"Tell me again how you found them."

The table shook when she dropped her backpack on it. The coffee in the cup sloshed, spilling out. Cagney grabbed a napkin and wiped it up.

"I'm glad you like them. You can have them."

"You don't like them?" Molly headed toward the coffeemaker.

"I do. But I really didn't pick them. They picked me. Like I said, Alex is the cousin of Dr. St. Clair."

"She seems awfully devoted to Blake. I didn't know women in the twenty-first century displayed that kind of, well, I don't know what to call it."

Cagney recalled how Alex hung on every word Blake had spoken and how she literally hung on him.

Molly placed the cup in the machine and hit the button. "But they seem like the perfect couple, if you ask me. They could be models for a romance novel."

Cagney gagged. "Y-y-you think so? No, I don't think. No."

"Are you all right?"

Molly grabbed a napkin from the pile next to the sugar and cream and passed it to Cagney.

"I'm fine." She forced the words out. "It just went down the wrong pipe. I think I'm okay now. It seems to be happening a lot to me lately."

"Good, I'd hate to lose my best friend." Molly retrieved her coffee and sat next to Cagney. "Speaking of friends,"—she dragged the word friends out—"I'm dying to know how it went for you and Brad. You two seemed to enjoy yourselves."

Of course, Molly would ask. *Honestly, I'm surprised she didn't lead with it.*

"It was your first date. Did you do anything when you left?" Molly lifted an eyebrow.

"He took me straight home. It was, after all, our first date. I barely know the man."

But he did kiss me on the cheek. In private. He didn't need to do that. And, oh, God. I didn't dislike it. And there may have been just a bit of chemistry. Where did that come from?

"You're right. You've got plenty of time for that. Didn't I tell you Brad's a good guy?"

Cagney swallowed hard. "Yes, you did."

"Cagney, all I want for you is what I have with Logan. I know you've just met Brad, but he's Logan's roommate. He's smart and witty and well, I know how important it is for you to date someone who's intelligent."

Molly had a point, there. She had been drawn to intelligent men in the past. Brainpower was sexy. But my God, his brainpower lay in a totally foreign area from her interests.

Molly picked up her cup. "Don't tell Brad this,"—Molly's lips touched the mug, and she gazed over the cup at Cagney—"but Logan and I have been talking about moving in together."

"I-I'm happy for you." Cagney thought back to when Molly first met Logan. The relationship started out rocky. Personally, Cagney didn't care for Logan when she first met him. Perhaps she had just been overprotective of her friend. He hadn't done anything horrible like killing anyone. And he made Molly happy. This was the happiest she'd seen her in a long time.

Molly sighed. "Are you really? Because that didn't sound like a ringing endorsement."

"I'm sorry. I was just thinking back to when you first met. He put you through some 'things.' " Cagney gestured air quotes.

"Yes, he did." Her friend's tone softened. "We've worked through that, and our relationship has never been better." She stared down at her coffee cup. "And thank you for having my best interests at heart." The words came out as a whisper.

"Always."

Cagney picked her phone up from the table. "Time for class." She rose and grabbed her cup. "Not sure I have enough caffeine for a group of freshmen."

"I've got to get some papers graded. See you later."

****

Relief flooded Cagney once her twentieth-century history class ended. The students actually seemed engaged. But then, the topic of the counterculture of the nineteen-sixties and -seventies always sparked curiosity and conversation.

Next up, yoga. Boy, did she need it. The lying that

accompanied her new fake relationship already overwhelmed her. She had thought she could compartmentalize it. You know, only on such-and-such days at this-or-that hour, she'd sit across from Brad and be his girlfriend.

She didn't realize how this bogus dating scam would color her entire world. Or that Molly would be so frickin' enthusiastic about it that would be the sole topic of conversation. She prayed her friend's interest would wane, so she didn't have to feign loving Brad every minute of every day.

She walked into class determined to push past her newly found status. It was time to focus on the moment. Then she saw him. Brad doing pre-session stretches. What was wrong with this picture?

For starters, his presence in class. Again. Why? Because that's what he believed boyfriends did. But that paled in comparison to the three women—good-looking women—who stood around him.

Wait. What did he have on? She couldn't take her eyes off of him. He bent at the waist and the blue skin-tight yoga pants hugged his butt. Wow. As he stood, she noticed the T-shirt of the same color hung a bit looser on him, but then anything would be looser than those pants. Her eyes glanced at his butt again. Wowsa. *Stop it. You're not some sex-deprived bimbo.* She sighed. *No, you're a sex-deprived graduate student. And his...don't even think those thoughts.*

She walked closer but couldn't get through the women admirers. Brad could fake date any of them. That would be fine by her. She'd have to mention it to him.

"Brad," she began. The three women turned at the

same time. They eyed her. Then Brad turned.

"Cagney."

"You beat me here."

"I thought I needed to get some stretching time in. They"—he pointed to the women around him—"were helping me do it the right way."

"I'm sure they were."

Brad's cheeks were bright red.

"We'll go back to our spots now, Brad," one of the women said.

"Thanks, Sarah, I appreciate the lesson."

"Anytime, Brad."

This was like the third time the man was in class and he knew her name. She'd been in class for more than a year and didn't know anyone's name.

He walked over to her, a tea towel in hand. He looked every bit the part of a yoga student. That curl behind his ear moved ever so slightly.

"What do you think? Am I dressed okay? I wasn't sure what to wear, so Blake and I went out shopping Sunday. He said this would be the perfect set of clothing."

She chuckled thinking about Brad taking Blake's advice.

"What's so funny? Is this outfit not proper?" He scrubbed the back of his neck.

She tilted her head and studied the clothes on him from the front. Her breath hitched. She didn't know what to say. She didn't think she should tell him he was sexy. But truly he was. The attention from the women should have already told him that.

"I think you'll be able to do all the moves much more easily." She hoped that was noncommittal enough. She remembered her astonishment on their blind date of how he didn't look like a nerd, but she had no idea what type of body really lay under those jeans of his.

"But do I look okay?"

He took a step forward and said in a whisper, "Do I look like I could be your boyfriend taking yoga with you?"

The sincerity in his voice made her laugh. "You make me look like the girlfriend of someone taking yoga." She shook her head. "Any woman would be willing to have you as a boyfriend."

She nodded toward where Sarah and her two friends were milling about and occasionally looking in their direction. "Especially those women."

"You mean, they…"

"Yes, they were sizing you up as boyfriend material. I'm sure. And not in the fake way. You'd be the real deal."

Brad's face paled. "No, I could not have a relationship with any of them."

"Why not?"

"Just look at them." He shook his head. "They're so beautiful."

She glared at him. She was initially insulted. "What am I, chopped liver?"

He touched her shoulder, and her breath hitched. *Dammit.* "No, Cagney, I didn't mean that. I could never have a real relationship with you either. This fake thing we're doing is traumatizing me enough."

She laughed. "I traumatize you?"

"Good afternoon, class." Harmony walked into the room. "We'll be starting, so limber up."

Cagney turned her back to Brad and strode to her mat.

"Cagney, I—"

"We'll talk about it later."

Chapter 18

Alex

"You should have seen him, Cag." Alex sighed. She never had to worry about her relationship. "I've never seen his hair quiver so much. I'm telling you he's lying to me. Something's going on between him and Mary Jean."

She shoved the fry into her mouth and chomped as if she had a grudge against it. She replayed the scene at the Quad in her mind. She had seen Blake and that woman on the way over to the café to meet Cagney to study together. She had psych homework to do. Now it seemed inconsequential.

Cagney tilted her head. "I thought you said her name was Mariah."

She waved a hand. "Mary Jean. Mariah. It doesn't matter. What matters is the woman is gorgeous." She paused, fuming at how close they had been sitting on a regular sized picnic table. "And what matters even more is that she's out to get my Blake."

"Wait. How do you even know this woman's name?" Cagney furrowed her brows.

"I met her. Once. Blake introduced us...she seemed to study me. I can't explain it. I felt as if she were scrutinizing me. Maybe to see if I were good enough for Blake?"

She picked up another fry and studied it. She had

come to like Cagney in the short time they were in JJ's world. She liked everything in JJ's world. Except that somehow she began to doubt Blake's love for her. She didn't understand it. Now that their love story was finished and published, she hadn't worried about it. Should she be concerned now? It sure felt like it.

She looked Cagney in the eye. "Is this the type of uncertainty you feel in your world about love?" She shoved the fry into her mouth. She had always thought of love as being simple. And a happily ever after. This was the first time she considered that maybe she and Blake didn't have a happily ever after. She didn't like the feeling. Not one bit.

"Yes, it's what everyone in the real world feels at some point in a relationship. Fear that the other person doesn't love them."

"Is this why you don't want to get involved with Brad?"

Cagney heaved her chest.

Perhaps she had touched a nerve. Even in all her distress, Alex wanted nothing more than for Cagney to know the type of all-consuming love she and Blake have. Or had? The idea that Blake might be romantically interested in another woman gnawed at the pit of her stomach. Yeah, she now understood, at least in some small way, why JJ had balked about committing to Dr. Cooper. It might be the reason why Cagney resisted getting to know Brad.

"No. You know very well I have nothing in common with that man. And I'm busy with my doctorate."

Hmm. These answers sounded similar to the excuses JJ had given her. She sighed. She had her own man problems, apparently. How could this even happen? Her love life had been perfect.

She had been staring down at her Chernobyl Chicken Wrap. She lifted her eyes and gazed at Cagney.

"Is it even possible for Blake to find someone else attractive?" She shook her head. "And act upon it."

Alex leaned back in the booth. "Is this the end of Blake and me?"

"Don't be ridiculous. JJ wrote your love story. And it's a great love story. And only JJ can break you apart. You know that. You're worrying for nothing."

"Really? Are you sure?" She stared off into space. She knew it worked that way in her fictional world, but…

"I just don't know. They were sitting so close at the picnic table." Tears rolled down her cheeks. Damn, she had tried so hard not to cry. "And Cagney." She looked at her friend. "She was playing with his hair."

"Don't cry, Alex. Please don't cry."

"That's easy for you to say. You're dating someone you don't even care about. You wouldn't care if Brad saw another woman."

She picked up a napkin and blew her nose. What was she going to do?

"What if Blake decided he loved this woman—" Alex saw Cagney's disbelief in her eyes. "Hear me out." She wiped tears from her eyes with the back of her hand.

"And he left me. And then I'd be stuck in this world forever. Without him."

"Then Dr. St. Clair can write another love story for you with someone even better than Blake."

"There is no one better than Blake. Not in my world. Not in this world. Not in any world. We are made for each other." She placed her arms on the table and lowered her head into them. "I'm doomed. I'm really doomed."

****

Cagney

Cagney stared at the out-of-control Alex.

"Alex, please don't cry."

"You told me that before." She raised her head slightly. "And did that help? No. Here I am still crying."

Cagney didn't know what to do. Her first thought was to text Brad. He had Blake's number. No, that'd only make things worse, and Alex was upset enough. And honestly, if she had a boyfriend and thought he was cheating on her, she'd be just as distraught as Alex. The woman deserved a good cry.

She pulled a small packet of tissues out of her backpack. "Here, Alex. Take these."

Cagney looked nervously around. Alex was calling attention to herself. Alvin looked their way. She mouthed, "She's okay." *I'm sure he doesn't want to get involved with a crying woman.*

But she was incapable of handling this situation. Apparently, Alex was inconsolable. She felt everyone looking at them. She shifted her weight in her seat as her mind raced with options.

"That's it. I should have thought of that earlier."

Cagney picked up her phone and began to text. "The hell with that." She deleted the little she had and placed a phone call.

"Sorry to bother you, but Alex is having a

meltdown. Can you help?" Cagney crossed her fingers. "At the café, yeah. Thanks."

Alex raised her head and glared at her. "I told you I don't want to talk to anyone. Didn't you hear me?" She let out a sigh and buried her head in her hands again.

Dr. St. Clair stood at their booth fifteen minutes later. "I'm sorry to bother you with this." Cagney waved a hand toward the sobbing fictional character. "But I truly didn't know what to do." She scooched over on the bench and her advisor sat.

"It's fine. I know all too well what my characters are like. It sounded like an emergency."

Dr. St. Clair's elbows rested on the table. She leaned closer to her character. "Alex, talk to me. What's going on?"

"Blake doesn't love me anymore. He loves Mary Jean."

"It's Mariah," Cagney said.

"I don't care if her name is Petunia. Blake loves her and not me."

"Tell me, from the beginning, what you saw." Dr. St. Clair leaned back in the seat.

"Do I have to?" Alex's whine echoed throughout the café.

"Alex Zurich, listen to me. You're going to sit up, wipe those eyes, and tell me exactly what you saw. I'm sure there's a logical explanation for it."

Yeah, Cagney thought, like Alex is going to listen to her.

"Okay." Alex sat up, pulled the last tissue out of the pack Cagney gave her and handed the empty package back to her. She wiped her eyes and exhaled. Deeply. Then she recounted everything she had seen.

Everything Cagney had heard before.

Dr. St. Clair sat silent for a moment. Perhaps Alex was right. Maybe Blake could...

"Alex, listen to me."

Alex nodded ever so slightly. "Yes, JJ?" The tone was small and hesitant.

"According to the rules we followed during your last visit, I don't believe it's possible for Blake to be interested in anyone else. Not unless I write it into your story."

Hmm, that sounded right. Just when did she start believing in this fictional world story?

"If that's the case, what's he's doing with what's-her-face?" Alex glared at Dr. St. Clair. "And why was she playing with his hair? Answer me that, JJ?"

Her advisor shook her head. "I'm sure there's nothing between them. You said they were in the same class."

"Yeah, art history." The words huffed out of Alex's mouth. She leaned back.

Cagney feared Alex didn't believe Dr. St. Clair. That meant Alex wouldn't let up on the issue until she either confirmed Blake was cheating on her—which Cagney felt highly unlikely—or she knew why Mariah seemed fascinated with his hair. Either way, she didn't have time to babysit a heartbroken fictional character. Her own fake relationship already occupied too much of her time. And then she had to work on her dissertation. What had happened to her priorities?

Chapter 19

Brad

"I know it's not a real relationship. That would never work between us. We have nothing in common. But I don't want people whispering behind our backs, 'Why are they even together? They're such an odd couple.' " Brad took a sip of coffee and shook his head.

Blake sat across from him, nodding at his words.

"I need to know why women date. And then I want to become the man women—well, Cagney—would like to date. Because our pretend dating has to look real."

"Am I understanding you correctly?" Blake leaned in over the booth. "You want to make yourself more attractive to Cagney, but not because you want a real relationship with her."

Brad slapped the table. "Exactly. I knew you could help me. You have the perfect relationship with Alex. You too were made for each other."

"That's because…we were created…yes, we were made for each other. If you only knew."

"What do women like, Blake?"

Just at that moment, Craig Anderson, the quarterback for UNO's Fighting Fingers, sauntered into the café, wearing a T-shirt with the school colors of lime green and purple.

A collective sigh rose among the women.

"Man, he even looks good in our hideous school

colors." Brad shook his head. "And did you see the way he strutted? That man exudes confidence."

Blake turned to see what everyone was looking at. "All the women swoon over him."

Brad nodded. He wished he had the looks of the quarterback, and definitely the confidence.

"What makes—"

"Sports." Blake's hair bounced wildly. "That's it, Brad. We're joining a sports team."

"I'm a PhD student. I can't be joining any team. Besides, I've tried sports before. And I really don't want to wear the school colors. Please."

"What sports have you tried and not liked?" Blake had taken out his phone and appeared to be rapidly looking for something. "That way we can eliminate them right from the start."

Brad sighed. Reasoning with Blake appeared futile. He had to admit in high school, the jocks got all the girls. If he took up a sport, he would look like a guy that women—no, Cagney—would want to date. He shrugged. What could it hurt?

"I joined a community baseball team when I was nine."

"Baseball." Blake nodded. "The all-American sport. That's great."

"No, it wasn't great. I was waiting for my turn to bat. The kid ahead of me was on the plate. He swung, made contact with the ball, and threw the bat in my direction as he went to run the bases. It hit me right in my gut and knocked the air out of my lungs. I couldn't breathe. I thought I was going to die."

Blake winced. "Too bloody bad. Scratch baseball. What other sports have you attempted?"

"Basketball." Brad sighed. "My career in basketball in high school was short-lived. Like all of one practice." He took a sip of his coffee. Just the memory of it made his arm ache.

"What happened?" Blake put the phone down and gave the man his full attention.

"I was dribbling down court—at least, I think it was down court—lost the ball and somehow kept running and couldn't stop." He paused and bit his tongue. "Until I hit the wall."

"Bad luck."

"Yeah, it was. I broke my arm. It was in a sling for months and I couldn't enter the science fair." He didn't realize the pain had stayed with him all these years. "And Doug Dalton won first place." The injustice of it all.

Blake picked up his phone again and appeared to be scrolling. "I've found it," he said, perhaps a bit too loud, since nearby customers glared at him. He shook his head. "I've got it," he whispered and leaned over the table. "Tennis. Tennis is the perfect sport. Nobody's going to throw a bat at you and there are no walls to run into." He straightened up and smiled as if he had just discovered a new classification of rocks.

Brad ran a hand over his beard. "Do you know how to play tennis?"

"No, I don't. But we'll learn together. How hard could it possibly be?" Blake's hair shimmied with enthusiasm. "You're the one who wants to be a—"

"Yeah, yeah, don't remind me." Brad raised a hand. "Okay, I'll give it a try."

"Great. Meet me tomorrow morning at eight in…" Blake looked confused. "How about your office?"

"Fine." He didn't have office hours or yoga tomorrow, so he could waste his time learning to play tennis. This fake dating was sure taking up more time than he originally thought it would.

****

Blake

"Are you ready?"

Blake stuck his head into Brad's office.

This would redeem him. Alex would see he wasn't cheating on her. He had spent too much of last evening explaining to her he loved her and only her. His words rang hollow even to him because he couldn't reveal what he and Mariah had been up to. And yes, they had been up to something. But not what Alex thought. He lied badly. Disastrously, even. He only had to deceive Alex—he winced at the thought—a little longer.

Once Brad acknowledged him, he trudged in, carrying several large bags.

"What in the world is all that?"

"Tennis equipment and apparel, my dear man."

He dropped the bags on the floor and then dropped himself in a chair.

"I didn't realize how much energy one expended shopping." He ran a hand through his hair. "Ugh." He struggled to pull it out. He caught Brad smiling at him.

He disliked shopping, but this was for a good cause. Beyond getting Brad and Cagney together, this would get him back in Alex's good graces. Oh, God, at least he hoped so.

"But we're on a mission. To make Cagney fall in love with you." He rose.

"No, the mission is to make me look as if I could be her boyfriend. There's no way she'll ever fall in love with me." Brad paused. "Not that I want her to. We're just pretending. I want to make this all look as real as possible."

"Righto. I misspoke." Frankly, he couldn't see the difference for the life of him. Brad wanted to look like Cagney's boyfriend, but he didn't want to be her boyfriend. This world was so confusing.

"Nonetheless, I do believe I've purchased everything we need to make you look like you could be her boyfriend. Her tennis-playing boyfriend."

Blake picked up a bag and placed it on the desk. The handles of two tennis rackets stuck out. He pulled one out and handed it to Brad.

"Try it on for size," he said. "See how it fits you."

Brad twisted the racket in his wrist back and forth several times.

"Since I'm not sure how it should fit in my hand, I guess it's good."

"Great. Great."

Blake took the other racket out and tossed it from one hand to the other several times. "Yes, I think this will work...oops." The racket hit the lamp on Brad's desk. *Thunk.* It fell to the ground. "Sorry," he whispered. He looked around. "I didn't realize how small your office was."

Brad shook his head and set the object upright. "Don't worry. I've had this thing since middle school. I think it's indestructible."

"I've got the tennis balls in here." He picked up the bag and set it on the second chair in front of Brad's desk.

"Here we have our official tennis outfits." He lifted the other bag and set it on the desk. He pulled out a white collared shirt with three buttons at the neckline.

"What do you think?"

"It's a white shirt. What am I supposed to think?" Apparently, Brad didn't grasp the significance of the item.

"You'll look like a professional tennis player in this. And like an athlete. Which in turn will make you look—"

"Like Cagney's boyfriend." They recited the conclusion together.

Brad sat down. "Blake, I appreciate everything you've done. And I know it was my idea to become someone who Cagney would be seen dating. But honestly, I'm having second thoughts about this."

"Trust me on this one, Brad. This will work. Everyone will find it totally believable that Cagney is dating a tennis star."

"Whoa. I'm no tennis star. I'm barely a tennis wannabe."

Blake flicked his wrist. "Doesn't matter. A mere technicality. You only have to look as if you can play tennis."

Brad didn't answer immediately.

"I guess you're right. I do want to look like Cagney's boyfriend."

Blake pulled two pairs of white shorts out of the bag.

"Stop. Right. There. What the hell are those things?"

"Tennis shorts…no need to panic."

"Blake, I don't wear shorts. Ever." He rubbed his beard, his eyes wide. "I've never worn shorts…okay, one time." He held up his index finger. "Remember my disastrous basketball career in high school? All one day of it?"

Blake nodded. Where was this heading?

"I stepped out on the court. In shorts, because that's what basketball players wear, right? Well, I already I felt super self-conscious. Then I heard giggling. Female giggling. I looked in its direction and there were three girls pointing at me. Me!"

Brad sat down and put both hands on his head. "I had a crush on one of the girls. I was never so embarrassed in my life." He paused and looked up at Blake. "Actually, it was a blessing of sorts that I broke my arm and never had to wear a pair of shorts again."

"I'm sorry. That had to be awful." How was he going to get Brad in these shorts? "Brad, no one is going to laugh at you. All sorts of men wear shorts." He racked his brain for a better answer. "Besides, this makes you look like you're Cagney's boyfriend, right? And that's the whole purpose of this exercise."

"I guess you're right." Brad reluctantly picked up the clothes.

"That's the spirit." Whew, what a relief. "Let's go into the men's room to change. Then we can head over to the café. Alex said she and Cagney would be there."

Blake couldn't wait for Alex to see him. He had actually done something right. If their mission were to get Brad and Cagney together—and it was—then he had just taken a decisive step in the right direction. Alex would be proud of him. He was sure of it. And with any luck forget about seeing him with Mariah.

Chapter 20

Brad

"Look, Brad." Brad flinched as Blake slapped him on the shoulder. "All the women are looking at us. Women do like athletic men. I told you."

The two had entered the café in their new tennis apparel, rackets in hand. Brad's face warmed as he realized everyone was watching them. Of course, they were looking.

As Blake took long, confident strides toward the booth where Cagney and Alex were, his hair bouncing with every step, he whistled and twirled the racket like a majorette's baton. He appeared a man confident in his actions. That is, until he dropped the racket. *Ouch.* Brad bit his lower lip as he felt for his friend. He never realized how far one of those things could bounce.

"Oops. Bloody bad luck." Blake scrambled to retrieve it, seemingly unaware of the spectacle he had made. It landed near a booth occupied by two young women. One bent down, grabbed it, and handed it to him. She giggled as Blake took it.

"Sorry to disturb you, ladies." He nodded at them, his hair bobbing, and returned to Brad's side.

Now it was official. If every single person in this place had not been staring before, now they were watching their every move. His cheeks burned. A knot formed in his stomach.

Blake strutted over to where Alex and Cagney sat with a confidence that belied his hairy legs.

Brad followed, hesitantly. He couldn't figure out how this would help him look like he should be Cagney's boyfriend. But Alex loved Blake. That much he knew. And if that sort of thing worked for them, then perhaps this experiment had some merit.

"Blake." Alex jumped out of the seat and hugged her man. "You look so handsome. When did you take up tennis? It's not part of our story, is it? This is so exciting." She scrutinized the man, whose hair was still flouncing.

Cagney's lip was curled in a smile. "I didn't know you played tennis."

"I don't."

"What he means," Blake said, "is that we're still learning. It's a difficult sport in which to become proficient, but we can. Right, Brad?"

"Yeah. What he said." While this sounded good when Blake suggested it, the concept definitely lacked something in its implementation. If only he owned an invisibility cloak. If this was the attention jocks received, he'd rather stay a rock nerd.

"We want to invite you to one of our practice sessions."

What the hell did that man just say? No, he couldn't have…

They hadn't stepped foot on a court yet. Hell, they'd been in these stupid clothes for less than an hour. No. Hell, no.

"Don't you think it's rather soon for an audience?" Brad tightened his grip on the racket.

"No, no. Alex and Cagney will get to see master

sportsmen in the making. It'll be exciting." He waved his racket. Brad jumped backward to avoid getting hit in the gut.

Cagney gagged. Was it the master sportsman phrase? Because it made him want to gag, that's for sure.

"Dr. Townsend, I didn't know you played tennis."

That voice. It jangled his already strained nerves. When had Piper crept up on them? Brad's cheeks grew hot and he was momentarily speechless. "It's just something I'm fooling around with."

"I didn't mean to interrupt anything." She stared at Cagney. "I saw you here and thought maybe you can help me with…oh, Blake. I didn't recognize you dressed like that."

Piper stared at Cagney and then Alex.

"Oh, Cagney, this is Piper Kutte. She's a student with Blake in my geology class."

"Nice to meet you." Cagney smiled.

"Oh, where are my manners?" Blake shook his head. "This is my fiancée, Alex Zurich."

"Have you been playing for a long time?" Piper addressed the question to Brad.

"Playing?" What? "Oh, you mean this?" He raised his racket. "Not that long, no." He gripped the racket so tight his palm hurt.

"Piper, we're practicing tomorrow at the courts by the stadium. Three-ish?" Blake looked Brad's way evidently to confirm the time.

Brad nodded. "Yeah," he said quietly. "Three-ish. But we're really not—"

"Oh great. I'll be there." And she ran off.

Brad groaned. "Why did you do that?"

"Because she seemed interested that we played?"

"But we don't know the first thing about tennis. And besides, she's my student. I think we're blurring the lines of the teacher-student relationship."

"Oops. Sorry…wait, I'm your student too."

When did a simple pretend relationship get so complicated? Yoga? Tennis? Fraternizing with students?

"It's different with you," he finally admitted. He tried to think on his feet. "I met you before you were my student." He smiled. "Remember, we go way back," he said, referencing Blake's words to Piper, "and you're only auditing the course."

"Oh, yes, I had nearly forgotten that."

****

The following day at three-ish on the dot, Blake and Brad were standing on opposite sides of one of the several tennis nets the University of Northern Ohio's sports center on the south side of campus. Alex, Cagney, and Piper stood on the sidelines. Oh, no. Nearly three-quarters of the class came out to see this fiasco.

"Yay, Blake. You go."

"Take him down, Blake."

Brad wasn't sure how Blake had managed it, but he had befriended just about every one of his classmates and they all felt a distinct loyalty to him. Was he doing something wrong?

Blake strutted to the net, his hair bouncing, and waved at him. Brad had just opened a can of tennis balls, stuffed two into his pockets, and trudged over to meet him.

"Uhm. Do you know how to do this? I didn't think

we'd have such an audience," Blake said.

"Why did you make an announcement in class, then?" Brad's legs shook.

"The spirit just overtook me?" Blake's face was flushed, and it wasn't because of the April weather.

"I watched some videos last night." Subtext: Brad stayed up half the night studying videos out on his small balcony practicing his swing and stance. For a ruse that started because he thought Cagney should be seen with an athlete…

No use worrying about it now.

"I'll serve first. Then you just try to hit the ball back. Okay?"

Blake nodded, his hair bouncing.

Brad pivoted and strode toward the base line. Once in place, he nodded to Blake who had assumed a pose that at least looked like he knew what he was doing. Knees bent, elbows close, and the racket positioned in front of him diagonally.

Brad tossed the ball into the air with his left hand, just like he saw in the videos, and raised his right arm with the racket, first to the side and then behind his head. He mumbled the words to himself as he did it.

"Don't forget trunk rotation." He brought the racket down on the ball and pleaded with the gods of tennis it made contact. "Then the follow-through," he muttered, as he finished the swing.

The serve proved better than expected. The ball flew just inches above the net—just like in the videos. But he didn't have time to bask in a job well done. Once it made the single bounce on the other side, Blake met it, his hair dancing in all directions, and returned the volley.

The crowd cheered. Brad scrambled to his right to meet the ball and when his racket made contact and let out that sweet sound he had read about the night before, he breathed a sigh of relief.

They volleyed several times, each round greeted with delight. Brad swore he could pick out Cagney's voice out of the small group.

When Blake failed to hit a shot over the net, someone shouted—he thought it was Piper—"Fifteen, love."

Brad froze in place and shouted. "Practice. This is practice. We're not keeping score. I thought we made that clear."

The crowd booed. What crowd? These were his students. "That's it. We're done for the day." He had just played tennis in front of his students. What if a professor found out? Would he be kicked out of the program? Shit, his opponent, as it were, was one of his students. How did he let himself get in over his head like this? All over a fake relationship. Maybe he should rethink his priorities.

The crowd, no, the students, groaned and slowly began to disperse. "You were robbed, Blake," the surfer dude called as he turned to leave.

Brad strode to the bench at the end of the court and reached for a bottle of water. As he drank, Alex dashed to Blake on the other side of the court and threw herself at him. "You were wonderful out there." He smiled. True love, huh?

"You were amazing on the court, Dr. Townsend."

He had been so mesmerized by Alex and Blake he didn't see Piper approach him. "Were you ever a professional player?"

"No." He caught someone out of the corner of his eye. Cagney. She stood back and eyed Piper.

"Cagney, what did you think?" He smiled. A genuine smile he realized. He also realized he wanted, no, needed, to know her opinion.

"Is that your sister?" Brad had forgotten for a moment his student was still there.

"No, she's my girlfriend." The words came out easily and felt right. *My pretend girlfriend*, he reminded himself.

****

Cagney

Cagney blushed when Brad referred to her as his girlfriend. She also felt the heat of Piper's stare.

"When you introduced me to her yesterday, I thought she was your sister. You didn't introduce her as your girlfriend. I didn't know you had a girlfriend."

He doesn't, Cagney thought.

"Why should you? You're my student. I'm your instructor. You really don't need to know anything about my personal life."

The anger in his voice surprised her. She had never seen this side of him.

Piper pivoted and walked toward Cagney. "He's mine," she whispered as she brushed her shoulder against hers. "Stay away."

"Brad, Cagney." She turned to where Blake's voice was coming from. He and Alex were surrounded by several students. "We're headed for the Physics Café. You guys coming?"

Brad looked to her. "You go, if you want, but I'm tired. I'm going home." He slid his gaze to Cagney. "I hope that's okay."

"That's very okay. I'm going home, too. You get some rest, you tennis star."

****

Cagney

Cagney plopped onto her couch and stared at the ceiling. "What a long day." The tennis practice. "What was that all about?" Why had Brad taken an interest in tennis? It had to be Blake's influence. She was sure of it. But to what end?

She counted the cracks on her ceiling as she tried to push everything out of her mind. Especially Piper. She didn't need the jealousy she threw around. Piper could have Brad, as far as she was concerned.

"No." She shook her head, her mind still tallying up the broken lines of paint. "Piper isn't the right girlfriend for him." She stopped herself. "Why do I even care if he dated someone who wasn't right for him?"

She had serious academic work to contend with. She didn't need to be wasting her time with Brad's choice of girlfriend.

Just a few short weeks ago she didn't even know Bradley Townsend existed. And for the first few days she did know of his existence, she referred to him by another name. What had changed?

Come to think of it, when the hell were Alex and Blake going to whoosh off to their own world? She had been fake dating long enough. She found herself fully entrenched in the outlandish experiment. They could leave any time. Maybe she'd talk to Dr. St. Clair about that.

There seemed to be more cracks in the ceiling. Or maybe she was tired and seeing double. She pushed herself up from the couch and went into the kitchen to make macaroni and cheese for supper.

Chapter 21

Brad

"Dr. Townsend, you were awesome on the tennis court the yesterday."

Piper's praise as he walked into class the next day shouldn't have startled him, but it did.

"Blake was a worthy opponent."

That was surfer dude. He looked toward Blake in the seat in the next aisle and nodded as he said, "You both were good."

Blake turned and high-fived the surfer dude. "Thanks."

"When are you playing again?" Piper asked.

"Excuse me?" Brad looked at Piper then Blake.

"I want to watch. I love watching men play tennis." She smiled and tilted her head.

"Uhm, I'm not sure." He looked to his new British friend, the one who got him into this mess, hoping he would offer assistance.

"Any time you're ready, Brad." Blake's hair bounced as he nodded. "I think we're developing nicely in our tennis prowess."

Damn, that wasn't the response he wanted.

"That's enough talk about tennis. It's time to talk geology." He should never have lost control of the class. Again. When would he learn to keep control of it? There must be an online on the subject he could watch.

"We're talking about plate tectonics." He realized he hadn't even set his backpack down. He did so hastily, then strode to the whiteboard to write the topic down. "Can anyone tell me what it is?" He pivoted and looked at his students. Most of them had their heads down scribbling something into their notebooks. He prayed it was class related.

Blake raised his hand. "Blake, go ahead."

Blake shifted the weight in his seat. "It's the theory that the Earth has layers, a rigid outside layer that covers another more moldable inner layer."

"That's exactly right."

Piper raised her hand. Brad winced. "Yes?"

"From what I read last night, is it correct that the outer layer is called the"—she bit her lower lip and looked up at the ceiling—"the lithosphere?" The word came out slowly as if she were recalling each syllable.

"Yes, Piper. Very good. That's exactly what it's called." Maybe she was attending the tutoring program. He always loved it when people understood the earth.

Piper sat up taller in her seat and gave a quick glance to the woman who sat to her left. Brad couldn't help but notice she pulled her already too-low blouse down just a tad more.

"Does anyone know what the lower layer is called?"

"I know. I know." Piper raised her hand and shook it. She probably did get the tutoring. Good for her.

He nodded toward her. "It's called the"—she hesitated only a moment—"as-then-o-sphere." Her head bobbed with the pronunciation of each syllable. Maybe he didn't suck at teaching.

****

As the students filed out of class, Blake hung back. "Meet you at the café." He nodded. Brad smiled at the man's hair. He wondered who told him it looked good on him. Then he thought, it must be a good look; Alex loved it. "I'm meeting Alex at her psychology class and we'll be at the café soon."

"Absolutely. I'm looking forward to talking to Cagney." Wait. Did he just say that? The man who couldn't talk in front of women. The man who barely spoke to her on their blind date. When did that happen?

As he shoved the textbook and his notes in his backpack, he wondered what she thought of the tennis practice. He endured that torture so he could be the type of guy a woman, no, Cagney would date.

****

The moment Brad opened the door to the Physics Café he sensed something felt amiss. Several steps in and he heard it. A low-level murmur permeated the air.

"There he is." "That's him all right."

He glanced around to see who "he" was. But he didn't see anyone.

"God, he's even more handsome in person."

Brad walked up to the booth that he and Cagney had claimed as their own and placed his laptop case on the table.

"I want to take tennis lessons now." A women's voice said from…where exactly? And why?

He glanced around again, only this time self-consciously. He searched the tables and booths for Blake.

"You're being paranoid. It's just a coincidence they mentioned tennis. Lots of people play tennis." No

129

one outside of his class knew he played yesterday.

"Go on up and talk to him."

They're looking this way. They can't be looking at me. No, they're not. He sat down. Where was Cagney? Why wasn't she here yet?

He opened his laptop and waited for it to boot. The murmuring continued. He called up a document and stared at it.

"It really is him. Did you see that form of his on the court?" Where was that coming from? He wished Cagney would arrive.

"Oh, look. There she is." He worked hard to concentrate on the journal article on soil erosion, but dammit, that voice was loud.

"That's his girlfriend." While spoken in a hushed tone, it certainly was loud enough for everyone to hear. Whose girlfriend? He promised himself he wouldn't look up again. Nothing made sense.

"Hi, Brad." Relief washed over him. It would be all right now.

"Cagney." He stood and kissed her on the cheek.

"Oooh." Women's voices chorused.

Cagney's cheeks grew red. Did he do something wrong? She hadn't blushed like that since that first time, when he couldn't decide how to greet her.

"What's going on, Cagney?" he asked as she settled into the other side of the booth. "Ever since I stepped in, people have been making references to tennis." He scanned the room again. It seemed like far too many people appeared to be looking at them.

"You didn't see it, then?" She took her laptop out of her backpack.

"See what?"

"The video." Was she purposely not looking at him?

"What friggin' video?"

She sighed as if she were annoyed.

"I'm sorry. But I don't know what you're talking about."

She pulled her phone out of the pocket of her jacket and started scrolling.

"This one." She handed him the phone. Was she smiling?

He stared at the video in disbelief. It had already begun to play. Someone—he probably knew who—had recorded him playing tennis yesterday. He watched it once, then again. He winced at his serve. He watched himself run across the court.

He handed the phone back to Cagney with only one word: "Piper."

While he hadn't wanted to believe she wanted more than just tutoring, her comments in class earlier seemed to confirm his worse fears.

"Did you read the comments?" She handed the phone back. "Read the comments."

He took the phone and clicked the proper section. "Where has this man been all my life? And you mean he's here at the University of Northern Ohio?" His cheeks burned.

"Wow. He's perfection." He looked up at Cagney. He wondered what she thought about this.

"I don't know what to say." He gave her the phone back. This time she stuffed it in her pocket.

"Why would Piper do that?" He sighed. He couldn't judge Cagney's reaction. He had only taken up tennis to be a believable boyfriend. Fake boyfriend. He didn't need this type of attention.

"She's infatuated with you." Her answer was flat. He couldn't gauge her feelings. She could be anything from bemused to angry.

"I'm sorry." He didn't know what else to say and the silence bothered him.

"Don't be. It's not your fault." She almost smiled.

He looked at the keys of his computer, then met her eyes. "Did I embarrass you?"

Cagney laughed. "No, but I knew you would be mortified when you saw it. Are you okay?"

"I'm embarrassed, that's for sure. But other than that, I'm fine."

She put her elbows on the table and cocked her head. "Can I ask you something?"

He shrugged. "Sure. Anything."

"Why did you take up tennis? Did Blake talk you into it?"

He leaned back in the bench and considered his reply carefully. "I'll tell you, but it's going to sound stupid." He raised a hand. "Please keep your judgment to the end." That brought a smile out of her.

"I wanted to do something so people thought I was your real boyfriend." He explained the conversation he had with Blake. "Blake came up with the idea of tennis. Before I knew it, I was so far in I couldn't get out."

She nodded slowly. "I'm not sure I understand the logic, Brad." She scanned the room. Interestingly, the murmuring had quieted some.

"You did accomplish one thing." She raised an eyebrow.

"What was that?"

"You are the boyfriend every woman on campus

now wants."

He groaned. "That wasn't what I wanted. I just wanted people to believe we could be a couple. All I've done is called attention to myself." He paused. "In shorts, yet."

"It's social media, Brad. By the weekend, some other video will grab people's attention and go viral. Mark my words, come Monday, no one will be talking about it. You'll be back to being an anonymous PhD student."

"You're probably right. Of course."

****

Cagney

Cagney arrived at her yoga class early Monday. She needed a bit more stretching time after her sedentary weekend at the library. They really should rent out cots for grad students, she thought, as she sat on the floor, legs extended out. That way—her right hand reached for her right knee—she could just camp out Saturday night.

"There he is." "Finally." "I thought he wouldn't show."

Cagney turned to see who they were talking about. Could it be? Brad had just entered the room. Just entered. The man wasn't more than two steps beyond the door when Sarah and her two friends who typically fawned over him led the group of women that met him there.

"Brad, you never told me you played tennis." Sarah's voice sounded sickeningly sweet.

"You know, I love to play tennis," another woman said.

"Do you think you can teach me to play?"

She stared at what could only be called a mob scene, her mind not fully absorbing the situation. Brad looked as if he tried to move forward. Some woman in deep purple leggings and a sports bra blocked his way.

"I've got to help him." She jumped up and sprinted toward the group.

When she got to the fringe of the mob, she cleared her throat. "Excuse me, ladies." Everyone stopped to look at her. "I hate to burst your romantic bubbles, but"—she inched her way into the group and closer to him—"if anyone is taking tennis lessons from this man it's me."

She now stood next to him. She had turned on her full fake-girlfriend mode. She stood on her tiptoes and gave Brad a kiss on the cheek. His beard tickled her lips. In return, he put his arm around her and pulled her closer. Her heart hitched.

"After all," she said, "I am his girlfriend." She took a deep breath. Fake girlfriend, she reminded herself. "Now, if you'll excuse us, we have a yoga class to attend."

She took a step and the women allowed her through. Most were dispersing, but not without some griping. "How did she get that guy?" "What makes her so special?" "I'm sure she was just in the right place at the right time."

"I tried to get through, Cag." She felt his soft breath in her ear. "They wouldn't let me."

They had made it to her mat safely. No woman approached them. She felt as if she had just saved a wounded, stray puppy.

Brad dropped to the ground and sat cross-legged. He shook his head. "I thought you said everyone would forget about the video over the weekend. It appears these ladies didn't get the memo." His lip lifted slightly as if he were trying to smile.

"Apparently not." Cagney sat next to him. "But I think your experiment worked." She touched his knee, and her hand tingled.

"Really? How did it work? This has been nothing but a disaster from my viewpoint."

"Tell me again. Why did you take up tennis?"

He sighed. "To look like the boyfriend a woman would want."

She laughed.

"Oh. My. God." He scanned the room. While many of the women were busy stretching or talking among themselves, several still eyed him. "You mean all those women would take me as a boyfriend?" He shook his head.

She nodded. "It appears your experiment worked beyond your wildest dreams."

Chapter 22

Cagney

"It's happened. It finally happened."

Cagney had just taken one sip of her morning I've-got-freshmen-to-teach coffee and barely had one eye open, when Molly burst into the graduate student lounge. It was a Monday morning. Whatever happened had better be good. She was not ready to be social.

Molly sat herself next to her at the card table and stared at her with those green eyes. They sparkled this morning. Nothing should sparkle this early on a Monday morning. She looked like a puppy expecting a treat.

"What happened?" Cagney barely got the words out.

"You're not going to believe this." Molly bounced in her seat. She hadn't seen her this excited since…she and Logan decided to become serious. This has to do with Logan, then. Had she more coffee in her she probably could have guessed, but she hadn't had her quota of caffeine yet.

"Logan and I found an apartment we both love and we're moving in together."

Cagney felt her friend's eyes bore on her. She put her mug down and leaned over to hug her friend. "That's wonderful news, Molly. I'm so happy for you."

And she truly was. Molly had a lot to live up to

academically. With both parents award-winning historians, she had to be under considerable pressure to excel. Cagney smiled as she thought about her friend's milestone in her personal life. She knew her friend thought Logan was "the one." The one she would marry and have children with. Cagney had never seen her this animated.

"Where is this amazing apartment?" She held her friend at arm's length. With Molly's red hair wrapped in a ponytail, she looked young and idealistic. Cagney hoped this next step in her friend's life proved to be positive. Something in the back of her mind niggled that this might be where Molly gets her heart broken. She thought back to the beginning of her friend's relationship with Logan.

Cagney shook off the idea. Why would she think that? Was she jealous? No. Did she wish her friend misfortune? Certainly not. But Molly went into every new adventure with such high hopes. Like the time she applied for a grant to study suffragettes of the early nineteen hundreds. She should have been a shoo-in. She had an extensive background. And of course, she had the name. Her parents' name.

Another grad student had won the award, probably equally as deserving, but the loss devastated her. Molly convinced herself her academic career had come to an end and her mom and dad would disown her. Cagney didn't want to see her friend go through a crisis like that again, especially when it involved her personal life.

"It's off campus. On Buell Avenue. It's not far of a drive. We decided we wanted something far enough away from the university so we felt like adults. We want our parents to take our relationship seriously and

137

that's hard to do when you live above a bar."

Molly had a point there.

"Our apartment complex is at the end of the street. Most of it has modest homes. The last two blocks have these amazing fourplexes. I think it will be perfect for us."

"I'm so happy for you both."

"You and Brad have to come to our apartment-warming party. Brad agreed to help Logan move the furniture Saturday, so the following Friday evening we thought we'd have people over and show it off."

Molly's words rolled out of her mouth, as if she wanted to share her joy as quickly as possible.

"I'll be there." That, Cagney thought, tested their friendship. She hated parties, but she couldn't very well decline her best friend's event.

But with Brad? Molly had just assumed Cagney would be going with him. But of course, she did. That's what everyone saw. So far, not a single person questioned their so-called relationship. Not one person thought it odd they were dating and had nothing in common. Absolutely nothing in common, she reminded herself.

Cagney hadn't been fake dating Brad that long. It still didn't feel completely comfortable. She wondered if it would ever feel right. She doubted it. So much deception. And Molly and Logan's apartment-warming party wouldn't help her feel at ease in this charade.

"I know you're not a party person," Molly said, as if she had read her thoughts, "but I'm inviting Alex and Blake too. You guys seemed to have formed a real bond. And they're so much fun to be around."

"Yeah, that they are." She tried to manage a smile,

but even she thought it weak. She knew she didn't fool Molly. Not only would she have to pretend to be Brad's girlfriend for the night, now she had to deal with two fictional characters who wanted the relationship to get real.

"I've got class to teach." Cagney rose and grabbed her coffee. She hoped teaching freshmen about Watergate would take her mind off her own issues. "I'm so happy for you, Molly."

"Oh, my." She pulled her phone out of a pocket. "I have a meeting with Dr. Conrad about my thesis." She rose so fast the chair nearly toppled. "Oh, Cagney, if you see any good boxes around here for moving, would you save them for me?"

And she was out the door.

Hopefully, Molly wasn't making a mistake.

Chapter 23

Alex

"Cagney, look. Look over there."

Alex stopped dead in her tracks as she and Cagney were crossing the Quad to meet JJ. She clenched her teeth.

She pulled at Cagney's arm to physically position her in the right direction. "There"—she pointed at a picnic table under a large maple tree—"that's my Blake with that woman." She took several deep breaths. Her chest ached. "Again."

"That's the woman he calls Mariah." She took another deep breath. "See, I didn't imagine anything. You can see it with your own eyes now."

Her universe had cracked. Wide open. How could this have happened?

The first time she had caught Blake with that woman he said they had been just studying. That's all it was, she told herself. Two people studying. After all, their love story was written. And printed. And shipped to hundreds of thousands of readers. It included no beautiful, blonde woman named Mariah sitting on a picnic table with Blake, their knees touching.

Blake said something Alex couldn't hear and the woman laughed. "She's laughing a bit too hard, don't you think?"

She turned to Cagney, who stood frozen, her mouth

open. "Well, what do you think?"

"They're a good distance from us. That doesn't look like Blake to me."

"Cagney, don't lie." She stomped a foot. "That's Blake. Look at that hair." Her body quivered. "What am I going to do?"

"Okay, it's Blake." Cagney sounded exasperated. "But he told you they're studying. That's all. Nothing else is happening."

"You can't say that. Look at them! It sure looks suspicious to me." She glanced over at the two of them. They looked cozier by the minute. "I thought we had a happily ever after together." She bit her lip. She felt lightheaded. "What happened to that?" The words came out slowly and quietly.

The Mariah woman pulled a notebook out of her backpack and wrote something down. She handed it to Blake. When he saw it, he smiled. Much too widely for Alex's liking. He handed it back to her. They still sat too close.

She sniffled. When did she start crying? She strode in their direction. "I've got to see what's…" Her feet moved but her body didn't.

"Cagney. Let go of me." Alex tried to shake herself out of the hold.

"No. You're not going over there." The grip only tightened.

Alex glared at her. "You can't stop me. That's my boyfriend who looks like he's a bit too friendly with…Oh. My. God. She's playing with his hair. She can't do that. I am the only person allowed to play with his hair."

She tried to wriggle out of Cagney's hold again but

couldn't. For a short person she was strong.

"Listen to me, Alex Zurich. You are not going over there. When you get home tonight, you'll mention—in a calm and sane manner—that you saw the two of them again. I'm sure he'll have a perfectly good explanation."

Alex thought this over for a moment. "Yeah, maybe you're right. Maybe I should wait till tonight. That way, there won't be any witnesses when I kill him."

Cagney sighed. Dramatically.

"What the hell was that about? Do you think I'm overreacting?"

"I didn't say that."

"No, but that sigh did. It sounded like something straight out of a romance novel." She tried to smile. "And you know I'm the expert on romance novels. You just better tell me what you really think."

Alex took her eyes off Cagney to see what Mariah and Blake were up to now. Again, those knees were touching. They had a book open in front of them and appeared to be enjoying its contents immensely. What were they reading?

"This is getting worse by the minute." She whipped her head toward Cagney to be sure the woman saw what was happening. First the hair and now this…this…whatever this was. "That looks intimate to me. How about you?"

Cagney let go of Alex's arm. "I can't say what it looks like." Her words were quiet and evenly paced. "Not knowing the full context of the setting."

"For crying out loud, Cag. I don't believe you." Warm tears streamed down her cheeks and reached her mouth. Salty.

"Can't you at least admit it looks a little suspect? It looks like more than just studying. He knows I'm concerned with this." She waved her hand in the direction of Blake and Mariah still looking far too friendly on the picnic table. "He's never talked about her. Why do you think that is?" She crossed her arms over her chest.

"Because she's not important to his life." Cagney nodded.

"Oh, no, you're not getting away with that line."

"I think I am, Alex. Let me tell you something." The woman pointed a finger at her. Not exactly in Alex's face because of the height difference, but that finger wagged away.

"Every single time I'm with Blake, he talks about you. Every. Single. Time. He doesn't talk about that person. Whoever the hell she is." She pointed toward the picnic table. "That tells me everything I need to know about the man's priorities. Or should I say priority? Singular." Alex swore heat radiated off Cagney, she was that intense.

"You. You are Blake's priority. His only priority. Do you understand?" She paused. Alex snuck another peek at what was happening at the picnic table. They were gone. Blake and the blonde had left while she was arguing with Cagney.

"Darn, they're gone. Now I can't follow them. See what you did, Cag?"

Cagney laughed. "I didn't do anything. You'll talk to Blake tonight in a calm and adult manner."

Alex sighed. "Yes, you're right." Could it be she was overreacting? Cagney made a good point. Their love story was written and printed. Nothing could reverse that, unless…

"What if JJ is working on a sequel of our story where Blake leaves me? Maybe that's what we saw?"

"That is the stupidest…" Cagney began. "…wait. There's only one way to find out. Where were we going? Dr. St. Clair's office. Let's get over there and see if she's writing Blake out of your life."

"Brilliant idea, Cagney. Let's go." She pulled Cagney as she headed for JJ's office.

****

Cagney

"JJ. JJ. You need to help me." Alex stood in front of the professor's desk, hands on her hips.

"Please, Dr. St. Clair, you need to help me too. This woman physically dragged me across the Quad to get to you." Cagney straightened her T-shirt.

"What's wrong, Alex? You look upset."

"That's the understatement of the century." Cagney glared at the fictional character.

"I'm choosing to ignore that comment." But she wasn't beneath sticking her tongue out at her.

"Both of you, just stop." Dr. St. Clair took a deep breath. "Now, tell me what's going on."

"Are you working on a sequel to Blake and mine's love story?"

The professor cocked her head. "You mean the one where you want me to make you a psychologist."

"No, I'm talking about the one where Blake leaves me for some blonde." She slammed her fist on the desk. "Because I just saw it play out in the Quad moments ago." She pointed toward the door, then the window, then just threw her hands up in the air. "I'm not sure what direction the Quad's in."

Dr. St. Clair sighed. Deeply. "Haven't we been through this before, Alex? First, I couldn't write that story even if I wanted to. You two are the most popular couple I've ever written about. My fans would kill me."

Alex took a step back from the desk. "Are you sure?"

Dr. St. Clair pinched the bridge of her nose. "I'm sure. I know what I'm working on now and it has nothing to do with you and Blake."

Alex opened her mouth.

"Don't even say another word. I'm not breaking you and Blake up. And that's the only way Blake would be unfaithful to you. You have to believe me." She took a deep breath. "And have faith in Blake. Do you really think he could be happy with anyone else?"

"All right, JJ. I'm trying to believe you. And Blake."

Chapter 24

Blake

"You told me the other night in bed she meant nothing to you."

Alex's appearance, apparently out of thin air, startled Blake. He jerked his head up, which caused him to completely forget the factors needed to determine plate tectonic movement.

She hovered above the booth Blake and Brad sat in. If he didn't know and love her, he would say she looked menacing. His brows raised, he opened his mouth to speak, but didn't get the chance.

"You told me she was someone from your art history class. But I saw you guys again. In the same damn spot. Same damn picnic table. And you guys looked way too friendly for just classmates."

Blake didn't pick up on a lot, but he knew the word classmates came out sarcastically.

Damn. Not again. This could ruin everything.

"Like I said—"

"What the hell are you doing with her?"

He ran a nervous hand through his hair only for it to get tangled in the underbrush. "We're studying, love." That wasn't a total lie. They were studying. It just wasn't the class materials.

She crossed her arms and tapped her foot. His words did nothing to allay her fears. And hell, why should they? He had to admit that his actions looked suspicious. Immensely suspicious. He was sure he'd doubt Alex if she'd pull a stunt like this. He wanted so much to tell her the truth.

Instead, he slid his body down the bench and patted the place he had occupied. "Art class is fascinating. Did you know that Van Gogh studied books on color theory and that's why—"

"I don't care about Van Gogh and his colors. I care that I saw you with a woman—a beautiful woman—on a picnic table. Again. And it looked like you were having fun."

"I'm sure you're hungry. Brad and I were just about to order."

"You're distracting me. I learned about this in psychology class. You're trying to make me forget about what I'm mad about."

Blake's cheeks grew hot. "I may be. But I know you're hungry. And I'm trying to say you have nothing to worry about. I love you. And only you."

He did. He loved her with every ounce of his soul. This woman couldn't be more his soulmate than if someone had handpicked her…wait. Someone did handpick her. JJ. She knew exactly what type of woman he needed.

"I love you too much to hurt you."

She sat slowly. "I don't know. You two looked—"

He turned his head. "Didn't you have a study date with what's-his-name from your psychology class not too long ago?"

"Greg. Greg Melfour."

"And did I get jealous and ask you what you two were doing?" He crossed his arms and glanced at Brad to see if he was watching. Of course, he was. If his smile was any indication, the man found his troubles quite enjoyable.

Alex shook her head. "Of course, you didn't. Because Greg is three inches shorter than me, wears two-inch thick glasses, and makes Alvin and the guys look like Hollywood leading men."

She did have a point there. Absolutely no competition.

"See. I wasn't jealous. No need for you to be either." Bloody hell, she didn't buy that.

Alex huffed out some unintelligible word. He was scared to ask her to repeat it. He tried so hard to be circumspect. Not once, but twice, she'd spotted them on the Quad. At different hours of the day. The first time he thought Alex would be in psychology class. And this time? She should have been in her journalism class.

How did he misjudge the timing so badly? Twice. *Blake, you need to be more careful.*

"Love, I'm sure Brad doesn't want to hear about this. Why don't we all get something to eat?"

"You're doing it again, Blake Teesdale." He recognized the controlled anger in her voice. "Trying to distract and appease me." She ran a hand through her hair.

"Tell me you'll never see Mary Jean—"

"It's Mariah."

"Tell me you'll never see Mariah again."

Blake closed his eyes. "How can I promise that, love? She's in my class. I see her every day."

He pulled her close. Her body was tense. "You've got to know I only have eyes for you. It's you I love. And always will. Need I remind you our love story is complete?"

Alex sighed. Her face softened. "It is, isn't it?" She looked up at him and kissed him on the cheek. "JJ made sure of that." His body trembled. He didn't deserve a woman as beautiful as Alex.

"What does Dr. St. Clair have to do with your relationship? I'm lost." Brad's question startled him.

He froze. Alex's body stiffened in his arms. She held him tighter. "Well, uhm, it's just that…"

Come on, brain, start working. You can come up with something.

"She introduced us. And she told us we'd be perfect for each other. Didn't she Blake?"

He looked down at her eyes. He loved her beautiful emerald eyes. "Why yes. That's right. She introduced us."

"I know you're Dr. St. Clair's cousin." Brad pointed at Alex. "But how did you meet her?"

Brad's index finger felt like a dagger to his heart. First, he was lying to Alex. Now the lies were multiplying and he had to lie to Brad. *Will it ever stop*? Of course, on a fundamental level he lied to everyone who thought he was a real person. He lived a charade in this world.

"I met JJ at a history convention. That's right. I was working on campus and was curious about her theories." He ran a hand through his hair. Damn. It got caught in there. Again. He carefully disengaged it as he continued. "I'm sure Cagney has told you about her exceptional ideas on conspiracies in American history. They're groundbreaking."

Brad bit his lip. Hopefully, the man was considering the matter. Perhaps, he was just paranoid.

Nothing good ever came from lying. He hoped he didn't have to do it much longer.

Blake spoke before the man could call him on the statement. "How about a cup of Manhattan Project Clam Chowder, love? Brad, are you ready to order?"

Chapter 25

Brad

Sweat dripped from the tip of Brad's nose. The old sofa grew heavier in his arms by the minute. He and Logan carefully navigated the steps to his friend's new apartment. Logan pulled the piece of furniture up the stairs, while Brad held up the rear.

"I guess you couldn't find an apartment on the street level." He huffed out the words. He hated moving.

"I tried." Logan's words came out ragged. "I really did. Just to avoid this."

Logan sounded just as exhausted as he did. Luckily, after this, they could crash.

The narrow stairwell made it all the more difficult to navigate the large piece of furniture. Logan paused. Brad craned his head around the couch to determine why. He couldn't see much except the old upholstery tacks in the garish yellow flowered arms of the sofa.

"It's the turn. I have to readjust my grip."

Brad sighed. What he didn't do for friends. One day, I'll be moving and I'll need help, he thought.

Brad bent and lowered his end of the couch while Logan fixed his grip. In a matter of moments, he was climbing the stairs again.

"We're in the hallway now," Logan announced.

As if he couldn't figure that out.

"Last leg here."

"I'm glad because I'm ready to drop it right here."

Molly waited for them at the door. As they brought the furniture in, she backed up.

"Right here. I think it would be perfect, don't you, honey?"

Logan grunted. "It's heavy. I'm happy to have it anywhere but in my arms." He nodded to Brad, and they maneuvered themselves and set the sofa down.

Logan immediately fell into it and Brad followed.

"I can't wait for our apartment-warming party next Friday." Molly seemed quite indifferent to their exhausted plight.

"Honey, do you think you could get Brad and me a bottle of water? We're too tired and sore to move."

"Of course. How inconsiderate of me." She strode to the galley kitchen adjacent to the living room.

"She's excited," Logan whispered. "New place and all. She's nesting."

"I heard that, Logan Adams. I'm right here." She pivoted and glared at the men over the counter that divided the rooms. Each hand clutched a bottle of water.

Were they kidding each other or was this a real squabble? Because if it were real, he might die right here from thirst while they had their stare-down. *Don't be stupid, Brad.* Were most couples like his? Certainly, he and Cagney didn't carry on like that, but they weren't a real couple. *Would we be like that if we were really dating*? Wait…where did that come from?

"Brad." Molly's voice interrupted his thoughts. "The water. Take it."

"Sorry. I was thinking about other things." He took

the bottle and wasted no time in opening it and chugging it.

"Were you thinking about the time when you and Cagney would be sharing an apartment?" Logan jabbed him in the arm. Molly sat on the arm of the sofa next to Logan.

"N-no." Brad choked. "T-that wasn't on my mind."

"Don't put any pressure on him." Molly slapped Logan's arm.

"You and Cagney are coming to our party, right?" Molly's words came out more like a command than a statement. He couldn't do anything but agree.

He nodded. "Of course."

"And I invited Alex and Blake because you two seem so close to them. Besides, they're a fun couple." Was that an evil gleam in her eye? No, he was just imagining it.

"And so that you can't say you don't know anyone."

She knew his typical modus operandi. He always got out of parties by saying he didn't know anyone. His mind raced with all the reasons he didn't feel comfortable in groups. It seemed Molly ambushed that plan.

"It's going to be so much fun, Brad."

Yeah, right. So. Much. Fun. He sucked in a deep breath.

****

Cagney

Brad took a deep breath. "I'm stuck behind this stupid truck that won't go over thirty-five miles an hour. It's a good thing I'm a patient man."

Cagney didn't mind the situation. Just the thought

of attending Molly's party stressed her. And going as Brad's girlfriend, well, the situation blew her stress meter off the charts. Her imagination ran amuck with the possibilities of people approaching her expecting her to talk about her boyfriend. Let the big, slow truck delay them. Even if it's only by a few moments.

His knuckles turned white on the steering wheel. "That's an awfully quirky sign of your calmness."

"What? Damn truck driver. I bet we'll have to follow him all the way." His eyes were focused on the road. Or probably the truck. The patient man was cursing the truck mentally.

"This is my life, you know." He glanced at her. A bottom lip turned upward ever so slightly. She decided it was a smile. "And my sister tells me that things like this"—he nodded, apparently at the semi—"are meant to teach me a lesson."

He looked at her again. He now wore a genuine smile that actually looked handsome on him. "In this case, she would say the Universe is teaching me patience."

He took in a deep breath. "Can't he go any faster?"

"The road has curves," she said as the car just navigated one. "And he's big and has a higher center of gravity than we do."

His head turned quickly and ever so slightly toward her. "You know what a center of gravity is?"

Damn, just when she was beginning to find him moderately attractive. "Of course. I took high school physics. I may have gotten a C in it, but I learned some things."

"Oh." His voice was low and thoughtful. "I'm sorry. I guess I just thought girls in the liberal arts knew nothing about the sciences."

"First off, any college-aged female is past the 'girl' stage. They're women." She shook her head. "We're women."

"Oh, I know you're a woman. I just say girls…I better shut up. I'm digging myself into a hole. I'm sorry if I offended you." He tilted his head as he seemed to study the semi. "We're probably going to be doing this for a while, this pretend relationship. I don't want you to be any more uncomfortable than you already are."

"I'm not uncomfortable with you." She focused on that one curl near his ear. The one that always caught her eye. "Not anymore."

"Really?" The truck slowed down to nearly a stop. "What's his problem?"

"Center of gravity. He can't take the turn that fast."

He ran a hand through his hair. She was pleased it didn't disturb that curl. Then immediately chastised herself.

"I knew that."

"I knew you knew that. You're a patient man."

The truck had finally turned. "Look, he's gone." His smile, this time, consumed his entire face. His blue eyes shone. "And I learned to be patient."

"I don't think you learned anything."

His laugh caused the curl to wiggle. "You're right. I didn't learn a thing. But don't tell my sister. She thinks she's converting me."

"Converting you to what?" She tilted her head. This man was more entertaining every time she saw him. At least this fake dating wasn't as awkward as it was in the beginning. How dare he say she was uncomfortable.

"That is yet to be seen. She's trying to tell me the Universe unfolds in its own time and my trying to rush it is futile."

"She's probably right."

"What?" He took his eyes off the road. That curl was temporarily hidden. Darn it.

"Now hear me out. The Universe undoubtedly unfolds in its own time. And it may be futile to rush things." He had his mouth open, no doubt ready to argue. "But it's also human nature to push our timeline on it. And truthfully"—she held her hands palms up—"who can say we don't influence the timing."

"Oh no. My sister is going to hate you."

"It's fortunate then that I'll never meet her." Brad's lips curved downward.

"Probably," he said softly.

Chapter 26

Cagney

Cagney let out a sigh as Brad parked his truck.

Brad chuckled and turned toward her. "What's that? It doesn't sound like a noise a party animal makes."

"I dread walking into that apartment." She wrapped her arms around her chest.

"I'm not feeling the party spirit either, if it makes you feel any better."

She turned in her seat to look at him and that damn curl. "You know everyone in there thinks we're dating. And Molly will introduce us as a couple."

He nodded. "Yeah. And that was our intent. Wasn't it?"

He touched her arm. Even though she had her light lavender jacket on, his touch helped to calm her. "I'm every bit as nervous. I have this fear one day everyone will find out. They'll discover we've just been pretending. And going in there now, I expect someone to point at me and say, 'Hey, you two aren't really dating. What's up with that?' "

Cagney laughed. "I know what you mean. I'm afraid I'll let it slip in front of Molly. She would be furious with me if she knew our relationship was a sham."

"So how do you want play our big entrance

tonight, pretend girlfriend?" His genuine smile put her at ease. "What would a real couple do at a party like this?"

She nodded as she thought about their options. "Do we stay together? Play the inseparable couple madly in love."

Brad let out a laugh.

"Do we play the confident pair who enters together, go our separate ways as we mingle with everyone, then end up back together at the end of the night?" She dipped her chin and fluttered her eyelashes.

"Why don't we play the madly in love?" Brad suggested.

Chills sprinted down her spine.

"That way, Molly can think her romantic thoughts when we have to slip out early."

She shook her head and laughed. "Brilliant. I promise not to leave your side." She took her hand and crossed her heart as if she were making a pact with her best friend in third grade.

Brad imitated the motion.

A knock at the window startled her. She turned to see Alex, her hands up against the window, cupped around her face, peering in. A second knock came from Brad's side. Blake waved his hands like the mad man she had come to think he was, his hair flouncing away.

As Cagney opened the door, Alex moved to the side. "Come on. What are you two doing just sitting there? This is my first apartment-warming party. I asked JJ. She had said my backstory never included one."

Excitement radiated from this tall, beautiful woman. Cagney realized that Alex did everything with a fresh zeal as if it were her first time. Now, she realized that at least this event was a first for her.

By the time she had exited the truck, Blake and Brad were waiting for her.

"Ready?" Brad's blue eyes looked directly at hers. Gorgeous blue eyes, really.

She walked next to him as she watched Blake and Alex walk arm-in-arm through the parking lot to the building. They looked so in love. But of course, they were. They were fictional characters. People didn't act like that in real life.

Alex and Blake entered the apartment first. Molly greeted them, hugging them as if they were old friends. Molly was, in fact, in a full embrace with Alex before she noticed them. "Cagney, Brad, so glad you guys made it." She released her hold on Alex.

She gave Cagney a quick squeeze. "Get in here. I've been waiting for you both."

Cagney took a deep breath before stepping over the threshold. Her feet wouldn't allow her to stray much farther. Her fictional friends, though, mingled like pros.

She took a step closer to Brad, who placed a hand on her shoulder. "This is more crowded than I expected. I didn't think this place could hold so many people." His breath tickled her ear.

"All the more reason to call it an early evening." She glanced up at him. He nodded.

Then Logan waved at them. "Brad, come over here, I want you to meet someone."

"I won't be long, I promise," he whispered in her ear before he removed his hand from her shoulder. She shivered and felt a sense of loss as he left her.

She didn't have time to think about it because

Molly called her. "Cagney, here, I want you to meet somebody." She cringed but turned to the sound of the voice and smiled.

Cagney didn't dislike people. They were fine—within boundaries. She lost the ability to talk without stammering in a group. Except for teaching. She excelled at that. But then she knew what to say. She knew what was expected of her. She didn't know what people expected of her at a party, especially people she didn't know well. She sighed. Let's face it, she thought, aside from talking about Harding, she sucked at making conversation.

"This is Michelle. She's in my—"

"The food's here." There was no denying Blake's British accent as he shouted over the voices of the others.

"Did you know the guys from the Physics Café started a catering business?" Molly bounced on her heels. "I think we're their first customers."

Alvin, Ted, and Simon carried the trays of food into the small kitchen, and Cagney wondered why anyone would go through that much expense for just a party.

"There's more in the truck, too," Ted said, "if anyone wants to help us. Hint. Hint."

Simon dropped his load off and headed toward the door. Brad followed. Of course, he followed. She had come to learn in the short time she knew him that was the type of man he was.

Molly made a beeline for the kitchen where Alvin and Simon were depositing their trays. "Thank goodness you made it. I was beginning to worry you weren't coming."

Alvin ran a hand through his crew-cut hair. "You said eight o'clock. It's literally ten till."

"I know." Molly's voice was low, and Cagney strained to hear it. "But I forgot I told everyone else seven."

Alvin laughed. "You should have called us."

Logan appeared at Molly's side. "No harm, guys. You're awesome." He lifted the aluminum foil off one of the deeper trays. "This looks like the makings of a Philadelphia Experiment Cheesesteak."

Simon beamed. "It is. Except we didn't bring the particlizer so there's no chance of the onions disappearing."

Blake groaned. He had been riffling through two other dishes. Alex slapped him gently on the arm. "You've never gotten a free cappuccino anyway."

Ted returned, Brad following him, each carrying a tray. Alvin rearranged the other trays to make room for the new arrivals. Brad deposited his.

"Brad, thanks." Alvin nodded toward him. "And by the way, why can't you take electricity to a party?"

Brad grinned widely. Yeah, this was their schtick. Cagney sighed and waited.

"I don't know. Why can't you take electricity to a party?"

"Because it doesn't know how to conduct itself."

Brad, Alvin, Ted, and Simon laughed. Everyone else just groaned.

As guests lined up to fill their plates, Brad got closer to Cagney.

"Sorry about leaving you. Duty called. But now we can navigate the party as the love-struck couple everyone believes we are." Cagney laughed nervously.

"Should I hold your hand?" She nodded her consent, and he gently placed his hand in hers. "Maybe we should just roam?"

She didn't get a chance to answer because Logan came up, slapped Brad on the back, and dragged him off. "Sorry, Cag," Logan said as they took off toward what she assumed was a bedroom. "I'll bring him back soon."

Brad's sudden departure saddened her in a way she couldn't understand. Part of it, she knew, was the fact she had to face these people alone. But there was another aspect to her emotion, something she couldn't put her finger on.

She found a folding chair in the living room and planted herself. She didn't want to mingle. If Molly saw her, she'd chastise her, but she looked like she'd be mingling for a while.

She smiled as she saw Alex lead Blake by the hand. It appeared she was determined to meet every person. Blake didn't seem too upset. He'd start talking and his hair would bounce. Cagney took it as a good sign. It felt odd to watch JJ's fictional couple interact with everyone. And she was the only person in the room who knew they were fictional. She wondered when she had resigned herself to the impossible. That characters from a book she read had come to life. She could never explain this to anyone. Not even Brad.

She watched as the fictional heroine whispered something in Blake's ear. He nodded, then looked her way, and waved. *Is he waving at me?*

Evidently he was, because he wouldn't stop waving until she waved back. She watched as Alex kissed him on the cheek and headed…oh, no, her way.

"Cagney, isn't this a great party? I'm glad this is my first." She helped herself to the seat on the end of the couch next to her.

Cagney nodded because what else could she do?

"Look over there." Alex pointed toward Molly and Logan, arms wrapped around one another.

If Logan wasn't with Brad, Cagney thought, where was he? Why hadn't he come back so they could make their apologies and leave? She scanned the room quickly. She didn't see him anywhere.

"Do you see Molly?" Alex's question interrupted her panicked thoughts.

"I see her. She looks like she's enjoying herself."

"She does. And do you know why?"

"She loves to entertain."

Anyone could see Molly was in her element. She enjoyed being around people. Cagney believed Molly gained her energy by interacting with others. Unlike her. Parties and other social functions drained her. And right now, her battery was running low. She'd like nothing better than to find Brad and leave. Maybe someone ambushed him?

"That's part of it." Was there irritation in Alex's voice? What was the purpose of this conversation anyway? What was so important that she dragged herself away from Blake?

"She told me she loves living with Logan. She said she's never been happier in her life."

Cagney nodded. "Yeah, she told me she's enjoying it. I'm happy for her."

"Someday, you can have that kind of happiness." Alex sighed as she gazed at Molly kissing Logan on the cheek.

"Excuse me? What are you talking about?" Cagney twisted her body so that she faced Alex. "What kind of happiness?"

"That kind." She pointed at the couple. "Look at them. They're in love. And living together. Does it get any better than that?"

Cagney shook her head. Did Alex just imply…

"Does what get any better? What are you—"

"Cagney Adler, you know exactly what I'm talking about. You and Brad need to move in together."

Alex sighed. Cagney thought the fictional woman was imagining a happily ever after for Brad and herself.

"No! What are you thinking?" Several people nearby looked at her.

"We're fake dating." She took a deep breath. Only fake dating, she reminded herself.

"And that's all it's going to remain." The words came out slowly and she hoped controlled.

"I didn't mean like tomorrow," Alex said. "I mean once you realize you two love each other and start thinking about the future."

"We do not love each other."

"So you say." The fictional character smiled. "But the day will come when you and Brad will move in together and you'll be as happy as Molly."

****

"Can I put my arm around you?" he whispered in her ear when he sat next to her. "I think they"—he nodded toward where Molly and Logan shared a chair—"may expect it."

The plan, Cagney reminded herself, was to pretend to be madly in love and duck out early. So what was she doing sitting a bit too close to Brad on the couch at least an hour after all the other guests, except for Alex and Blake, had left? Where had their plan gone awry?

"I guess we're far enough in our fake relationship for you to do that," she whispered back. Without any more encouragement, he slid his arm along the back of the couch and wrapped it around her. She didn't feel uncomfortable, like she thought she would. Instead, it felt right. Oh, what was she saying?

"You two whispering sweet nothings in each other's ears?"

Cagney's cheeks grew hot at Logan's remark, but Brad shrugged it off easily. "Wouldn't you like to know?" He pulled her closer.

"You two make a good couple," Alex volunteered. She sat on Blake's lap on a chair next to Molly.

Cagney trained her sight on her in the hopes she'd get the message the statement was ill-timed and unnecessary—and so much more. But then she took a good look at how Alex and Blake had stuffed themselves into a single chair.

Cagney didn't know how the two tall individuals could look so comfortable in such a small space. But heck, they were in love. And fictional, she reminded herself. Fictional. Maybe they could warp the laws of science. Maybe it was all an illusion. Hell, she didn't know what anything was anymore.

"They do." Molly's agreement knocked Cagney out of her thoughts.

Cagney tried to put some space between her and Brad, but he kept a firm grip on her. Hell, they didn't look like a couple. "Don't panic," he whispered in her ear. "We'll leave soon."

She let out a breath knowing that he might have a

plan to get them out.

"Brad, I never thought I'd say this," Logan said, as he pulled Molly even closer, "but I've never been more content. You and Cagney should think about living together."

****

Brad

"Has the whole world gone mad?" Cagney tried to buckle her seat belt but kept missing the mark.

Brad looked over at her and took her hand. She stopped fiddling and looked at him. "Calm down. It's okay."

"But they don't know this is just fake." The whine in her voice hurt him. But he couldn't understand why. What he had with Cagney wasn't real, only an illusion.

He buckled her seat belt. "But we want them to think it's real. And the fact that they think we're enough of a couple to be talking about our future, our fake future"—oh good, that made her smile—"means we're fulfilling our mission."

He started the engine. Before he put the car in gear, he asked, "Do you miss those blind dates?"

She laughed. God, it was good to hear her laugh. He knew the party had stressed her as much as it did him. He wanted to leap off the couch and punch Logan in the nose when he suggested he and Cagney live together. He could just imagine how upset she was to hear that.

"It's been a long evening. I'm sorry about Logan's remark. Our plan of playing love-crossed lovers and leaving early didn't work out." He looked at the dashboard clock. It was after midnight.

"It's late. I hope this doesn't interfere with your

study plans for tomorrow. What's on your agenda?"

He talked to calm her some. He could tell by her stiff pose she was still upset. But he also genuinely wanted to know what she planned for Saturday, one of the two days they agreed upon they wouldn't make contact. He wanted to feel connected to her on the weekends. Knowing her plans helped keep that connection. The desire, though, mystified him.

"You do know how to sweet talk a lady." Cagney smiled. "I'm disappearing into the library tomorrow to take a second look at old newspaper accounts of the Harding administration."

He heard the enthusiasm in her voice.

"I think I may have missed something the first time around. I have a gut feeling that the answer to my…"

He glanced to his side when she quit talking in mid-sentence.

"I'm sorry. Again." She shook her head. "I know I'm boring you with the details. But I'm excited about this. I think it's the breakthrough I need. That is, short of going to DC to research."

"You're fine." He meant it. He had grown to love to hear about her research. "I'm learning history from you. That wasn't one of my better subjects."

"But I bet you still got As in it." Cagney's voice had her lilt back.

Chapter 27

Cagney

"I should have been at the library hours ago. One o'clock on a Saturday and I'm lying on the couch. I'm never this lazy."

But the night before she and Brad had stayed at Molly's party way too long. Whatever happened to her and Brad's exit strategy of love-crossed lovers needing to leave to...well, whatever love-crossed lovers do.

Okay, she knew. She knew. But she couldn't imagine doing any of those with Brad. Could she? No. No.

She stared at the ceiling, utterly void of her usual energy and her enthusiasm for research. She could only muster the strength to count the damn cracks. Were they multiplying? No, it had to be her imagination.

She took a deep breath, realizing she had to get off the couch, out the door, and to the library. "This could be the break I need in my research."

With that bit of encouragement, she rose and trudged to the dining room and picked up her backpack already filled with everything she needed.

She hadn't taken two steps toward the door when a deep, loud rumbling shook the apartment. Her body vibrated from the sound. She lost her footing momentarily and tightened her grip on the backpack.

"What the...?"

She pivoted. The ceiling in her living room had collapsed. Dust enveloped the room. Her mind flashed to newsreels of the World War II Blitzkrieg of London. She coughed, choking on the dust.

"What the hell?" She took a step closer, unsure whether it was safe to step into the area. The couch from the apartment above had fallen on hers, smashing it. The force of the crash had broken a leg of the coffee table, and everything on it had toppled to the floor. Pieces of the ceiling, varying in size from tiny to large chunks, had been strewn everywhere, covering her neighbor's couch, the coffee table, and the floor. She had just lain on that couch moments before. She could have been injured or killed. Her legs trembled. She pulled a chair from the dining room and sat, as her mind tried to grasp what just happened.

"Mary Ann, upstairs. I wonder if she's all right."

A knock at the door made her jump. "Who's there?" she asked as she rose.

"It's me, Mary Ann."

Cagney hurried to open the door. "Are you okay?"

Mary Ann looked like Cagney felt. "Yeah. Just shocked."

"I was so worried you were on your couch."

"Want to see the damage?" Cagney asked.

"Yes." She led her the few short steps to the living room. Not all of the dust had settled yet, and it glinted in the afternoon light from the window above the couch.

"I told the landlord the floor seemed to give out in places. I could feel it sink when I walked on it."

"Have you called him yet?" Cagney didn't relish this call.

"No, I was worried about you."

Cagney pulled her phone from her jeans pocket and hit speed dial. She had put the landlord's number in there when she first moved in and, boy, had she needed it. From the bathroom pipes bursting last winter to the refrigerator dying.

Surprisingly, he picked up on the third ring. "Mr. Jackson, this is Cagney Adler, apartment two-oh-seven." Like she needed to identify herself.

"I have a slight problem. The ceiling fell and I have three-oh-seven's couch on top of mine."

"I told her to walk gently in that room. She didn't listen."

"Mary Ann is here now if you want to—"

"I'll be right over." He disconnected the call.

"He says—"

"I heard him. I'm going to wait upstairs for him. I'm not sure where I'm going to stay while he repairs this." She walked into the kitchen. "I'm glad you're not hurt."

The door closed and it struck her. "Shit, I need a place to stay too. I can't live here."

She had to think. It's not like she had family in Bell Wyck. Well, it's not like she had family at all. There was Molly, of course. She still held the phone and positioned it to hit Molly's speed dial number. Wait. Molly couldn't help her. She was blissfully living with Logan.

Cagney sighed. "I'm homeless." She didn't know who to call, but Brad popped into her mind. "I can't call him. That's stupid," she argued with herself. "Besides, this is the weekend. We agreed. No contact on weekends."

They'd already gone to a party together the night before. Even though this violated their unwritten contract, so did that party. She needed to talk to someone. How sad was it that the only person she could call was her bogus boyfriend? He couldn't help with accommodations, of course. But she knew he would listen. Maybe he had some ideas. She didn't have money for a hotel.

She hit his number and held her breath. She stared into the living room as she explained her situation.

"Are you sure you're not exaggerating. I mean plaster falls, but it's unusual for the entire ceiling to come down." Cagney huffed. Men.

She stepped back into the living room and started to cough. Plaster dust covered every square inch. "Excuse me. Not all the dust has settled yet." She craned her head upward. "No, Brad, it's a real hole. It's just not the plaster crumbling. I can see into the apartment above me. And well, their couch is like on top of my couch, so I suppose that tells you something."

Her eyes welled with tears. It was bad enough that her apartment was probably unlivable—where else would the ceiling fall next for no apparent reason?—but now Brad, Mr. Science, doubted her story? Did he think she was out for attention or sympathy? She was no Piper.

She sniffled, trying to head off a flood of tears. "Let me take a picture of it." She disconnected the call, even though she knew she didn't have to, because she didn't want him to hear her cry.

She took a deep breath and aimed the phone's camera at the stacked couches and hit the button. Then she snapped a shot at the hole in the ceiling. What a disaster. Where was she going to live? She sent the photos to Brad. *There, you arrogant science nerd. I didn't make this up.*

Almost immediately, her phone pinged. "Are you hurt? Were you anywhere near it when it collapsed? What's your landlord going to do about it? When will he fix it?" The words rolled out fast and the man sounded panicked.

Tears rolled down her face. She couldn't stop them as much as she wanted to. "He's on his way over. And I hope he fixes it soon, because…"

She couldn't believe this. "I can't live in this apartment with the ceiling gone." She walked into the kitchen and pulled a paper towel off the roll.

"Of course, you can't. Do you have a friend or family you can stay with?"

She winced at the word family. No, she didn't have family. It still stung after all these years.

"No, Molly was the only one I felt comfortable imposing on." She wiped her cheeks with the towel. She knew she should have bought tissues. And she had just been at her apartment-warming party the night before. Stupid timing.

Brad mumbled something, then said, "You can stay with me."

She thought she must have heard him wrong. Certainly, he didn't say what she thought he did.

"Excuse me?" She massaged her neck with her free hand.

"You're more than welcome to stay with me until your ceiling gets repaired."

By golly, he had said that. What in the universe was he thinking?

"No, I couldn't do that." She grimaced. She couldn't imagine sharing a place with a man, let alone Brad.

"Yes, you could. Remember, Logan was my roommate. Now I have an extra bedroom."

"That's sweet, but I could never—"

"Where else are you going to stay? Any hotel a graduate student could afford wouldn't be safe. And you certainly wouldn't be able to study there. Have you ever gone past the Crimson Canopy?"

Cagney choked out a laugh. She had been past that motel along Albert Street. It was not family-friendly. "I could never stay there."

"Right. I'm glad you see it my way. Pack up a few things for tonight and I'll be over in a bit. I'd like to be there when your landlord gets there." He disconnected the call.

"He didn't leave me any choice." Cagney was still in a stupor from the disaster, but even if she had been thinking straight, she didn't know of anywhere she could go. Brad, her fake boyfriend, had now become a very real hero of sorts. She had a place to sleep, thanks to him.

She trudged to her bedroom. As she pulled the duffle bag out of the closet, a ripple of tears tickled her cheeks. She wiped them off with the back of her hand. She closed her eyes before turning and plunking the bag on her bed.

She didn't know Brad well enough to be rooming with him, even for a day, let alone for the length of time it would take to repair her ceiling. What would that be? Days? Weeks? No, not months. Definitely not months. Okay, she didn't know how fast her landlord would act.

The man wasn't a beacon of efficiency.

She pulled several T-shirts out of her drawers and shoved them into the duffle. She strode to the closet to retrieve her jeans. She didn't have much of a wardrobe. It appeared to be a blessing right now.

She flung the jeans onto the bed. My God, she couldn't think of anything more uncomfortable than Brad being the first person she saw in the morning. She had a difficult enough time making conversation with him during their fake dates.

She stuffed the jeans into the bag. Underwear. And bras. She had to pack them. She had to dress in the same apartment as that man. How exactly would that work out? Sure, he wouldn't see her, but she'd know he would be on the other side of that bedroom door.

And he'd undress in his room. He'd take off those tight jeans he always wore that showed off his cute butt. The one little curl by his ear as it fluttered as he…where the hell did those thoughts come from? She shook her head as if that would help get the image of a near-naked Brad out of her mind.

Chapter 28

Brad

The ping of the phone interrupted Brad's research. He didn't have many friends. Not friends to call him at—he looked at the lower right-hand corner of his laptop—one in the afternoon on a Saturday. Certainly, it couldn't be Logan. The man had other things on his mind. Let's face it, that would be the only person…

He looked at the caller ID. Holy moley. It was Cagney. *Why would she call me? We agreed she didn't need to pretend on weekends.* Besides, she had planned a full day at the library. That he knew for a fact.

She'd talked about Harding and the strange circumstances of his death. She'd said she'd scour old newspapers again on microfilm. Her entire face glowed when she talked about her dissertation. So that's exactly where she should be. In the library that makes her happy. Not calling him.

He shook his head. He hadn't answered her call yet. That was the only way he would find out what she wanted.

"Cagney, what's up?"

"I'm sorry to bother you. I just had to call someone."

He strained to hear her. It sounded as if she had been crying. What had happened to make her cry? That woman shouldn't have to cry over anything.

"What's wrong?" The short wait for her to answer hurt him.

"I just, well, the ceiling in my living room kinda fell in. There's dust everywhere." She sniffled.

"Are you hurt?" God, please say no.

"No, I'm just shaken. It's not every day there's a hole in my ceiling that allows me a view of the apartment above me."

"Are you sure you're not exaggerating? I mean plaster falls, but it's unusual for the entire ceiling to come down."

Whoa. She didn't like that suggestion. "What I mean—"

The call disconnected. He pulled the phone from his ear and stared at the screen as if that would explain why she hung up on him. "Damn. I said the wrong thing. She's already upset, and I made it worse."

She called him for support and what did he do? He screwed up. No wonder he didn't have a real girlfriend.

His phone pinged again. He opened it. She had sent pictures. Two. He couldn't believe what he saw. She had not exaggerated one bit.

His finger swiftly hit her speed dial number. "I'm so sorry." He made sure she hadn't been in the room when the ceiling fell. "No, of course, you can't live there."

Where would she go? "Do you have family you can stay with?"

He could hear the pain in her voice. She didn't have family close. Come to think of it, she never talked about her parents. Or brothers or sisters. *Damn. I probably shoved my foot in my mouth again.*

"You can stay with me. Stay with me until your

landlord repairs the ceiling." He didn't know where that suggestion came from. He was pretty sure it was bad form to ask your fake girlfriend to live with you in real life. Especially when the fake girlfriend was genuinely beautiful, even if she didn't know it.

She couldn't stay in the fleabag of a hotel Crimson Canopy and told her so. Relieved when she agreed she wouldn't be safe there, he didn't give her any other option.

"Pack some things. I'm on my way. I want to be there when the landlord gets there."

She mumbled something he didn't understand, but he took it as a yes. He disconnected the phone and headed for the kitchen.

****

Cagney

Cagney sucked in a deep breath as she crossed the kitchen to answer the door. She knew her landlord stood on the other side. The man normally grew irritated with minor repairs. She knew he would be irate with the situation. And he'd try to blame it on someone.

"Brad." Definitely not the person she expected. At least, not so soon.

"I got here as fast as I could. Are you okay? You're not hurt, are you?" He scrubbed the back of his neck.

"I thought you'd be the landlord."

"Oh, good. He's not here yet."

She opened the door wider and stepped aside. "Come in. Do you want to see the damage?"

He nodded and followed her into the living room. As he looked up through the hole into Mary Ann's apartment, he let out a low whistle. "You're lucky you weren't in here when it happened."

He pivoted and gazed into her eyes. Her spine tingled at the apparent scrutiny and her brain went back to a half-naked Brad. *Don't do that.*

"I know," she whispered. "I had just left the room not moments before."

An awkward silence hung between them. Certainly, they had gotten beyond this stage. So why was she just standing there looking into his eyes?

"I appreciate your coming over," she said, trying to keep her voice under control, "but I can talk to my landlord on my own."

If he didn't look so concerned, she'd be upset with his apparent arrogance at her not being able to handle the situation.

"Oh, I know you can. But I'm just going to sit right over there." He pointed in the general direction of her dining-room office. He walked past her, their shoulders barely touching, and pulled the dining room chair she had sat on earlier closer to the living room. "You're going to do all the talking. I'm just here to stare at him so he listens."

Cagney tilted her head and slowly shook it. "I'm not sure—"

Brad sat down. "If he's sexist, he'll try to blow you off. I know how some men work. My sister took her car to the mechanic. They gave her a line of bull. I went in the next day with her and she said the exact same thing and they listened to her."

He crossed his legs. "It's a shame some men treat women like they're idiots. You're a very smart woman and I won't let any man treat you like that."

"Wait one minute. Didn't you just do that to me? I mean you didn't believe me when I said there was a hole in my ceiling. I had to send you pict—"

"Whoa. I did. I'm so sorry." He uncrossed his legs, stood, and took several steps toward her. I'm guilty as hell." He ran a hand through his hair.

She looked up at him and smiled. "I guess it's just part of the male DNA." She was still mad at him for not believing her, but those eyes looked sincere.

"And all those times I doubted you knew anything about science. I'm one of those sexist jerks. And I thought I was so enlightened."

"Enlightened?"

"Yeah, it's the word my sister uses all the time. She thinks I should be more enlightened." He used air quotes. "She might be right. If what I said earlier to you is any indication, I do need to be enlightened."

He scanned the apartment as if he were looking for something. "If you want me to leave or hide in the bathroom when he arrives, let me know. I won't try to be—"

"No, honestly. I think I'd like you to be present. You know, my landlord just might be that type of jerk."

A knock at the door interrupted their conversation. "I guess that's him." She strode to the door and opened it. Mr. Jackson pushed his way past Cagney without a greeting. Brad stood, fists balled. She shook her head. She didn't need him making a scene.

"I don't see how this could have happened. You college students are so irresponsible." He stood at the edge of the living room.

Cagney bit her tongue.

"I'm not sure what that Mary Ann person above you was doing, but the structure of this apartment is strong. This didn't happen without a reason." He took a few steps and stared at the couches.

"Do you have any idea how long it will take to fix it?" Cagney stood what she felt was a safe distance from him just outside the living room area. The landlord had climbed over the detritus and was staring up at the hole.

"I can't say." He shrugged. "This shouldn't have happened."

If she heard "this shouldn't have happened" one more time she would deck the man. Who cared if he was six-something friggin' feet?

"But yet, it did happen." She tried to control her voice. "And I clearly can't live here with the ceiling gone, so you need to tell me that you're going to get it repaired as soon as possible." Her fingernails dug into the palms of her hands. "Because of course it's in your best financial interest. Next week the rent is due and I'm not paying for an uninhabitable apartment."

Jackson spun on his heel. "Where do you get off telling me what to do?" His eyes grew wide. "You can't talk to me like that. I'm the—"

Oh, she had had it with men. "You supply a service. I'm your customer. And if you don't want me taking you to tenants' court, you'll repair this as quickly as you can. And once it's repaired, I'll pay for the pro-rated portion of the month. But you're not getting a full month's rent if I haven't lived in the place for a full month. And you're getting no rent money until the apartment is livable. If I have to, I'll put the rent money into escrow. But there's no way you're getting a single cent from me until this is fixed." She crossed her arms.

"You can't do that you little—"

"Don't go there, sir." Brad appeared next to her.

"The woman knows her rights. You're not about to intimidate her."

Damn. I could have handled this.

"Cagney. I'm sorry." He placed his hand on her shoulder "I know you didn't want me to share this, but the poor man needs to know what he's up against."

She resisted asking what he was talking about.

"Cagney's brother is the assistant Ohio state attorney general." He looked down at her. "Sorry. But he needs to know."

Cagney hoped the landlord couldn't see her body shake as she tried to suppress laughter.

"And he's the lead investigator of Project Off-Campus, which is looking into housing violations and indicting negligent landlords. I'm sure Cagney would never mention this to her brother, but..." He raised an eyebrow.

Color rushed out of Jackson's face.

"Oh, in addition to fixing the ceiling, you will replace my couch and coffee table as well as Mary Ann's couch and any other of her furniture that was ruined." She suppressed a giggle. "Won't you?"

"Give kids a little education—"

"And we know our rights," Cagney interrupted. Brad's large, comforting arm wrapped around her shoulders. She leaned into him. "It's either that or you can talk to my brother."

Jackson walked toward them, and Brad's fingers tightened. He had a secure grip on her. While she should be upset that he acted protective, she liked it.

"I'll call my guys and get them on it." He walked through the kitchen and grabbed the doorknob. "I'm going upstairs now. I suppose I'll get the same song and dance routine from her."

He exited and slammed the door. The apartment shook. Cagney burst out laughing. "What a jerk." She turned to Brad. "Where did you come up with that story?"

"I keep telling you scientists are creative."

Chapter 29

Cagney

"I still feel uncomfortable about this," Cagney said as they lugged the last of her books into Brad's apartment. She had told him she didn't need everything, but he had insisted that she make his place home. And as a fellow doctoral student, he intuitively knew the value she placed on her books.

The move had taken most of the afternoon with the exception of them stopping to grab a pizza. And now the sun had gone down and she never did get to the library.

"Where else would you go?"

She shook her head. Brad's question interrupted her thoughts. He was right, of course. She had no other place to go. The only other option would have been to crash at her advisor's. Dr. St. Clair was the only other person she even remotely felt close to. But she knew fictional characters occupied that room. How absurd.

She sighed. "Am I that sad of a person that I really don't have any friends I know well enough that I can stay with?"

Brad tilted his head as if he were considering an answer. "You do have a very close friend. Molly. But she's recently taken her relationship to the next level."

"But there's no one else. They are plenty of grad students in the history department. Why have I never befriended them? What's wrong with me?" She sat on the edge of the bed. She didn't want to cry in front of Brad.

"I've always suspected it," she said, blinking away tears, "but this confirms it. I really don't fit in anywhere."

Brad ran a hand over his beard. "Come with me. I want to show you something."

"If you're trying to distract me—"

"Nope, I want to show you something. I promise it's not a distraction."

She slowly rose. She wished he'd just go into his bedroom and allow her to adjust. She felt foolish being here, needing his help. He shouldn't have been this close to her. Just a pretend boyfriend. Just someone whom she met once or twice a week. How did she end up like this?

She followed him through the dining room and onto a small balcony. The spring breeze caressed and comforted her. This was good for her.

"I love this balcony." Brad went to the railing and looked at the sky. "I can see the stars from here."

She stood next to him. "They are pretty." She sighed. "Is this what you wanted me to see? That my troubles are tiny in comparison to the stars in the universe."

"Technically, these are only the stars of the Milky Way we can see from our small sliver of the universe."

She froze. Why did he have to make her feel stupid? At her most vulnerable moment? She looked up at him and he had a smile on his face. "Just kidding. Sorry."

"No worries. A scientist I'm not. But if there are

this many stars"—she nudged him—"and I know many of them are planets, imagine how many there are in the universe. And how insignificant we are."

"I didn't ask you on the balcony to make you feel like you didn't matter. Quite the opposite." He moved toward the telescope. "Let me hone in on"—his one eye was already planted against the scope—"here it is. Venus."

He motioned for her to come closer. "Oops. I need to adjust this. I didn't factor in the height difference." He bent his knees until he was her height. And somehow that made him closer to her. She watched his large hands as he meticulously focused the telescope again. "Now, look at Venus."

She moved over as he placed his hands on her shoulders to help her align herself properly. His touch, she admitted, comforted her. She closed one eye and gazed into the night sky. It took her a moment to find it. "It's beautiful, simply beautiful."

She twisted to look at him. "Thanks for showing me." She sighed. "I still don't see how this isn't a distraction, but it did help."

"Let's sit." He pointed to two café chairs to their left. "I have a story to tell you. There's more."

She sat and he moved the second chair so he could see her face. "You said you don't fit in."

She shrugged. "I don't. I can't seem to make close friends."

"There's Alex and Blake. They seem to love you."

Cagney shook her head. If she could only tell him. "They just feel obligated. You know, being related to my advisor." She wanted to cry. Again. "I'm different, that's all. I do a lot of things alone. And that's okay."

She shrugged.

She laughed softly. "Until you need someone to help you when the ceiling crashes in on you. Literally."

"But you're not different. You shouldn't feel alone." He shifted his weight in the chair. "Sometimes I feel alone. In fact, I felt like that constantly in middle school and up until my freshman year in high school. Then my science teacher taught me something."

"About being alone? In a science class?"

"Yeah, but he didn't realize it helped me overcome my feelings of not being enough and being different."

"What did he say?" Cagney leaned forward. She gazed at the curl that hugged his ear.

"Every star in that sky, every rock on this earth, is composed of the exact same elements as we are. You and I have every element, albeit in different proportions, in your body that the North Star has and Venus has." He paused and glanced at the sky. "We are very much a part of this world, this universe. We belong here.

"When I realized that, it didn't matter that the senior jock made fun of me. I was meant to be here. I was made of star stuff. Even if no one else realized its implications, I did. And it inspired me to become a geology major and it made me less lonely." He looked at the sky. "How can you be lonely when the stars and planets—gazillions of them—are your cousins?" He sucked in a breath, as if he were thinking about it.

"Look." He stood and shoved his hand in his jeans pocket. When he pulled it out, he had it curled in a fist. He sat again, extended his arm between them, and then unclutched his hand. "I'm sure you know what type of rock this is from your childhood rock collection."

"Of course, that's a quartz." She squinted. "I told you about my rock collection on that disastrous blind date we went on…and you remembered."

Brad blushed. "I remember stuff when it comes to rocks." He turned the rock over in his hand. "But we're off track."

"Cagney Adler, the point I'm trying to make is that you belong here just as much as the stars and planets of the sky and the rocks of the earth. Your presence makes a difference and you fit perfectly in this world. If no one else appreciates you, your cousins in the sky do." He touched her knee. "And I do."

Chapter 30

Cagney

Cagney woke up the following morning disoriented. Her eyes barely open, she scanned the bedroom. It felt like her own, but where were the posters of dead presidents? *That's right. I'm at Brad's.* She groaned. Her calamitous circumstances rushed back to her. The ceiling—or lack thereof. The humiliation.

She swung her legs off the bed and took a deep breath and sat for a moment. *Nothing's changing my circumstances. I might as well start the day.*

She stood, walked across the room, and rummaged through her duffle bag until she found a T-shirt and jeans. She dressed. "I'll worry about a shower later." Because truthfully, she didn't know the man's schedule and well, felt weird about taking a shower in another person's home.

She sat at the desk in the room. Hesitancy engulfed her. How awkward would this get? The only way to know, she thought, was by getting out there. She took another deep breath to fortify her resolve.

As she crossed the living room, the toaster popped. "He must be up and getting breakfast." She stood on the threshold to the kitchen. "Oh, my heavens." He was slathering peanut butter over a bagel.

And he was doing it without a shirt—in his bare

chest. She tried hard to process this.

She knew his shoulders were broad, but without a shirt they looked even broader. Maybe he did work in a quarry. He turned and he was—chiseled. She couldn't believe that was the first word to pop into her mind. And those arms. They certainly didn't get that muscular from buttering bagels.

Who knew what was hiding under his button-down shirt on their blind date?

"You're not wearing a shirt." Her cheeks burned.

Brad turned, half a bagel in one hand. He looked down. "Oh, I'm sorry. I'm—" His arms darted to his chest and the bagel slammed against it. "Shit." He moved his arms and peeled the bagel off him. Peanut butter covered his pecs.

"I'm so sorry." Cagney hurried to him and picked up a towel from the counter. She dabbed his chest. His hard chest. "Damn." She took a quick step back. "I'm sorry. I don't know what I was thinking. Here." She handed him the towel. "You can do it."

He accepted the towel and laughed. "It's okay." He looked down and wiped off the peanut butter. "I haven't taken a shower yet."

"Uhm, is that how you prepare breakfast every morning?" Her voice cracked.

"Yeah." He rubbed the last of the food off him. "It was. I'll start wearing shirts."

"No." Her answer was too quick. "I mean, I don't want you to change the way you do things. No, you can butter your bagel without a shirt on. I don't want you to think…"

She ran a hand through her hair. He was staring at her. He probably thought she was a babbling idiot. Who could blame him?

"I'll think about it. I just don't want to make you feel uncomfortable. It's a habit I developed a while ago." He turned to the sink and ran some hot water over the towel. He patted himself again. "I'm pretty messy in the morning. And this saves me staining my shirts even before I go out."

"You don't need to explain yourself in your own home. I'm—"

"Hungry, perhaps?" He quirked a brow. "I have more bagels. And more peanut butter. It's not a fancy breakfast."

She took a deep breath. Her world had changed. In an instant. She had to get used to it. Her stomach rumbled. "You know what? That sounds perfect."

"I'll go get a shirt on."

"No. Don't. It's okay."

"Are you sure? I don't want to make you—"

"Uncomfortable. I know. I'm fine. Please don't change how you do anything because I'm here. I'm imposing upon you enough."

He laughed as he pulled two bagels out of the freezer. "I don't think I want to eat that one." He nodded to the one on the counter. After he placed the bagels in the microwave to thaw, he threw the old one in the trash.

****

Cagney slipped into their booth at the café. She thought of Brad every time she sat here. After she opened her laptop, she sipped her mc^2 coffee. The name screamed energy. The guys had named it after Einstein's equation, E equals mc^2. And the E, she knew, represented energy.

Extra energy never hurt any doctoral student. Brilliant marketing. Alvin and the guys were more than just science nerds, they were smart businessmen.

The weekend had drained her, both physically and mentally. Her muscles burned from moving the books and other items she needed to Brad's apartment. Her brain throbbed at the full realization that if it weren't for her fake boyfriend, she'd be homeless. She still regretted not making it to the library Saturday, though she knew she had no choice.

Dr. St. Clair would arrive any minute. She looked up and there she was. Punctual, as ever. Dammit, Alex tagged along behind her. She didn't want to deal with the woman.

The professor smiled broadly and slid across from her. Alex sat next to her. "How was your weekend?"

"It sucked." Cagney envisioned Dr. St. Clair having a glorious weekend with her boyfriend. The boyfriend Alex had seemed to have chosen, by the way. She shivered at the thought. History would not repeat itself.

"Do you want to talk about it?" Her advisor sounded genuinely concerned.

"It has nothing to do with my academic life." She shook her head ever so slightly. "Not directly at least."

"Doesn't matter. Our relationship, I hope, is more than just academic."

She quickly glanced at Alex. She knew the woman would jump on this.

"My ceiling fell in Saturday afternoon."

"What? Really?"

"Yeah. There's a hole where the couch from upstairs fell onto mine." She fought back tears as she retold the story.

"Were you hurt?" Dr. St. Clair leaned forward.

"No. Just shaken." She sucked in a breath. "And now I can't live there until it's repaired."

"You know you could stay with me. My spare bedroom is occupied at the moment,"—she waved a hand toward Alex—"but there's a couch in the living room and one in my office. I don't want you living out of your car."

"Thank you, Dr. St. Clair, but I've found a place."

"Where?" Her advisor held her gaze.

"Molly's?" She jumped at the sound of Alex's voice.

"No, you know Molly moved in with Logan. We were at their party. I'm staying with Brad." She sucked in a breath and waited for the inevitable fallout.

"That's awesome." Alex bounced in her seat. "That's the universe saying you two were meant to be together. Signs don't get much clearer than that. You've taken your fake relationship to a new level." She leaned back and placed her hands behind her head. "That's so romantic."

"Is that so?" Cagney leaned forward, her hands on her laptop. "If we've taken our relationship to the next level, as you say, then why haven't returned to your own world?"

She glanced at her advisor, hoping she didn't take offense. She wasn't sure how the relationship between an author and her characters worked. Would Dr. St. Clair be insulted she wanted them out of her life?

Her advisor's smile reassured her.

"I guess you're not securely set in your relationship." Alex's eyes sparkled.

Cagney didn't dare tell her about the balcony incident, because that did seem almost romantic. And she definitely wouldn't tell either of them about the shirtless breakfast. Not in a million years.

****

Brad

"No, Blake, it's not like that. Not. At. All." Brad ran a quick hand through his hair. Class had ended and they were at the Physics Café. Cagney couldn't meet him today. She needed to spend some quality time with the library—understandable considering the weekend.

"But you two are living under the same roof. Something's going to happen. It has to. It's the universal law of romance novels."

"Blake, I think you've been spending too much time around Dr. St. Clair and Alex. Life isn't a romance novel. We're two adults who happen to be sharing the same apartment. Separate bedrooms. Separate lives."

Blake nodded. "If. You. Say. So."

"I do say so. Why is it so hard for you to believe?"

"You may be an expert in rocks, Brad, but you don't know the first thing about human nature."

I know my human nature. And I think this is about to become more complicated than I anticipated.

Chapter 31

Alex

"Alex Zurich, I don't have time to wander aimlessly through a bookstore today."

Alex herded Cagney into A Likely Story bookshop despite her whining. She had something special she wanted to show Cagney. Something that would make her reconsider her relationship with Brad.

"We are not wandering aimlessly. We're looking for a good book to read."

Cagney had only taken several steps into the store when she stopped. Alex nearly collided into her.

The woman pivoted and looked her in the eye. "I'm hopelessly behind on my research. I haven't seen the inside of the library in who knows how long. I've got to get serious about my studies."

Alex took a step back and raised her hands. "I know. I know. You keep telling me that. But you can take a few minutes and help me out here. You can study later. You study history, for crying out loud. Dead people. They'll still be dead when we're done here."

Cagney mumbled something under her breath Alex couldn't make out. It was probably better that way.

On the way to finding a romance novel, Alex stopped at the history section and sighed.

"What's that all about?" Cagney asked.

"This section right here"—Alex made a flourishing

gesture with her arms—"is where JJ met Dr. Cooper."
She sighed, thinking about the encounter. "Right here."
She gazed at the shelves and wondered what books they
held then.

"Really?" Cagney took a step toward the twentieth-
century section and studied a book. "Hmm. This one
looks pretty good. I didn't think Lankford had come out
with this yet." She picked it up and thumbed the pages.

Alex couldn't believe the woman. How could she
stay calm when she was in the presence of JJ and
Kenn's origin story? The origin story she and Blake
initiated. And she so wanted to do the same for Cagney.
Except this woman seemed even more stubborn than JJ
had been. Imagine that.

"Don't you see the implications here?" Alex knew
her impatience showed in her voice.

"What are you talking about? Implications of
what?"

"Are you blind?" Alex saw the parallels between
JJ's romance and Cagney's. Even if Cagney hadn't
caught on yet she was in the middle of a romance.

"If JJ and Dr. Cooper could overcome their
differences and find true love, then you and Brad can
too. And your love story isn't nearly as tumultuous as
theirs was, you know." She chuckled. "JJ hated Kenn
the first time she met him."

"What frickin' love story?"

Alex could tell by her friend's defensive tone that
she had struck a nerve. She wanted to tell her that but
knew better.

"Brad and I have no love story. Our bogus dating is
nothing more than deception and me staying with him
temporarily is merely a matter of convenience."

"Exactly." Alex couldn't quit smiling. Cagney loved Brad. She knew it. It was a given.

"You really are still thinking I'm going to fall head over heels in love with Brad?"

"Haven't you already softened to him? I mean, you wanted nothing to do with him when you first met him."

"Let's go look at the romance novels, Alex. I have work to do." And she headed in that direction.

The woman was in love, obviously. She didn't deny it. Alex so wanted to lecture her about getting in touch with her feelings. It wouldn't do any good. Not yet, at least. Cagney needed a little more time, that's all.

"Okay. I'll stop talking about it." For today. Alex hurried to keep up with her. The woman may be short, but when she was on a mission those legs worked overtime.

She followed Cagney and perused the romance novels. One looked promising and she picked it up and flipped through the pages. What do you know? A fake dating plot, go figure. She needed something to read, but she couldn't concentrate. At first, she thought her irritation with Cagney distracted her, but that didn't seem quite right.

No, she had the eerie, uncomfortable feeling someone was watching her. She looked up from the pages.

"Cagney? Is it my imagination or is that woman over there"—she pointed to the in-store café—"staring at us." She grabbed her shoulder. "Wait. Don't look. Don't make it obvious."

Too late. Cagney had already looked in her direction. Alex fumbled the book. It fell. She hastily bent to pick it up, all the while keeping an eye on the woman. "That's Mariah," she whispered. "The woman Blake is having an affair with."

"He's not having an affair." Easy enough for her to say. "They're just in the same class."

Before Alex could say anything, the woman headed their way. She pivoted and stared at the shelf again. "So, Cagney," she tried to remain calm and sound casual, "do you think I'd like this romcom."

"Alex? Alex Zurich?"

Alex looked up from the shelf. She felt her blood rise. How dare this woman approach her.

"Do you remember me, Mariah? Mariah Hopper. I'm in Blake's art history class." She extended her hand. *Do I have to shake it? This woman is hitting on Blake. I'm not even sure they haven't had...shit.*

She took it and shook. "Oh, yes. I remember you."

Cagney jabbed her ribs. "Be nice."

"He's such a nice man. You're a lucky woman. He talks about you all the time."

Does he now? Really?

"And you must be Cagney." Mariah nodded. "Blake's mentioned you too. And Brad."

"Nice to meet you."

"Well, I won't keep you. I saw you and I just wanted to say. You're a very lucky woman, Alex. Blake is a wonderful man. So funny. And handsome."

Alex watched as the woman turned on a heel and left the store. "What the hell was that about?"

"Shh! Everybody's watching," Cagney whispered.

"I really don't care if they are. Who does she think she is?" Alex huffed.

"Let's go over and sit. Maybe have a coffee. Bring

that book with you."

Alex didn't want to go sit. "I'd rather follow that woman and pummel her."

"I think mine is the better option."

Alex shrugged. "I know it is. It's just not the most satisfying one."

They strode to the other side of the store. Cagney pointed in the direction of an empty café table. "Go. Sit. I'll bring the coffee."

She didn't have any choice. Since when did this woman get so assertive? She took deep breaths while Cagney ordered their coffees.

Her friend plunked one in front of her. "Take a sip. It'll help."

She did as she was told. *I'm not in the least bit happy, but Cagney will never admit Blake is having an affair.*

"I'm sorry. I guess I acted a bit immature," Alex apologized.

They sat in silence for a moment. "I'm buying this." She held up the book. "And then we can leave. Thank you, Cagney, for helping me through this."

And when I prove he's cheating on me, I'll pummel him to within an inch of his life.

Chapter 32

Cagney

Cagney tested the water one more time. Finally hot enough. She stripped off her pajamas and laid them on the commode. She pushed the shower curtain to the side and stepped in.

"Ahh. Nothing like a hot shower in the morning." As she reached for her shampoo, she hesitated. All her toiletries sat next to Brad's. She experienced a level of sharing she was pretty sure exceeded the bounds of a fake girlfriend. And it felt weird.

She was in the middle of washing her hair when she heard the door open. Didn't she lock it? Why not?

"Oh, I didn't think you were in here?" Brad stated it more as a question.

Cagney froze, two fistfuls of shampooed hair on either side of her head. Her first urge was to cover herself.

"Didn't you hear the water running?"

"I guess I did. Or not. I don't know. I was thinking about the erosion of sedimentary rock in South Africa, and I guess I blocked everything else out? I'm sorry. I just wanted to trim my beard and brush my teeth. Of course, I shouldn't have done that earlier. It's just I'm not completely used to this routine, not that I don't enjoy your—"

Cagney heard herself laugh. The man was so

caught up in his work. Not unlike her and Harding. "It's okay." She released her hair and pulled the shower curtain back just a bit so she could see him. She imagined his horror. But she wanted to see it in his face.

"It's okay." She couldn't believe she was saying this. "Go ahead. I promise not to look." She closed the curtain.

He laughed. "I'm so sorry. I'll leave."

She whipped open the curtain again, this time so fast the plastic rubbing together caused Brad to turn. "Bradley Townsend, this is your apartment. This is your bathroom. Get yourself in front of that sink and do what you need to do. Act like I'm not even here."

"O-okay. If you're sure."

"I'm sure."

"So tell me about the erosion of sedimentary rock in South Africa. Are your studies going to lead to a research trip there? That could be exciting." She rinsed the shampoo out of her hair.

He didn't answer right away, but she heard the buzz of his electric clippers. Maybe men didn't talk while they trimmed their beards. Well, of course not, silly. If they talked, that could lead to all kinds of facial disasters.

"No, I don't think I'll need to visit there." *Buzz. Buzz.* "It's a shame. I'd love to go." *Buzz. Buzz.*

"What's on your agenda today, Cagney?"

She had been rubbing conditioner in her hair. She stopped. "Same as every day. Teach. Grade papers. Research. Nothing exciting."

He laughed. She hadn't heard the clippers so maybe he had finished trimming his beard.

"And yoga, right? It is Wednesday."

"Yes, we"—she emphasized we—"have yoga today. I certainly wouldn't want you to miss it. Sarah and her friends would be so disappointed." She positioned herself to make sure the water fully rinsed out the conditioner.

"By the way, is that why you're trimming your beard? To make a good impression for Sarah?"

He groaned. "They're so intrusive. Why do they bother me? Can't they just leave me alone? They already know you're my girlfriend...I mean they believe you're my girlfriend. So why are they still bothering me?"

"They're surrounding you like that precisely because of it. They're hoping to break us up...you know...they're hoping to break up the relationship they think we have."

****

Brad

Brad knew he shouldn't be trimming his beard. My God, there was a naked woman in his shower. If he were a gentleman, he would have excused himself and walked out, closing the door behind him. That's what he should have done. Why didn't he?

But then she didn't give him much of an option. He feared if he didn't stay, she would have marched out of the shower and dragged him back. She was short, beautiful, and determined.

Still, that was no reason to invade her privacy. He'd have to be more aware of his routine. When Logan lived with him, they interrupted each other. It was no big deal just to walk in to use the toilet while he was in the shower.

Brad recalled Logan had barged in on him once when he was showering to tell him he had found the perfect date for him. Right now, he couldn't even remember the woman's name. But Logan had burst in, pulled the curtain back, and shoved his phone under his nose to show him her photo. He chuckled. He should have expected it to have ended as disastrously as it did.

To be truthful, he found it hard to concentrate. It was bad enough she was only feet away from him. Did he mention she was naked? And covered in soap.

Brad definitely knew he shouldn't be trimming his beard. And now he was rushing through it. Well, he was trying to hurry the process. She kept talking to him. Not that he didn't love talking to her. She knew very little about geology, yet she always—always—asked how his research was going. And she always—always—appeared interested in the answers. She didn't need to do that.

Finally, he thought as he caught the last stray hair sticking out. He tilted his head to the left, then the right. Not bad for quick once over when his concentration on the task sucked. He clicked the razor off.

"Cagney, I'm done now. I'll see you, uh, in the living room, or maybe the kitchen? But I'm leaving now. So you don't have to feel like you're trapped in there. I'll close the door on my way out."

She laughed. "I don't feel trapped. But I am almost done. I'll see you in a bit."

Brad exited, closed the door behind him, and stood just outside it. "How could I not have seen this coming?" He rubbed his beard. "I'm in big trouble."

Chapter 33

Cagney

The loud, forceful thud broke Cagney's concentration. It sounded like it came from Brad's bedroom. The bloodcurdling scream that followed jolted her out of her chair. Without thinking, she rushed to his room. She stood frozen outside the closed door wondering whether to knock. Maybe it was something he did routinely. It could be some type of ritual he did before he started reading about rocks. Damn. She didn't know the study habits of geologists.

She summoned her courage, took a deep breath, and knocked. Okay, it wasn't so much a knock as her hand almost making contact with the door. She tried again. This time she succeeded.

"What?" Brad snapped. "Who's there and what do you want?" His pure anger intimated her momentarily.

"It's me, Cagney, and just wanted to know if you're all right. I heard what sounded like a book hit a wall." Her voice trailed off.

No answer, but in a moment the door opened. Brad's hair looked like he had tried to pull it out and his blue eyes were dull.

"I'm so sorry, Cagney. I didn't mean to yell at you, I'm just…" He rubbed his beard.

"Frustrated with your studies?" She raised an eyebrow and tried to smile.

"Exactly." He heaved out a sigh. "I promise not to do it again." He started to close the door. Cagney didn't know why she did it, but she put her foot over the threshold. When he pushed the door, it reverberated off her foot.

He narrowed his eyes. His frown told her everything she needed to know about his state of mind.

"What do you think you're doing?"

Had she miscalculated? "I think it's time you take a break from the books. The Society Against Book Abuse called. They think you need to step away from the room before any more books get harmed." She crossed her arms, hoping it showed him how confident she was. Which she wasn't.

His lips curved slightly. "Somebody reported me to the society?" He raised his brows. "It's not my first violation."

Cagney took a step back and gasped, holding her hand over her mouth. "Oh, no, you may be in deep trouble then, Mr. Townsend."

He opened the door wider. She stepped aside for him and followed him to the living room. He collapsed on the couch and she sat on the chair. And waited for him to talk.

"Geology sucks sometimes." He put his legs on the coffee table. "I'm stuck on this one piece of evidence." He rubbed his beard. "It has the potential to derail my entire dissertation."

"No, I'm sure you're mistaken." She hadn't the foggiest idea what he meant, but she knew his science skills wouldn't let something like that happen. "You need a distraction."

She rose. "I'm going to make some popcorn. You

find us a movie to watch on whatever streaming service you have. I'm going to make sure you don't think about rocks and erosion for the rest of the evening."

She didn't give him a chance to argue. She headed for the kitchen and pulled out a pot. He followed. "What are you doing?"

"I'm making popcorn."

"They have microwave popcorn these days."

"No. Never microwave."

She had already reached for the oil—"Olive oil, that's healthy."—and the bag of kernels she had bought the other day.

"What's the difference?" He ran a hand through his hair. It did little to tame it.

"What's the difference?" She mocked his tone. "You'll see. This will be the best popcorn you've had in a long time. Especially if you've been eating that garbage from a grease-stained bag. Guaranteed." She turned on the burner and poured just enough oil to cover the bottom. "You go find us a movie."

He shrugged and left the room.

She poured the kernels in and put the lid on the pot. She shook it and the satisfying *pop, pop, pop* began.

"My God, that smells delicious," Brad said as she placed the bowl between them on the piece of furniture they called the couch. While not small enough to be a loveseat, it desperately needed more space to be called a couch. Cagney thought it put just the right amount of space between them.

He stuffed a handful of popcorn into this mouth. He smiled.

"Did I not tell you it would be the best you've eaten in a long while?"

He nodded with small rapid movements of his head. "The best I've ever eaten. Hands down."

He stood. "Where are you going?" She feared he would go back to his room. Though he did seem content with the popcorn.

"Going to grab us a couple of sodas. Can't eat popcorn without soda."

He returned and handed her the can. As she opened it, she asked, "What movie are we watching?"

"Remember the movie we watched with Logan and Molly on our first fake date?"

She nodded.

"This is the first in that franchise, *Sawdust Man: Forest of Flames.* I'm going on the assumption you were telling the truth when you said you liked it."

"I was and I did. Let's start."

Neither of them talked for the first forty minutes of the movie.

"Brad." She touched him on the shoulder, his muscled shoulder. "This is really good."

What's going on here? She was roommates with a man, who several weeks ago was a stranger.

Now, she was sitting perilously close to him, sharing a bowl of popcorn and their love of superhero flicks. This bogus relationship slipped every day into a solid friendship. And maybe more?

She snuck a glance at him.

"What?" He winked, as he grabbed another handful of popcorn.

Her heart hitched.

"Nothing. Just enjoying the movie. Thanks for choosing it."

Damn.

Brad clicked off the television when the movie ended. "So very good."

She stood, collected the cans and empty bowl, and headed for the kitchen.

"Brad," she called to him, "all I see is a trash can. Please tell me you recycle and are hiding the container."

He pulled himself from the couch and strode toward her. "Right here. Open this." He opened the door to the closet. She noticed how close he was. Living together, no rooming together, hell, whatever she called it, meant that she was physically closer to him. Nearly all the time.

"Good man. I knew you recycled."

"I try. Logan wasn't good at it. I was always going through the trash to see what he had thrown out."

"Not surprised."

"Oh. My. God." Brad's exclamation startled her.

"What? What's wrong?"

"Nothing. I've got it. You know that piece of evidence I was stuck on?"

She nodded. "Yeah? The one that had you throwing books at the wall?"

"One book. Just one." His lip turned up in an almost smile. "It won't derail my dissertation after all."

"It won't?"

"Nope. I can actually use it to help prove my point." He took a step closer to her and kissed her on the cheek. "I'm going to write this down before I forget. I couldn't have done this without you."

He left the room. She shook her head slightly and brought her hand to the spot he had kissed. There was no pulling her heart out of this.

Chapter 34

Cagney

Cagney wondered why she and Brad still met several times a week at the Physics Café. Her friends—all two of them—and her advisor knew they shared an apartment. Wasn't that enough for them to believe they were dating? Yet, here they were.

She stole a glance at him as she opened her laptop. It felt comforting in an odd way to know she would be sitting across from him on certain days. She looked forward to seeing his one stray curl. And she liked that she could talk to him about her studies. Even though he didn't know much about history, he appeared to be sincerely interested. At least he asked intelligent questions. She appreciated that.

She needed to shift gears and think about Harding, though. The real man in her life. She sighed as she opened her email and scanned the inbox. The problem with a digital mailbox, she thought, was that it could theoretically contain an infinite number of emails. And she thought her box was near that number. But then, she'd subscribed to every newsletter that was even tangentially related to history conspiracies. She never realized how many conspiracies there were until now.

She began to methodically go down the list, searching for something relevant. Then she saw it. "I don't believe it." She put a hand to her mouth and laughed. "I think it's a miracle." She wanted to jump out of the booth at the Physics Café and do a happy dance. She didn't think anyone wanted to see that.

Brad looked up from his laptop. "What can't you believe?"

"He finally returned my email."

"Who?"

"Alonzo Reichard. He's the reigning expert on Harding. I sent him an email...wow, even before we had our blind date. I remember because he was on my mind that evening."

Brad closed his laptop and leaned over. "You were on a date with me and thinking about another guy? I think I should be insulted."

Cagney thought back to that disastrous night. "No, because as I recall, you had little interest in me." She paused. "And we agreed we had nothing in common."

"Yet here we are." He waved a hand. Just like he did on their first date. Only date, she reminded herself. Only real date. The rest of this, all these weeks, had been pretend.

"So, what did your Harding expert say?" He smiled and ran a hand over his beard.

"I haven't opened it yet." She looked down at the inbox. "I'm afraid he'll tell me my dissertation topic is baseless."

"Why would he do that? It sounds fascinating to me. The theory that Mrs. Harding killed him. Wow. There's a movie for you."

She gazed at that curl hugging his ear. "Sarcasm doesn't become you, Bradley Townsend."

"I'm not being sarcastic. Your dissertation is a daring concept, I'll admit, and I don't know much about history, but that's how breakthroughs occur. You look at a situation from a different perspective."

"That makes sense—in a theoretical world." She hoped he appreciated her throwing around a science-based word. "But reality sometimes halts those breakthroughs before the first rock could be split."

"You'll never know unless you open that email you've waited forever for." He rested an elbow on the laptop and the palm of his hand on his chin. "Until you open it, you've got a Schrodinger's black box situation on your hands." He nodded to the wall to the right of him.

She looked. Damn. They were sitting in the Schrodinger booth. The portrait of the physicist on the wall along with a cat poking its head out of an open black box. How fitting. Erwin Schrodinger created the thought experiment to show the paradox of quantum superposition. She didn't really understand the concept, but knew it had to do with the cat in the box either being dead or alive, depending on your consciousness.

"Okay, I guess it's time to see if the cat's dead or alive." She sighed and waved her hand over the mouse. Suddenly, she pulled it away and pointed her finger at Brad.

"If the damn cat is dead, it may very well be my entire academic career gets killed right along with it." She couldn't bear to be told her research had been all for naught.

"I mean what would I do with my life? I'd have to leave the university and eke out a meager life for me. I don't think I can waitress. God, I'd get the orders all screwed up. And forget bartending; that's just as bad." She sighed.

"Whoa. Calm down." He reached across the table and placed his hand on hers. It felt warm and comforting, just like every other time he had ever touched her.

"Do you really believe your advisor, what's her name?"

"Dr. St. Clair."

"Yeah, you don't think Dr. St. Clair would let you go on a flight of fancy with something as important as your dissertation topic, do you?"

Cagney thought about it. "No, you're right." Leave it to Brad to talk her off the ledge. "Reichard may not agree with my hypothesis but that doesn't mean my career is ruined." She quirked a brow. "Right?"

"That's what I'm trying to tell you."

"Right." She nodded. "Exactly."

He looked handsome when he smiled.

"I'm doing it." She shook her hand and hovered it over the mouse. "Here goes nothing." She grabbed it like it was a life preserver and clicked the email.

Dear Cagney, she read silently.

"For heaven's sake, read it out loud. I want to hear it, too."

She looked up, terrified all over again. "No, I can't do that. What if it's bad?"

"Stop that. If it's not what you wanted, I'll let you run to the restroom and cry for ten minutes. No more."

"What?" She'd need to cry forever if it were bad news.

"I read in some study that ten minutes of sobbing is the perfect amount of time to purge the grief from the human system. And then you can get on with your life."

"You're making that up. I'm sure there was no

study that said that."

"You're right. But I did read that crying washes out stress hormones and releases endorphins. So you'd at least feel better." He tilted his head as if he were a puppy waiting to be told he was a good boy.

"Read it out loud please. I'm sure it's good news."

She laughed and shook her head. "Okay, but I'm warning you."

Thank you for reaching out to me concerning your dissertation topic. You have constructed an interesting thesis. It's original and thought-provoking.

"Come on," she mumbled, "get to the part where you say it's stupid." She noticed Brad watching her, his lip slightly curled up. Sure, he enjoyed this, she thought.

I'd be happy to correspond with you regarding Harding's death and give you my thoughts. If we could find an agreeable time, we should probably arrange an online video meeting to get to know each other. I have the feeling our professional relationship is just beginning.

Of course, the best way for you to research the topic is to come to DC for yourself and peruse the stacks. And that way we could meet in person.

Looking forward to working with you,
Alonzo Reichard
Professor

It was more than she had hoped for. "Woohoo!" Brad shouted. Customers at nearby tables looked. "Oops, sorry. But I told you. The cat is alive and kicking."

She felt tears stream down her face. Evidently, Brad saw them. "Stress-relieving tears." She laughed and nodded. "Thanks for the pep talk."

"No problem. So when are you leaving for DC?"

She took a deep breath. "I've applied for several travel grants, but I haven't heard back from any of them. I need to do hands-on research in DC to give this dissertation credibility."

"It's not that far of a trip. Can't you just take it out of your stipend?"

****

Brad

The moment the words came out of his mouth, Brad regretted them.

"Of course, you can't. It's still a lot of money. What an ass I am."

He forgot two important things. Humanities majors did not get funded at the same rate as the sciences. And she probably didn't have anyone helping her through school. Not everyone had a grandmother who had money. His parents refused to help him because of his choice of major—"The sciences don't pay enough."— but his grandmother gave him occasional cash because she loved him. And believed in him. Period. No questions asked.

"No, I do not have the money." She grew defensive. He didn't mean for that to happen.

"I know it's not a lot, but it involves several nights of hotels. In DC." Cagney's voice rose. People were watching.

"I've apologized. I'm sorry. That was rude and insensitive. You wouldn't have applied in the first place if you had the money."

Cagney rose. "I'm going to the restroom now for that cry."

He turned and watched as she left.

Fake dating just got real. Again. Far too real for his taste. He realized he cared that she was crying because of him. That shouldn't have happened. She shouldn't be crying because of him. And he shouldn't care about it. It wasn't in the game plan.

This arrangement was meant to be purely ornamental. It was supposed to have all the appearances of a relationship, but without any feelings or commitments. Now again Cagney was crying because of his stupidity. Wasn't this how real relationships worked?

And he felt badly about it. Because he cared about her feelings. He cared? But it was supposed to be…

"Brad." Blake. He knew the English accent anywhere.

"Where's Cagney?" Alex came into view. "I thought you two would be together."

"She went to the rest room. She'll be out soon." *In about ten minutes.*

Alex and Blake slid into the booth where Cagney had been. "We're waiting for our order. I'm glad you guys are here." Alex was her perpetual cheerful self. She almost didn't seem real to him at times.

Blake waved his element placard, 80Hg, as if to prove that was the true purpose of their appearance.

"You know what? I'm going to go to the restroom too." She slid out of the booth, kissed Blake on the cheek, and left.

"It must true." Blake shook his head.

"What must be true?" Brad watched in amazement as the man's hair bounced.

"Women can't go to the restroom alone. They

always go in twos."

****

Cagney

"Cagney, are you in here?"

Alex's voice bounced off the walls of the ladies' restroom.

"Alex, is that you?" This was the last person she wanted to see. *And why in the hell did she come in here looking for me? What did Brad tell her?*

"Of course, it's me."

There was no way around it. She would have to come out of the stall. She flipped the lever to unlock the door and took a step out, a wad of toilet paper in one hand.

"Hi, Alex, fancy meeting you."

"Oh. My. God. Have you been crying? Why? What happened?"

The words tumbled out of her mouth.

"Nothing happened. I'm fine." She took a deep breath. "Allergies. That's all. Allergies."

"No, you're crying for another reason. Now spill it."

Cagney scanned the small restroom. Only three stalls. Walls a pale green. This wasn't the place she wanted to unpack her emotional baggage. And clearly that's all it was.

"I totally overreacted, that's all." Damn, Brad was right. Ten minutes of crying was cathartic. "Brad made a comment and I took it the wrong way."

Alex nodded. She looked thoughtful. "What kind of comment?"

"Do we have to talk about it in a public restroom?" Cagney glanced at the door. She feared someone would walk in at any minute.

"Actually, do we have to talk about it at all? Because it's all in the past and it doesn't matter." She took a deep breath and coughed. She could feel the tears coming again.

"That's where you're wrong, Cagney Adler."

"What are you talking about?"

"Think about it. You're crying because of something Brad said."

She rolled her eyes. "Yes, my bad. End of story."

"No, no." Alex bounced on her toes. "It's the beginning of the story."

Cagney ran a hand through her hair. "Listen, as much as I'd love to play guess where this conversation is going, I need to return an email. That professor I contacted about my thesis actually got back to me."

Alex went from bouncing to full out jumping. "I'm so excited for you. I know you've waited for this for a long time. JJ will be so excited for you too."

Cagney had to smile. As frustrating as the woman was, she was also a solid friend. It almost made her feel guilty that she had been trying to chase her back to her own world.

She hugged Cagney. Then out of nowhere, released her and took a step back. "What could Brad say that sent you to the restroom to cry?"

"He didn't mean to." Cagney told her the story.

"You know what's happening? Like I was going to tell you. You're crying because of Brad."

"Yeah, so what?" Cagney had a feeling she didn't want to hear this.

"You care enough about what Brad says that it hurts you. That means you have feelings for him. You guys have gone beyond the fake relationship stage. You love him."

"That's crazy." Cagney wiped a tear with the wad of toilet paper. "I'm just over sensitive. Everyone tells me that."

Chapter 35

Cagney

Cagney shook her head. "Excuse me? What did you say?" She couldn't believe her advisor was talking and she wasn't listening. That's because she was thinking about Brad's…what the hell was happening?

"I said I think I found funding for your DC trip." Dr. St. Clair leaned back in her office chair.

"Don't toy with a homeless person." Cagney shook her head. "I'm emotionally fragile at the moment."

"No, seriously. I've already laid claim to the money. It's yours."

"What money? How'd you do that?"

So many questions ran through Cagney's mind.

"This is so exciting, Cagney." Alex bounced in her seat. When did it become normal to have a fictional character attend meetings with your advisor?

"The history department has a fund earmarked for graduate student research travel. It's for worthy students who need to travel but haven't the money to do so."

"It does? How come I never knew that?" Wasn't she a worthy student?

"Because there hasn't been enough money in it to send anyone to the store for a loaf of bread, let alone travel on it."

Cagney wasn't surprised. In the short time she'd

been in the department, funding from the university had been sparse, to say the least. Studying dead people apparently didn't have the appeal of say, the planetarium, or physics. Or even rocks. *That's exactly why Brad receives a larger stipend than me.*

"It's funded through donations of professors and former students. The other day, we received notification that someone had donated a substantial amount to it. Apparently, anonymously." She shrugged. "Even Dr. Chare doesn't know who it is."

"The moment I heard about the money, I reserved it for you. You're worthy and you don't have the funds to travel on."

"Dr. St. Clair, I don't know how to thank you. This is the nicest thing anyone has done for me in a long time." That wasn't a lie.

"I know how excited you are about meeting Dr. Reichard, and confidentially, he's equally excited about meeting you from what I hear." She leaned forward and said softly, as if she were conveying confidential information, "I also know you're still not in your own apartment. Going on this trip may help take some of the stress off living with your fake boyfriend. I'm sure it's got to be, well, awkward, at times."

"And you know what will happen when you return?"

Alex's voice startled Cagney. With the news of having money to travel on, she had forgotten she was even in the room.

"No, what will happen when I return?" Cagney didn't even try to hide her irritation.

"When you return home, you'll realize how much you've missed Brad and learn how much he missed you. And you both discover how much you love each other."

Silence filled the room. "Don't roll your eyes, Cagney. It will happen."

Chapter 36

Brad

Cagney sat on what had become what Brad had thought of as her end of the couch. He sat on his. The bowl of popcorn between them. Since that first time she had coaxed him out of his room before he destroyed every book he owned, they had developed an occasional routine.

"This is the fourth in the franchise," he said to Cagney, "and critics panned it. But I think it's the best. It's *Sawdust Man: Smoldering Embers.*"

He grabbed a handful of popcorn as he clicked on the remote. While he had asked her to stay with him because, well, where else would she go, he had grown to like her company. Maybe a little too much. He liked talking to someone over breakfast. No, he liked talking to *her* over breakfast. He enjoyed the times when their schedules allowed them to eat dinner together. And on weekends when they would order something delivered.

He wanted them to watch one more movie before she left on her research trip.

"So far, I've loved them all. I'm sure I'll love this one." She brought her can of soda to her lips.

He laughed.

"What's so funny?"

"I've never met a woman who appreciated these superhero movies before."

"I think it was Blake's interpretation that sold me. Being a metaphor for the desires of the common person."

He laughed even harder. "Yeah, right."

"Just turn the damned thing on already."

They watched in silence for a while. Then he paused the movie.

"What are you doing? It's just at the…"

"Just have to make a bathroom trip." He rose. He didn't really need to, but he wanted an excuse to pause the movie and get her talking.

As he crossed the room on his return he asked, "Are you ready for your trip next week?"

Cagney nodded. Not a nod of confidence, he decided.

"I'm nervous. I hope I make a good impression."

He sat. "Of course, you will." He reached for the remote and asked, "Do you have everything you need? You know supplies like pens and journals and such?"

She crossed her leg. "I guess. I mean how much stuff does a person need?"

"I went on a research trip once and the only pen I had dried up. Kapoot. I had to leave the library to buy new pens and then go back. By the time I returned the library had closed."

"Really?"

No, not really. I'm trying to make a segway here without sounding too obvious. "I'm very picky about my pens." That wasn't a lie, he thought. He was. "The first two stores I went to didn't have them."

"What kind of pens?" Good, her curiosity was aroused.

He told her. "Is it odd that I have a pen addiction?"

She laughed. "Nope, I have one too. I only do a certain brand and then the ultra-fine point in it."

"Really? What brand?"

She told him. Yay. That was easy enough.

"It's because I write so small, I need a very fine line."

"You know what they say about people whose handwriting is small?"

"No, what do they say?"

"Handwriting specialists say they are introverted, focused individuals."

"Wait." Her hand was in the bowl. "Are you quoting from a pseudoscience? I just can't imagine you endorsing it as a real"—she pulled her hand out and gestured air quotes—"science. Are you feeling okay?"

"I'm feeling fine. I can have as open a mind as the next person."

"Okay, what's your handwriting say about you?" She jumped up and grabbed the grocery list he stuck to the refrigerator. She sat back down and grabbed her phone.

"What are you doing?"

"Two can play this game. You think you're so smart diagnosing me on how I write."

He smiled. She'll never suspect the reason he originally asked the question. She's run with the idea.

"But what I diagnosed, as you say, was all good characteristics."

She didn't seem to hear. She looked like she was busy scrolling.

"You print." She looked up from the phone. He noticed how her eyes sparkled when she thought she had made a point. And she was about to make a point.

"And according to this, you're intense and intelligent."

"Intense?"

"I'm not the one who throws books at the wall."

"You've got a point there."

"Let's finish the movie."

Chapter 37

Cagney

"Are you sure you have everything?"

Brad stared at her suitcase, then her laptop case, and then her. When he got to looking at her, it was more of a gaze than a stare. And Cagney knew the look well enough that it was one of concern.

"I have everything. Laptop. Phone. Charger. Notebooks. Pens. What else do I need?"

He shrugged. "I don't know. It looks like you have it all. Did you go over that checklist I made for you?"

She laughed. He stayed up late the weekend before her trip and created a checklist, a spreadsheet really, of everything she would need for her research trip. How did he know this? Because he spent the week before asking random questions at odd times.

"How do you take notes?" he asked while he slathered peanut butter on his bagel one morning.

At the time, she thought he was just making conversation. He knew how much she looked forward to the trip. He stunned her, though, the evening before she left when he handed her a printout spreadsheet, along with a small package with silver gift wrapping covered in gold stars.

"If you check off each item as you pack, then you'll know you have all your supplies."

How sweet. "Thank you. I am notorious for

forgetting things." She nodded toward the package on the dining room table. "What's this?"

"Just a little gift in honor of your trip."

"Of course," he said in response to her raised eyebrow, "you can open it now." When did they start communicating nonverbally?

She carefully opened the gift, not wanting to destroy the paper.

"How thoughtful." Inside the box was a set of her favorite pens—ultra-fine point, her favorite—and two perfect-sized journals. Tears filled her eyes. "Thank you."

Now the two stood at Bell Wyck's train station—just a small wooden platform with a covering—in an awkward silence. Cagney's excitement was so strong she didn't sleep well the night before. But now a sadness enveloped her. In this silence, she finally figured it out. She would miss Brad. His stupid jokes. His questions about her topic. Even his complaining about Piper.

"While I'm gone, Piper will have you all to herself. She'll love it."

Brad groaned. "That woman will be the death of me."

The PA system announced that boarding had begun. "I guess I'm ready." Leaving him, even for a few days, was difficult. She hadn't expected this. Damn. She would miss him. She thought back to when she first met him on that blind date. She didn't want a relationship and especially not with Rock Nerd.

Brother, she decided. He was the brother she never had. That was it.

"Cagney?" Brad wore a look of concern. *How long*

has he been calling my name?

"I'm sorry. I was lost in thought."

"Of course. You have a big project ahead of you."

"Yes, I do."

He dug into his jeans pocket. "I want you to have this." His fingers were clenched around what? She couldn't see. He took her hand and turned it palmed up. He placed the object in her hand and folded her fingers over it. "Keep it with you at all times."

She opened her hand. No, it couldn't be. It was the rock he kept in his pocket for moments he felt disconnected from the world.

"May the quartz be with you."

"I can't take this. This is your grounding object. This keeps you going."

"I want you to have it. You're meeting several important people in your field. You may feel at times you don't belong with them. But you do. All you need to do is touch the quartz and remember both of you are made of the same elements. And you belong in this universe. Any damn place you want to be."

"But what are you going to do?" She felt tears rolling down her cheeks. The PA system announced last call for boarding.

"I have something to ground me." He picked up her suitcase and led her by the hand to the train car. The porter took her baggage.

"Text me when you get there." Concern flooded his crystal blue eyes. Was that a tear glistening in there? He held her shoulders then kissed her on the cheek quickly, then stepped back. "Don't forget to text me."

The conductor called her. "I'm coming. Bye, Brad. I…I'm going to miss you."

She boarded the train and found her seat. Holy Harry Truman. She almost told him she loved him. Where the hell did that come from? She still had the rock in her hand. Hell.

****

Brad

Brad drove home from the train station thinking about Cagney's trip. He knew she'd do well. She knew her stuff, after all. He had never met a woman who could not only rattle off dates but also tell you the implications of historical events. If that Alonzo Reichard guy couldn't see how very capable she was in her field, then he was blind. And stupid.

He unlocked the door to his apartment, put the keys on the hook on the wall, and…realized he was lost. Utterly lost. Okay, he had only stepped into his apartment, but he missed her already. Was it too soon to say the place held an eerie quietness?

Straighten up, Townsend. It's just your imagination. You can't miss Cagney already. Just what are you going to when she moves back into her own place? A heaviness settled into his chest.

Pushing that aside, he forced himself to see the advantages of Cagney being away for a week. "I'll have the bathroom to myself." He realized he hadn't moved from the kitchen. He strode into the living room and sat on the couch. "Now that she's not here, I can buckle down and do some serious research and writing on my dissertation."

He had recently submitted two chapters to his advisor. He debated about waiting to write any more. It might be best to see what Dr. Taylor thought about those before plowing ahead. But Brad wanted this process to be done already. "More writing it is, then," he said out loud, and realized how empty the apartment was.

After about an hour of staring at what essentially was a blank page—Chapter Three didn't qualify as substance, any more than the header with his name on it did—he slammed his laptop shut.

"Damn it. I do miss her. God, I'm in trouble."

He stepped out onto the balcony and scanned the sky. When had it gotten dark? Maybe he had been staring at that screen longer than an hour. He stepped up to the telescope and focused in on Venus, the planet he showed Cagney when she first moved in.

He sighed. He knew he had a place in the universe. And he hoped Cagney knew her place in the universe too. That's why he gave her his rock. He reached into his pocket. It was the first time in—God, he didn't know how long—that he didn't carry it with him.

He slowly raised his head from the telescope. "But I really don't need it. I have something to remind me of my belonging. Someone. Someone to remind me."

The knock at the door startled him. The longer he listened the louder and faster the pounding got. Had they been knocking for a while? He had a hard time hearing it on the balcony. "Come to think of it, who'd be visiting me?"

Chapter 38

Cagney

"Brad, look at this." Cagney carefully moved the phone around the hotel room, making sure he saw the bar, the microwave, and coffee pot. She then showed him the bed and immediately pulled away from it. Her cheeks burned.

"Isn't it great? I didn't expect it to be so nice. Dr. St. Clair made all the arrangements."

She saw Brad's wide grin. Evidently, he appreciated it. She didn't understand the urge to give him a virtual tour of her room the moment she had soaked it all in. But he was the first person she wanted to share it with. He had given her his rock. As she thought of that, she pushed her hand into her pocket. It was still there.

"That's so nice. At the end of the week, you won't want to come back to this apartment." It was Friday night and Brad sat in the wingback chair. That's odd, she thought, he has the entire place to himself. That's his least favorite spot. She thought it even odder she knew the seating preferences of her fake boyfriend.

"Wait," the voice on the other end screamed. The voice was shrill and panicked and definitely didn't belong to Brad. "She lives here? You didn't tell me that."

She had never seen cheeks turn red so fast, from

the top to bottom like Brad's were doing even with the coverage of his beard. "We're roommates, Piper. Yes."

"You're more than roommates." She could hear Piper's voice rise another octave, if that were possible.

"Is that Piper in our—your—apartment?" Cagney had to remember she was only Brad's guest.

"Yes, Cagney." Brad's voice was low. "She stopped by shortly after I got back from the train station."

"How did she know where we, uhm, you live?"

"I'm not dumb." Brad's face blurred and in a nanosecond Piper glared at her. "I told you he was mine. You didn't listen. I didn't know you lived here."

The woman, barely a woman, rambled. And she was pissed. "Give the phone back to Brad now." Cagney glared back. How dare this child chastise her. "Now." Cagney added emphasis.

Piper's face blurred then disappeared and all she saw was the quick peek at the dining room. She heard a door close and then Brad's face appeared in the screen.

"I'm sorry. I never would have called if I thought you had company." She paused. "Shit, that sounds like I think you're a hermit. Of course, you would have company—"

"Cagney." Brad's voice was stern but compassionate. "I was hoping you'd call. No, I was waiting for your call." He rubbed his beard. "I'm trying to kick her out. But she's like…I don't know what she's like. All I know is that I'm very uncomfortable with her here."

"Where is she now?" She felt as if she were talking about a home invasion.

"She's in the living room and I'm in my bedroom. I

can breathe in here."

"What are you going to do?" She felt Brad's pain, but at the same time she felt...jealousy.

Jealousy? Why? They weren't in a real relationship. It would be good for Brad to have a real girlfriend. Piper was sexy. Maybe she was the woman of his dreams. So why did she feel anger rise when she saw the woman in her—wait, no—his apartment? Her stay there was only temporary.

"I'm going to have to usher her out." Brad's eyebrows furrowed.

"What? You look worried." Cagney bit her lip.

"It looks like it'll be difficult. She's planted herself on the couch. And was disappointed when I didn't sit next to her."

"What are going to do?"

"I know what I'm not going to do. I'm not going to physically pull her from the couch and throw her out the door—no matter how badly the urge strikes me."

He shook his head and sighed so loudly she could hear him.

Cagney's imagination went to several scenarios. "I'll tell you what. Go chase her out right now. I'll stay on the video call. This way, I'll be a witness."

Brad rubbed his beard. "I guess." His voice trailed off.

"Are you afraid of her?" If the situation wasn't so dire, she would laugh. But she knew how Brad felt about fraternizing with his students, especially this student. He sincerely worried about getting thrown out of the doctoral program.

Just then she heard a knock at Brad's door. "It's probably Piper wondering where I am. Stay with me."

****

Brad

"Uhm, who's there?"

A British accent responded. "Me, Blake."

"And me, Alex. Piper told us you were in here talking to Cagney. Can I talk to her?"

Brad shrugged and opened the door, ushered the couple in, and quickly shut the door. Then he handed Alex the phone.

"I've learned not to argue with her." Blake shook his head.

Alex glared at him. "But you're still my love, love."

"Cagney, how are you? We miss you here," Alex said.

"I've literally been gone less than twenty-four hours."

"Why is Piper in your home?" Alex's voice was hushed and she furtively glanced toward the guys.

"It's not my home. I'm a guest of Brad."

"As long as you're here," Brad called, "it's your home. For as long as you need it or as long as you care to stay."

Brad looked at his bedroom. The three of them—four if you count Cagney via video call—were huddled in there while Piper was in the living room. What was wrong with this picture?

"I've got it." He grabbed the phone from Alex. "Stay on the call, Cag. Blake, Alex, come with me. I'm going to throw Piper out and the three of you are my witnesses. Then she can't say anything untoward happened."

"Untoward. That's one way to phrase it." Alex

knitted her brows.

Blake nodded, his hair bouncing to his apparent approval. "I'm ready. Let's go."

"The nerve of that woman thinking you would choose her over Cagney." Alex huffed.

"Alex, you do know…"

She knew Cagney wasn't really his girlfriend. But Brad didn't want to correct her. Cagney had grown into a good friend, and he had feelings for her he couldn't explain. He kept dismissing them. He tried to tell himself she was like a sister. But his brain wouldn't listen. What started out as an awkward fake relationship felt more real every single moment. Like right now.

"Yeah, let's go. I can't take her here another moment." The moment he opened the bedroom door, Piper rose from the couch. "It's about time you came out of there. Have you told Casey you're through with her?"

He swore he heard Cagney laugh at the name he used to call her.

"Her name is Cagney and she's still on the line. I'm escorting you to the door and Alex and Blake along with Cagney are witnesses to this."

"Well, I never."

"Piper." Alex walked up to her. "Brad is already in a relationship with Cagney. And they're in love." Goosebumps ran up his spine. Holy slate. Maybe he was.

"And it's time you go home."

"I don't see why I have to go home. I think it's you two"—she pointed at Alex and Blake—"who don't belong here. And neither does she." She wagged a finger at the phone. "She's nothing but a—"

"Enough, Piper. Even if I were attracted to you—and I'm not—we couldn't date because I'm your teacher. It's a gigantic breach of the rules." He sighed. He grew increasingly worried that Piper would plant herself in his apartment until Cagney came home. *Yeah, I said home.*

"No, we're going to see you to the door. You've overstayed your welcome."

She huffed. "I don't understand it. I've done everything I could to get your attention." Blake and Alex shepherded her toward the door like a lost sheep. "I even learned about the things you seem to love." She pivoted and stared at Brad who took up the rear. "Geology is the most boring thing in the world." She paused. "And you know what? Anyone who's into that stuff must be boring too. Come to think of it, I'm not sure why I was ever into you in the first place."

She stood at the threshold for a moment. Tears ran down her cheeks. Part of Brad wanted to push her through it and slam the door. The moment he thought that, though, he felt badly. But he did want, no needed, her to leave. Pronto.

"You're not worth it Bradley Townsend. Good riddance." She finally walked out the door and left. Alex bent her body in two around the door frame as she watched the woman walk down the hall.

"She's at the elevator now." She turned her head toward him as she spoke. Then she returned to her sentry duty. "She's…gone."

Brad breathed a sigh of relief. "I'm so glad you two were here." He scratched his head. "Why are you here, anyway?"

Blake sauntered over to the couch and sat down,

his hair bouncing. "To help you."

Alex followed him and sat next to him. Close. Not like he and Cagney sat.

"What?" He lowered himself into the wingback chair.

"I heard Piper talking to someone in class before you got there the other day," Blake said. "Evidently, she had heard from someone, who knows who, that Cagney would be out of town. She didn't know the two of you were living together. She was livid about that. She said that—"

"Focus, Blake." Alex placed her hands about six inches out, palms together, and shook them. "Focus."

"Why, yes. As I was saying, she discovered you'd be alone this weekend and decided she'd visit. And try to…"

His cheeks grew hot.

"Get you into a compromised position," Alex finished.

Brad let out a low whistle. "Thanks. I owe you…big time."

Chapter 39

Cagney

Cagney woke up and stretched. She looked around the room, decorated in blues and browns, and pushed her hair out of her eyes. "I'm in the hotel." She pulled the covers off and swung her legs to the side of the bed. "And I'm meeting Alonzo Reichard."

She jumped out of bed bewildered by her good luck and intimidated by the thought of meeting one of the leading historians in her field.

She showered quickly but tried to dress with care. She chose a business-like gray pantsuit. She had considered black jeans but decided she needed to look as mature and responsible as she could. While she ate a quick—and free—hotel breakfast of a croissant sandwich, coffee, and cranberry juice, she texted Brad.

—I'm heading toward my meeting in a few. Wish me luck.—

The response came back swiftly.

—You don't need luck. You've got talent and intelligence. Those men better look out.—

As she was typing a response, another text from him popped up.

—May the quartz be with you. You belong there just as much as they do.—

She smiled and immediately reached for her pocket. She had remembered to stash it. She had never thought of Brad as having any insecurities. Well, except yoga. Knowing that he had the same doubts she carried with her made him more relatable.

She texted him back.

—*Got it.*—

And added a thumbs up emoji. And in that moment, she felt as if she could conquer the historical academic world. Flushed with confidence, she quickly texted Dr. St. Clair.

—*I'm on my way...*—

She shoved the phone in the pocket with the quartz and left in search of the subway station.

She found herself standing in front of the office door of Alonzo Reichard. The subway ride had been a blur. All she could recall was she sat next to some guy who had his dog sitting on his lap. It was just as well. It distracted her.

Her heart pounded as she knocked on the door. "Come in; it's open." That was his voice. She recognized it from the video call they were on last month.

The door squeaked as she opened it and Dr. Reichard looked up as she entered. It seemed like it took a moment for him to recognize her. But when he did, he rose and walked around the desk. "So good to see you in person."

He extended his hand, and she shook it. "Please, sit down."

****

The meeting took less than an hour. "And I'll make sure you have my clearance for our school library. You'll find documents in there that most people aren't allowed to touch. Even our own doctoral students."

Cagney's eyes teared up. This access ensured her dissertation would have all the necessary academic qualifications. "Thank you, Doctor."

"Please call me, Al. And I'm having dinner tonight with Max Rayburn. Can you join us?"

"E-e-excuse me, the author of *Conspiracies Are All Around Us*?"

Reichard nodded. "I've already told him about you. And he's expecting you. I hope you can make it."

"Yes, of course."

"Great. Let me give you the address of the restaurant." He turned toward the desk, pulled a sticky note off a pad, and began writing. "The name of the restaurant and its address. And don't worry. It's casual. It's just a neighborhood dive. Jeans are fine. We'll see you at seven, then."

"Thank you. Yes. Seven."

Cagney thought she would burst as she walked out of the building. She found the nearest bench, sat, and pulled out her cell phone. It wasn't even noon yet. She could get in several hours of serious research before she met—oh my God, the second most important person in conspiracy theories.

She had to tell Brad. He'd be so happy for her. She texted him. "I'm sure he's in class or in the library. He'll see it sometime today."

No sooner had she stood and shoved the phone back into her pocket, it chimed. She smiled at the notification sound she had assigned to his text messages. She pulled the phone back out and read his reply.

—I knew it. They can't help but think you're the greatest.—

As she walked in what she hoped was the general direction of the library, it hit her. He was so supportive. He sincerely believed in her. And she liked him—a lot. And they still didn't have much in common.

She smiled at a couple on a bench holding hands and laughing. She thought about how their relationship had developed. It started out as fake, but now that she lived in his home, it was beginning to feel real. She didn't know when that happened or how she felt about it.

****

"Wow, this week has flown."

The resources she had found during her trip had catapulted her dissertation from a fringe conspiracy theory to a solid thesis with more than enough evidence to back it up.

Not only that, she had met so many professors, librarians, and museum directors who not only encouraged her, but gave her their email addresses should she need additional help. She didn't feel as if it were just her and Dr. St. Clair anymore. She had connections.

She giggled at the thought of connections. "I just may get my degree before I turn thirty. And after that, I just might publish my dissertation. Just like Dr. St. Clair did."

She packed the last of her clothes in the suitcase. She feared she wouldn't be able to close it. She amazed herself. Even in the digital world, she still photocopied so many documents. So many. Why hadn't she thought of that before she left? She could have packed a larger suitcase.

She pulled the lid up and over to meet the bottom.

Quite a gap. Okay, maybe it wasn't the documents that prevented the suitcase from closing. It might have been the four or five books she bought. Oh, who was she kidding? *Nine. I bought nine books. I may have overcommitted.*

She pushed the top down and reached for the zipper. It took a while, but she finally got it. "Now to get it off the couch and down to the lobby." She pulled the suitcase off the bed. *Thud.*

Thank God for wheels. She pulled it to the door. Then she went through the hotel room again making sure she didn't forget anything. Satisfied, she said goodbye to the room, luxurious by her standards.

****

As Cagney sat on the train, waiting for it to leave the station, she thought about the work she had ahead of her. It exhilarated her. This was it. She had what she needed to make the argument concerning Harding's death.

Cagney pulled her phone out of her jacket pocket and texted her advisor. Again. She had texted Dr. St. Clair every single day she had been in DC. She shared some of her findings. Her advisor always reacted positively.

—*Coming home today.*—

She hit the send button.

It took only a moment for the response.

—*Great. Can't wait to see what you have.*—

Then her phone pinged again.

—*Alex and Blake say hi. They miss you. Hell, we all missed you.*—

Cagney chuckled. She wondered who the fictional couple bothered while she was away. It was probably

Brad…

Brad. Her breath hitched and she swore her heart skipped a beat when she thought of him. He would be picking her up in Bell Wyck. Not a day of the trip had passed without one of them texting—usually several times throughout a day. From her showing him the hotel room, to him dropping an occasional photo of his morning bagel with some stupid caption that referenced the day she saw him bare-chested.

She texted him.

—On my way. Sorry, you've got to share your home again.—

She sent it off and nearly immediately he answered.

—Oh, no. The return of the fake girlfriend. LOL!—

She laughed and before she could respond he sent another message.

—I'll be there when your train arrives. It's been too quiet around here. No one in the shower to talk to while I'm shaving.—

Chapter 40

Brad

"Why the hell am I so nervous?" Brad said to no one in particular. At least, he hoped none of the other people waiting for the train heard him. But he was edgy. He had missed Cagney's presence in the apartment. Damn it. He had missed Cagney.

He saw her step off the train. God, she looked beautiful. Her honey-colored hair was up in a ponytail that allowed her beautiful face to glow.

He didn't think she saw him with the other people milling about. He waved, hoping that would catch her attention. And it did. He knew she saw him because she smiled. She flashed him that natural smile that hit the corner of her eyes. He liked to think she saved that one for him, but he knew that probably wasn't the case.

It still made his heart beat a bit faster. He didn't realize how much he liked being around her. Maybe that wasn't the best way to put it. He knew he liked being around her. He didn't know how much he would miss her while she was gone.

What did that mean for their fake relationship, then? *Maybe I can find a scientific study that analyzes the degree to which you miss a person.* Perhaps a scientist had created a love spectrum that would quantify your feelings and measure it on a scale ranging from bitter enemies to ardent lovers. If only there was such a thing to let him know if he loved Cagney. Because right now he felt like he might.

She also quickened her pace when she saw him, and Brad realized he had been jogging toward her. They reached each other and stood for a moment just a few feet apart. Then, she dropped her bag, took two steps, and flung her arms around him. He hugged her back and gave her the squeeze a doctoral student deserved after a successful research trip. Oh, who was he kidding? He gave her the bear hug that showed how much he missed her.

"I missed you." Her words tickled his ear and delighted his heart.

"I missed you, too."

They both released their hold on the other at the same time.

"I'm sorry," he said. "I just kind of got carried away." His cheeks burned. He hoped she couldn't see it underneath his beard.

"No, I'm sorry." She ran her hand down her ponytail. "I don't know what I was thinking." Cagney picked up her bag.

"No, let me get that." He reached for it and their hands touched. What was that tingle all about? "I insist," he added when she didn't let go of it immediately.

"Thank you." Her cheeks glowed red. He didn't mean to embarrass her. He didn't want her to feel awkward around him.

They walked to the truck in silence. He put the bag in the back of the truck as Cagney got into the passenger seat. They were out of the parking lot and onto the street before either one of them spoke.

****

Cagney

"So, uhm…did Piper ever visit you again?" Cagney asked. While he hadn't mentioned it, a second and even a third visit seemed to fit the woman's personality. She was nothing if not persistent.

"No, no, she didn't. I think she got the hint." Brad kept his eyes on the road.

"She is beautiful." She paused. "If you think, well, if you want to date someone for real, like Piper, I'd understand."

"What? Are you crazy?" His head turned toward her, his eyes wide. She didn't expect his forceful response.

"I don't want our relationship, our fake relationship, I mean, to stand in the way of you finding someone—"

"No, Cagney. Why would you say that? Our relationship, fake relationship, you know, is all I want."

Cagney sighed. What did that mean? Did it mean he had no interest in a real relationship with her? Why did she care? *Do I want him as my real boyfriend?*

While her brain told her no, her heart, if its excessive beating was any indication, seemed to think otherwise. *When did I start caring about this guy?*

Damn that Alex. Alex kept telling Cagney that Brad and she had something more so often, that maybe she began to believe it? Ridiculous. *The two of us still have nothing in common. Period.* A fake relationship is enough.

Her heart started pounding again. What? *At the thought of not having Brad in my life?* No, surely the pounding was for the research she uncovered in DC.

Why am I thinking about this nonsense of a relationship when I have so many new ideas to explore for my dissertation?

"Do you want to date someone? Because I could—"

Brad's question startled her. "No, no. I'm good. I have my dissertation to finish. I couldn't possibly think about committing to someone before I finish."

"Right. Of course not. Same here." He rubbed his beard.

They rode in silence for a while. Bell Wyck wasn't that large, so why did it seem like it took forever to get near campus?

"Are you okay?" She almost forgot about Brad's presence. Who else would be driving?

"Yeah, I'm fine. I just have a lot of stuff to digest," Cagney said.

"I bet you do. I'm glad the trip was such a success for you." Brad glanced over at her.

"Thanks. It was so much more than I expected it to be." She laughed.

"Well, we're home." Brad said as he pulled into the apartment complex lot. He put the truck in park and turned to her.

Home, she thought. This place is beginning to feel like home. Or is Brad beginning to feel like home?

Chapter 41

Cagney

"Holy crap." Brad put down his phone. "I've got to go to my dad's birthday party this weekend." He took off his glasses and rubbed his eyes. "I forgot all about his birthday."

Cagney looked up from her laptop. They sat opposite each other at the Physics Café. "You don't sound like you want to go." What she wouldn't give to be able to celebrate her parents' birthdays with them again.

He ran a hand through his hair and stared into space for a moment. He took a deep breath. His words came out low and slow. "My parents and I don't get along."

He heaved a sigh and put on his glasses. "That's not the worse part of it. Somehow, they've learned from someone I have a girlfriend." He gestured air quotes. "And they want to meet her, uhm, you."

Cagney gagged on her coffee. "No, I couldn't possibly go. It's one thing to fool our friends that we're dating. It's totally different lying to parents. I think my going is a bad idea." She pursed her lips.

"I wouldn't even ask you because my parents and I don't see eye to eye on a lot of things." He rubbed his beard. "Okay, we don't agree on anything." He massaged his forehead. "I can't tell them I'm just pretending to date, though. They think I'm a loser to start with."

"Wait. What did you say? Your parents don't really think you're a loser. I'm sure it's just a—"

"Believe me. They don't think I've made proper life choices." He rubbed his beard. "I figure it's a ritual all parents go through. It must be in their owner's manual." He met her gaze. "Don't your parents criticize your choices?"

Oh. He didn't know. But then how could he? "No, they don't. But they're not around anymore. My mom died first five years ago, when I was an undergraduate. Then Dad died about a year and a half later." She paused. "But I like to think that if they were still around that they'd be proud of me, not making me feel bad."

"I am so sorry, Cagney. I didn't know. What an ass I am. I never would have asked."

"I know. It's all right. How could you have known? Maybe we should have filled out fake dating forms so we had a briefing on our backgrounds. You know the kind authors fill out for their characters."

Apparently, Brad did not know, judging from the blank expression.

"Anyway, your parents don't know I'm your girlfriend." She stopped. "Fake girlfriend. So you can take Piper. She'd be glad to be your girlfriend." While she suggested the undergrad in jest, she thought it might be a workable solution.

Brad shook his head and opened his mouth to speak. Cagney spoke more quickly.

"Now here me out. You can take Piper home for the weekend and we can tell everyone on campus that you and I broke up and Piper can be your fake girlfriend." Cagney was smiling by the end of her spiel.

"Oh, no. You're not going to do that to me. You may not be my girlfriend, but I thought you were my friend at least. Not Piper. Never Piper. Besides Piper has already moved on. She and surfer dude have been dating, according to Blake."

He ran a nervous hand through his hair. She was glad he left that curl around his ear untouched. "Please. It's just for one weekend."

"I'm really uncomfortable with this." *Shit, I've been uncomfortable with this entire situation.*

"You'll get to meet my grandmother, Summer. She's wonderful. You'll love her. I promise." He raised an eyebrow. "She alone is worth the trip."

"I guess, I—"

"Thank you. Thank you. Thank you. I owe you one." Brad sat back in the booth.

****

Alex

"What do you mean you're meeting Brad's family?"

Alex did her best to keep her voice low, because they were in the library. But this was exciting news. It threw her plans for Cagney's love life into high gear. They were making progress she didn't know about. And she thought Cagney told her everything. What was she hiding?

"Brad's going home for his dad's birthday party."

"And he invited you to go along. How romantic."

Alex sighed at the thought of Cagney and Brad taking their relationship to the next level. This was the stuff of romance novels. This was her mission coming to fruition. Just like she had done for JJ and Kenn.

Except this seemed to be happening a bit faster.

"Not exactly. He was coerced into it." Cagney paused. "By the circumstances."

"It doesn't matter how you got invited. Can't you see this is big?"

"Shh! You don't have to be so loud. People are looking at us."

"Let them look. You're in love and you should let the entire world know it."

"Quiet down. It's not what you think." Cagney seemed irritated.

"What's wrong? You should be excited. Isn't this what you wanted?"

"Me?" She looked stunned. "No, it's what you think I want. And I certainly don't want to meet his parents under deceptive conditions."

"What are you talking about?"

"Shh! You're raising your voice again, Alex. Please calm down. You know darn well Brad and I aren't dating. Not in the traditional way. And I have to spend a weekend with his parents pretending to love his son. I don't like the deceit. I don't like lying to his parents." She closed the book she had been researching.

"What if we get caught? What if they find out it's all a big hoax? That our relationship is bogus?"

"Listen to me, Cagney Adler—"

"Shh! You're getting loud again."

"Listen," she whispered, "there is nothing bogus about the way you and Brad act around each other. You two are sincerely nice to each other. You look out for the other's interest. You are to the point in your relationship—"

"Fake relationship," Cagney reminded her.

Alex stuck her tongue out at her. The woman frustrated her. She didn't see what was right in front of her. Brad liked her more than just as a fake girlfriend. If the woman couldn't see that, she didn't know how to get it across to her.

"The only thing that's a hoax is that you're putting the label fake on it." Alex gestured air quotes. "You two are now living together—"

"Out of necessity. I didn't have anywhere else to go."

"You're still living together. He cared enough about you to offer you his apartment."

She paused. There was so much she wanted to tell this woman. "If it were strictly a fake relationship, he wouldn't have to do that." She stared into Cagney's eyes. "Right?"

"He had no choice. I called him—"

"And right there. You called him. If it were a fake relationship—"

"If I hear 'if it were a fake relationship' one more time…"

"What I'm trying to tell you is that you both do things for each other that go above and beyond the call for something that's not real. Brad has real feelings for you."

"We've grown into friends. I guess." Cagney tilted her head, as if she were trying to decide how she felt about the man.

"And you have real feelings for Brad. Feelings that go beyond the obligatory duties of pretending to be with someone."

"I suppose I count him as a friend. But that's it."

"Really, only a friend?"

"Don't be silly. I have nothing in common with the man. There's no basis for a relationship to even form. Quit trying to tell me otherwise."

"Shh!" a student a table over admonished her.

Chapter 42

Blake

Blake slapped Brad on the shoulder. "I didn't think you had it in you. I'm proud of it. And you're not even a tennis player or any other kind of jock."

Brad gave him a blank stare. "What are you talking about? I had what in me?"

"You and Cagney. All this time you tell me you're dating her only as a matter of convenience. And she only moved in because her apartment is out of commission—"

"And all of that is true. So what are you talking about?"

"You're taking her to meet your parents."

"How in the world did you find out about that?" Brad scrubbed the back of his neck.

"Alex. Cagney told her. Boy, that's big, bloke. And that takes a lot of courage. I didn't know you were that serious about her."

"I'm not serious about her. It's not like I'm introducing them to their daughter-in-law. I'm taking her because my parents discovered I have a girlfriend."

"And you do. And it's Cagney." Blake smiled. Alex had been right all along for the reason for their visit. And it looked like events had sped up.

"My parents don't know my relationship with my girlfriend"—he gestured air quotes—"isn't real. They believe someone could actually like me like that."

"Oh, I see." Blake looked thoughtful. "Wait. What was the last thing you said? About somebody liking you?"

"Blake, I don't have a British accent. I'm not a man of the world like you. And I just don't know how to talk to women. Cagney is the first girlfriend I've ever had." He rubbed his beard. "And it's not a real relationship. How much of a loser am I?"

"You're not a loser. Not everyone is lucky enough to have someone write…uhm, to meet their soulmate as easily as I did."

"I envy you." Brad slumped in his seat. "I don't have any luck at all with women. That's one of the reasons I keep getting my degrees. It doesn't look like I would know what to do even if I met someone I might like, so I bury myself in my work."

Blake narrowed his eyes. "Isn't that a self-fulfilling prophecy?"

"What do you mean?"

"You don't expect to meet a woman and have a relationship so you make sure you're not in a position by burying yourself in your work."

"Don't be silly. I'm just not…I'm not doing that, am I?"

"I don't know. You tell me."

"No, you know I love geology and rocks and everything about the subject."

"Lots of people are passionate about their interests, their jobs, but still make time for a relationship."

Brad sighed.

Blake couldn't figure Brad out. He was a great guy, had good personality and every single female student in his class wanted to go out with him. Only Piper acted on her desires. If Brad knew that, would that improve his self-esteem?

"What are you afraid of?"

Brad took off his glasses and rubbed his eyes. "I'm afraid of rejection, dammit, Blake. To be told you're not good enough to be around someone? That hurts. Deeply. It creates a chasm in you as big as the Grand Canyon."

He paused and took a deep breath. "Have you ever been rejected?" He didn't wait for him to answer. "Of course, you haven't. Look at you. You look like you've just walked out of a magazine. You're perfect in every way. Women love you. All women."

Blake sat back. Wow. The man was carrying a lot of emotional baggage. Before he could think of anything to say, Brad apologized.

"I'm sorry. I didn't mean to crap on you like that. These are my problems. Not yours. It's on me if I'm jealous of you."

"You're jealous of me?" Blake blinked several times as he tried to digest what he had just heard.

"Of course. What I wouldn't give to be more like you. Blake? Can I tell you something in confidence, though?"

The Brit shot up and leaned over. "Of course. Whatever you have to tell me won't go any further." He motioned as if he were zipping his lips shut and then throwing away the key.

"I'm afraid once Cagney meets my parents, she won't even be my fake girlfriend anymore. My parents are, well, difficult." He sighed. "And that's an understatement."

Blake had nothing to say in rebuttal. He couldn't get Brad to see Cagney as his real girlfriend and now it appeared she might not be his pretend girlfriend much longer. He feared disappointing Alex. And he thought they were progressing so well.

Chapter 43

Brad

"Cag, did I mention my sister will be home this weekend, too?"

Brad stared at the road. They were actually doing this. They were both in his truck, headed for his parents' home.

"You mean the one who's trying to convert you to enlightenment?"

"My only sister," he said without enthusiasm.

"Will she expect me to give her an update on your road to a higher consciousness?"

"She might."

"And what should I say?"

"Tell the truth. I'm failing miserably." He smiled.

"You and your sister sound like total opposites."

"Not really, Missy takes after Summer. A lot. She's all woo-woo. Me. I'm not against woo-woo, I just…I don't know."

"I understand. If she should happen to ask, I'll tell her you're exceling in yoga."

He glanced her way and quirked a brow.

"Not a lie. You have the best downward dog pose in class." Her lips quirked upward. He had grown to love that small smile. "Should I leave out the part where Sarah and her friends stare at you while you're in that pose?"

"Do they?" He whipped his head her way. She was smiling. "You mean when they're done crowding me before class, they stare...?" He turned his head in her direction briefly. This was not the thing to cause an accident over.

"You're making that up. No, they don't." He tried to focus on the road again, but he had an image of the tall, beautiful, self-confident woman and her friends staring at his butt.

"Not making it up. They do. I keep telling you those women are crushing on you."

She had said this before, but he still found it difficult to believe. Why would any woman look at him twice?

"Brad, you may find this difficult to believe, but you're an attractive man." She paused. "Handsome even." The words came out as a whisper. Despite himself, he felt his lips curl up slightly. No woman had ever told him this before.

"Women find you attractive. Naturally."

He didn't know what to say. But his curiosity got the best of him. "Do you find me attractive, Cagney?"

She's taking too long to answer, he thought. *I should never have asked her that. I'm the ultimate dork.* "You don't—"

"I do, Brad. I thought that the first time I saw you on our blind date. I couldn't understand why you didn't have a girlfriend."

Brad's cellphone buzzed. Phew, that was close. I almost had to explain myself. He clicked the button and his mother's voice came through the car speakers. "Son, are you at the house yet? I'm running late. Don't you dare go upstairs and hide for the night before I get there. And are you bringing that girl, Casey."

Damn his mother. "Mom, we're about ten miles away. I won't hide before you get home"—his ire grew with every word—"and yes, I brought my girlfriend. And her name is Cagney. Not Casey. And she's sitting right here and heard every word you said."

His mother disconnected without another word.

"I'm so sorry, Cag. She's…" He heard, what? He glanced over to see her bobbing her head with laughter.

"Casey, huh?" She paced her words through her laughter. "Does getting my name wrong run in your family?"

Relief flooded his body and he laughed too. "Apparently, it does."

****

Cagney

Cagney's jaw dropped open when Brad pulled his truck into a driveway. Was it a driveway? Maybe it was an alley? No, it definitely was a driveway. The Townsend family driveway. She knew that for a fact because the lamppost she saw as he pulled in distinctly said "Townsends."

"Brad, do you want to tell me something about the house your family owns?" Her words barely came out in a whisper. Her heart raced. She didn't expect some wildly extravagant mansion-like home, which from all indications it appeared the house would be.

"Like what?" He glanced at her. Then he stopped the truck. "What's wrong, Cagney? You don't look good."

"Why didn't you tell me your family was filthy rich? Why didn't you warn me?"

He twisted his body so that he faced her. "I don't

know. I just never thought about it. Does it make a difference?"

Did it make a difference? Shit, she already found herself lying to his parents. Now his rich parents? Living in a place like this...well, she wasn't sure what "this" was, but she had a pretty good idea...would only put more pressure on her. Why couldn't Brad have taken Piper?

"No, it doesn't matter. Not really? I'll deal with it."

Silence filled the cab for a long moment. "I'm sorry. I've lived here my entire life. I forget homes like my parents' aren't the norm. I should have mentioned it and given you the option to bow out."

She shook her head. "I don't think I would have not come because of it. I'm just worried I don't have the upbringing I now see you obviously had. I don't want to embarrass you. Because your parents think I'm your real girlfriend."

"You could never embarrass me. Literally minutes ago, my mother embarrassed me by calling you by another name."

"I need to reserve judgment until after I've actually seen your home. Let's go. I'll be fine."

Brad put the truck back in gear and drove the rest of the way up the driveway. It seemed like a long time before they reached the house.

And what a house. "Whoa, this isn't a house. This looks like a...ski lodge. Brad pulled around the circle to the front door. Windows. So many windows. Cagney didn't know what type of wood was used, but the dark color shouted money. It looked as if it belonged in the Swiss Alps, with those overhanging eaves.

Brad didn't just pull up to a home; he pulled up to

a commercial establishment. This had to be a mistake. Nobody lived like this. Did they?

"What do you think? You're quiet." Brad interrupted her thoughts. Thank God, because they were just about to career out of control. She was so close to jumping out of the car and running away. Nothing in her history prepared her for this.

"Truthful? I'm a bit overwhelmed. My parents never had a house like this. None of my friends' parents either."

"Oh." Silence. "Cagney, the last thing I want is for you to feel more uncomfortable than this situation already makes both of us."

She smiled. She didn't need Brad worrying all weekend about how she felt. "I'll be fine. Your parents don't know me. I'm not your real girlfriend. I can spend one weekend pretending that this lifestyle is mine. I'll do my best not to make any major faux pas." She flashed him a smile and hoped he believed her.

"Really? Because we can go in, say hi, and then you or I can develop some excruciatingly painful condition—appendicitis or something—that warrants us leaving." He shrugged. "Like pronto."

She couldn't contain her laughter. "No, I'll stick it out the entire weekend. Besides, I want to meet your grandmother and I have to give your sister an update on your enlightenment status."

"Sure?"

She nodded. She was anything but sure. But she would never throw Brad to his parents alone. "Let's do this."

Chapter 44

Cagney

Brad opened the driver's side door, and she followed suit. She took a first tentative step onto the driveway. Parking lot? Valet area? Whatever it was.

She reached the back of the truck just as Brad pulled their bags out.

He didn't smile and that curl by his ear trembled ever so slightly. "You okay? Are you going to be okay with your parents all weekend?"

He nodded. She didn't believe it. "If not, don't forget about that painful condition we can develop."

They walked up the sidewalk, then Brad stopped and turned to her. "Thanks for coming with me. I don't know if I would have been able to handle this alone."

Her heart broke. He couldn't handle his parents alone? Just how bad were they? What did she sign up for?

He rang the bell.

"You don't have a key?" Cagney's brow furrowed. She had always had a key to her parents' house after she moved out. She would just walk in any time.

"No, my parents made me gave my key back when I started graduate school."

"Oh. I see." *No, I don't see.*

"They said that—"

Just then the door opened.

"The prodigal son returns." The dark-hair woman laughed. "Summer and I had bets on whether you'd show."

"I showed. Who won?" Brad laughed. The woman took several steps and hugged him. Well, it's starting off well, Cagney thought.

"Summer. I thought you'd call at the last minute with appendicitis or a broken bone. Or something." She let go of him and stood back.

"Oh, I'm sorry. I'm ignoring the lady you have with you. I'm Missy. Brad's sister."

"This is Cagney." Brad took a deep breath. "My girlfriend."

"Missy, nice to meet you."

"It's a pleasure to meet you. I hope you don't think me rude, but I didn't think you were real." She shook her head. "He's never had a girlfriend. I thought you were imaginary."

Brad coughed. "She's real…a real person, all right. In the flesh."

"I see that." Missy glared at her brother.

"Come on in. Let's not talk out here." Missy ushered them into an expansive foyer.

"Wow." Cagney couldn't think of another thing to say about the spacious area.

"It's big, I know. When I was a kid, I wanted to put a ping pong table in here. Such wasted space," Brad said.

Her resolve to pretend to be accustomed to this lifestyle seemed to be fading.

"I just don't get what you see in him." Missy had positioned herself next to Cagney. "He's just a big rock nerd."

"That's what I thought when I first met him. But he grew on me." *What am I doing here? Can this get any more awkward?*

Brad stepped next to her, and she allowed him to wrap his large hand around hers. She welcomed the reassuring gesture. The man really was growing on her. How did that happen?

"Bradley, you're home, son."

Coming into view, was a tall man, who very well could be Brad himself in another thirty years. The similarities were remarkable. And scary.

"Father." Brad let go of her hand and took several steps toward him. The two shook hands. What, no hugs? She didn't have any siblings, let alone a brother, so maybe father and son didn't hug? Something, though, felt very stiff about their meeting.

She thought if she could visit her parents again, the reunion would be emotional. With hugs and kisses and tears. *Stop. Just stop.*

"This must be Casey," Mr. Townsend said. His tone sounded more like he was calling a witness to the stand in court.

Cagney bit her lip.

"It's Cagney, Dad."

She took a step toward his father as she extended a hand. He shook it, though he seemed reluctant. "Nice to meet you, Mr. Townsend. And happy birthday."

"You two must be serious. This is the first time Bradley's ever brought a girl home for us to meet."

"That's because it's the first time he's ever had a girlfriend, Dad." Missy laughed. "Don't put so much pressure on her."

She turned to Cagney. "Our parents think long-term. All. The. Time. They're always thinking about our future."

"Futures are important. You need to know what you'll do after you get out of college."

Cagney took a deep breath. He thinks we're serious? Did he just imply we would marry? This whole arrangement had reached the point of the bizarre. It's just a weekend, she told herself. Come Sunday evening it would be all over. The pressure of pretending would pass. Oh, how she wanted to tell his dad they weren't a thing. Why they were pretending to be dating, but his dad wouldn't understand.

She was so involved in her own thoughts she hadn't paid attention to the conversation.

Apparently, Brad had just told him he didn't have a plan in place for a job once he graduated.

The room burst with tension.

"Guys, stop it." Missy sounded experienced. Cagney wondered if she had to break up these arguments on a regular basis.

"Bradley, so good to see you. You and your father have had your first argument."

A tall woman came into view, golden blonde hair. She wore a deep plum business suit. "I just got home."

She paused. "Oh, you must be Casey." She smiled at Cagney.

"Mom, it's Cagney. Her name is Cagney."

Cagney wanted to crawl under a rock.

"I'm sorry," Mrs. Townsend snapped. Her voice revealed her irritation, not regret. Cagney was sure it was at being corrected and not about getting her name wrong.

"Nice to meet you." She heard her voice quiver.

She held out her hand, but Brad's mother had already turned her attention to Missy.

"When did you get home?"

Brad walked up to her and took her hand. She looked up at him and he mouthed, "I'm sorry."

She felt tears streaming down her cheeks.

"Mom, Dad, I thought Cagney and I would go up and get our stuff unpacked and get washed up before dinner?" The statement came as a question.

"Of course. Separate bedrooms, though. We prepared separate bedrooms for the two of you." Mrs. Townsend stared at Cagney as she said this.

"Of course, Mrs. Townsend. I wouldn't have it any other way."

Brad released her hand, pivoted to pick up the two duffel bags they left at the door, and nodded to her to follow as he strode toward the stairs. The stairway screamed privilege. There were oil paintings and portraits of people who looked like they'd been dead for a millennium.

"I'm so sorry about my parents. I didn't know how to warn you about them."

They reached the landing and Brad led her to the left. "This is the guest room." He opened the door to a room that was larger than her entire apartment.

"What the hell is this?" She looked around and burst out laughing. "I can't afford the daily rates for this fancy hotel, Brad." Tears were still streaming down her cheeks.

"Sorry. It's pretentious, to say the least." He put her duffel bag on the canopied queen-sized bed.

Canopy? "The bed has a canopy and it's not for mosquitos?"

Cagney sat on the bed next to her duffel bag.

"It's supposed to be romantic." He tilted his head. "I think."

"I'm sure in the right circumstances it is. Right now, it's just the last straw." She sighed.

"I'm sorry, Cagney. I really am. I didn't think my parents would act like that with you. They don't even know you."

"It's okay. It's not your fault. Your sister seems nice."

"She is. My parents don't approve of the way she's living her life either."

"What's wrong with your parents?"

"Too much to explain right now." He looked at his watch. "Dinner will be at six thirty. If you want to recover in here until then, I'll come and get you. No judgment."

"Where will you be?"

"I'm dropping my bag off in my room and then going back down. My parents will want an update on my studies." He adjusted the bag on his shoulder. "If only to let me know it's not too late to get into law school."

He turned on a heel.

"Wait. I'll go down with you. Let me throw some cold water on my face."

"You don't have to, Cag. I'd understand."

"I want to. I'll be fine."

Chapter 45

Cagney

I don't need to hear this, Cagney thought as Mrs. Townsend continued on her rampage against the sciences as a profession. She should have stayed upstairs secluded in the bedroom until dinner.

Claire Margaret Townsend—was it odd that she already knew her middle name and had been in their home less than an hour?—rambled on about how lowly the sciences were.

"And the pay?" She waved a hand. "It's dismal. I looked up the average salary of a geologist. Your pay would never be much better than an entry-level attorney position. Not if you work a hundred years. Doesn't that tell you something, son?"

Son? She can't even call him by his name?

"Mom, we've been over this. I'm not interested in the law. I'm interested in rocks and the earth. It's where I'm meant to be."

Brad had been sitting on the far side of the couch from her. He rose and excused himself. She watched as the man she knew to be fun, thoughtful, and kind appeared to wither away. How dare they do that to him?

She saw movement out of the corner of her eye. She was so absorbed in the arguing, she had forgotten Summer, Brad's grandmother, was in the room too. The woman tapped her on the shoulder.

"Come with me. We'll let them battle this out." Her voice was low and almost playful. Was she not appalled by this situation?

She nodded as if to reinforce the invitation and Cagney rose and followed the graceful older woman into the hallway. The rest of the house was just as intimidating as the living room and foyer were.

She passed a shelf lined with vases and several severe portraits and uninspired landscapes. The colors were muted and dull.

"This had to be professionally decorated," Cagney mumbled to herself.

"It was and it cost a fortune."

"I'm sorry. I didn't think you heard me. I didn't mean to—"

"No worries. The money my daughter put into this house could have saved a whale or two. Or maybe helped save parts of the rainforest. Did you know the hyacinth macaw is now a vulnerable species? The next step is endangered."

Cagney smiled. "No, ma'am. I didn't know that. They are beautiful birds."

Summer led her into a large bedroom. Another room in this damned house that was larger than her apartment. But it stood in stark contrast to the other parts. Instead of classic paintings and shelves filled with what looked like ancient artifacts, this had a definite hippie vibe.

Posters of rock musicians from the sixties and seventies adorned the wall above the bed. And Summer had a stereo in a corner and a shelf full of records. The woman still listened to vinyl. A poster of a psychedelic peace sign hung above it.

"Sit down. Make yourself at home." Summer pointed to a beanbag chair.

Cagney laughed. "This is so unlike the rest of the house." She plopped herself onto the bag and sighed. She felt comfortable here.

"You can say it. It's not stuffy."

"That's true. It's also vintage hippie." Cagney quickly covered her mouth. "Sorry."

Summer had been rummaging through a dresser drawer. She turned and said, "Don't be. I'm a vintage hippie."

Cagney was falling in love with Brad's grandmother. She had never known her own and wondered if hers, had she lived, would have been anything like this woman.

Summer sat next to her in a purple butterfly chair. Cagney thought it would fit nicely in her own apartment.

Brad's grandmother flipped the lid on a small, rectangular wooden box and pulled out a pack of...were those rolling papers? She pulled a thin paper out of it and then picked up the green...oh my God...marijuana.

Brad's seventy-something grandmother smoked marijuana. I guess you can be old and smoke. She laughed. Uncontrollably. So many ideas flew through her head.

"Uhm, Summer," Cagney started. The woman had the pot arranged on the paper and was licking the edge. "Does your daughter know you do this?"

"Yep. And as you might expect, she doesn't approve. She tells me I should grow up." She picked a lighter out of the box, lit the joint, and inhaled deeply. "But I figure she's busy getting on her son's case right now. It'll be a while before she makes her way in here."

She offered the cigarette to Cagney. "No, no, I don't. I've never tried." She held up her hands.

"Really? Give it a try. Just one puff. It'll relax you. I keep telling my daughter she needs to smoke these. It would settle her ass down a bit." She leaned closer to Cagney.

"I guess. Just one puff wouldn't hurt." She leaned over, took the joint, and put it to her lips. She inhaled. Then exhaled. She sat for a moment. "It's not what I expected."

"I thought you might say that."

Cagney handed it back to Summer.

"How did you meet Brad?" She took a long toke and exhaled and held it out to her.

"A blind date, if you can believe that." Cagney accepted the joint.

"I can tell he really cares for you." Summer ran a hand through her hair. "And you really care for him."

"Oh, no. He doesn't." She paused. "If I tell you this, promise not to tell Brad's parents?" Was it the marijuana talking? Did marijuana even talk?

But at the moment, perhaps under the influence of marijuana, she felt as if she could confide in Summer.

"I would never tell them anything about their son."

"We're not really dating. It's just a thing we're doing so we don't have to go on any more blind dates. There's really nothing romantic between us."

"Oh, honey. I think you're wrong."

Summer took a toke on the joint and passed it to Cagney.

"What? What do you mean?" She took a long drag on the cigarette and then slowly exhaled. She watched

271

as the smoke lazily floated to the ceiling.

"I'm saying this because I watched your eyes as he left the living room. And then when you caught sight of him when he came back in." She paused.

"I watched you as he talked to his parents. And I saw the hurt in your eyes when they told him he should dump his studies and enter law school and—"

"He is my friend." She recalled how horrified— yes, that was the only word she could use—at the thought of parents not supporting their son's dreams. "And what parents totally disregard their son's life's choices?"

"Oh, hon. You're more than friends. You love him."

Cagney nearly dropped the joint. Did she?

****

A knock on the door startled Cagney. "Is it your daughter?" she whispered. What would Brad's mom think of her sitting here smoking pot?

"My daughter knows better to come around after she's berated my grandson," Summer whispered back. "Come in. The door's unlocked."

The door opened and Brad entered. His shoulders were slumped and the twinkle she always looked for in his eyes was gone.

"You're smoking." He smiled at his grandmother. "She hates when you do that."

"Yes, she does. And Cagney just got her first taste of it."

Brad turned his attention to her. "Are you all right?"

Cagney giggled. She focused on the strands of hair that curled around his right ear. The curl she noticed on their blind date. The curl that she noticed in yoga class. "Yeah, I think so."

"Summer, why are my parents the way they are?" He sat on the floor next to Cagney.

Then, he turned his attention to her. "Sorry you had to hear part of that. It's standard operating procedure around here."

Silence hung between them.

"I come home. They tell me my choice of geology as a major is stupid and then they start telling me how Dad can get me into any law school in the country." He sighed. "Which he can't, but…"

"And every time, Brad," Summer said, "you get upset. But you know what, Cagney?"

She shook her head. "He never gives in to their ideas. He's never once asked anyone when's the next LSAT. He's never said, 'Wait, let me pull out my laptop so I can submit an application.' He knows his mind."

She sighed. "Enough of your parents. We're not giving them any more control over your life by talking about them." She nodded. "Darn. We've smoked it all." She put the joint out in the cigarette tray next to her chair.

"I was telling Cagney what a great couple you two make." She glanced at Cagney and winked.

"No, it's not like that." He tapped Cagney on the thigh. "You could have told Summer. She would understand."

"I did." Her cheeks grew hot. Was it suddenly hot in the room?

"Then you know it's just pretend."

"Yeah, right," Summer said.

Chapter 46

Brad

Brad gulped. What an ass he was. Why did he have to invite Cagney? He should have just come alone. Faced whatever remarks Missy and his parents had about an imaginary girlfriend.

Cagney didn't deserve to be treated like this. His mother already had questioned her choice of a doctorate in history. And he knew his parents well. Today, the big birthday party day, wouldn't be any easier for her.

He pulled on his gray button-down shirt. His only shirt that wasn't a T-shirt. He smiled as he closed the buttons. It was the shirt he wore to the blind date with Cagney. He couldn't help but laugh.

"For two people with absolutely nothing in common, we've been seeing a lot of each other."

He went to fetch Cagney. He took a deep breath before he knocked on the door. She answered almost instantly, with a smile on her face. He realized he had been staring at her when she asked, "Is this not appropriate for your dad's birthday party? I thought I should dress up at least a little."

She wore a white short-sleeved dress that hugged her waist and the skirt part flared out. It had small pink polka dots on it. It was low cut, but not immodestly so. He had never seen her in anything but jeans and a T-shirt.

Her dark blonde hair, usually back in a no-nonsense ponytail, flowed down her shoulders, bouncy and curly, and wow. She was so…so feminine.

"N-no, n-no, it's very appropriate." He ran a hand through his hair, not knowing what to say next. "It's just…I've never seen you in a dress before. You look…beautiful, Cagney." She blushed.

"You look good yourself. That's the shirt you wore on our blind date." She reached up and fixed the collar. He inhaled her fresh scent. "There. Now you're straight."

"Thank you. And I'm sorry. Last night was a disaster. Like the Titanic or something."

She squinted one eye. "Did you just make a history reference?"

"I guess I did."

"I'm impressed."

"Brad, Casey, are you guys ready? The guests are arriving."

"We're coming, Mom."

"Are you ready?" He raised his eyebrows. "I can't guarantee this isn't going to be another fiasco."

"I'm ready for it." She closed her eyes. "I think."

He took her hand. "We'll get through this together."

They made their way to the rec room, the room Brad had spent most of his time in growing up. He played video games here, did his homework here, and he'd bring in portions of his rock collection, polishing and admiring them. He recalled the huge television on the wall flanked by posters. Aside from his bedroom, this represented a place of refuge in the house. Every other room felt foreign.

As he walked in, he realized the room of his youth had vanished. He didn't know when his parents had renovated it. It had been a while since he'd been home and even longer since he had been in the rec room. His trips home from college involved little more than hiding in his bedroom, eating in the dining room, and hanging with Summer in her bedroom.

While the large television still hung on the wall, a respectable, and he assumed expensive, seating group replaced his old comfy couch. And on the far side, where he had a shelf that stored all his video games, now held a bar. A wet bar yet. He wondered how his parents managed that.

"Bradley, so good to see you. It's been too long."

Uncle Jonathan Jacob Townsend took several steps from the other side of the room and shook his hand. "You don't come around much. Glad to see you could make it to your dad's birthday party."

Brad sucked in a breath. What had his parents told Uncle Jon about why he didn't visit? No matter.

"And who is this?" Uncle Jon turned to Cagney.

"This is Cagney Adler, my girlfriend. Cagney, this is my Uncle Jon. He's my dad's brother."

"Nice to meet you, sir." She extended her hand.

He took it and shook it.

The buffet with food was set against the far wall. He barely touched Cagney's back to guide her. He took a plate and handed it to her.

They filled their plates of the lasagna, cavatelli, ham and cheese sandwiches, Caesar salad...

"There's enough food here, your parents can open their own restaurant. It would put the Physics Café to shame."

"This is my dad's sixtieth birthday. They went all out." He scooped potato salad onto his plate. "No, I'm lying. They go all out like this for every occasion."

"I'm not surprised," Cagney whispered.

The only seats available were by Uncle Jon. Not his first choice in seating arrangements, not after the snide remark about his lack of visits. Hopefully, the man would be busy talking to the several other nieces and nephews who came out for the party.

"So, Bradley, your dad tells me you've finally decided to take the LSAT and go to law school. That's a wise choice. You should've done that years ago. Think of how far you could have been by now."

Uncle Jon threw back another gin and tonic. By Brad's count it was his third. His words weren't as crisp as when the party first began.

"Jonny, I hadn't told Bradley about the surprise yet." His dad shifted his weight in the folding chair and ran a hand through his hair.

"What surprise, Father?" The last word came out as an accusation. "What type of plans are you making behind my back?"

"I just did what you should have done a long time ago. I enrolled you in the latest LSAT testing. It's June fourteenth at eight a.m." He stood and pulled a paper out of his back pocket. "And conveniently, it's at that joke of a school you go to." He took several strides and handed Brad the paper.

Brad took it. Silence filled the room. Everyone stared at him. Waiting.

Brad stuttered. "Father,"—he strung the word out—"we've talked about this. At length." He pursed his lips.

"Son, you're young. You don't know what you want. I'm just helping you not make the mistake of your life."

Brad sat motionless. Cagney looked at him. He knew she was waiting for him to say something more. Anything. He shook his head.

"I've made a great life as a lawyer. Hell, you're going to school partly because of the fruits of my labor. Your entire life has been built upon what I've done for you. Do you expect me to continue to support you your entire life? Because if you continue in the direction, going with that ridiculously irresponsible degree of yours, that's what's going to happen. It's about damn time you grew up and took responsibility for your own life."

Chapter 47

Cagney

If Cagney didn't know better, she would have thought a strong wind had blown Brad back in his seat. The movement so swift, he almost lost control of his plate.

"Father, we've discussed—"

"You're right, son. I've discussed this matter with you until I'm blue in the face. Nothing seems to get through to you. And now you bring this young lady who I assume you'll be marrying. You can't even afford to make a life for yourself, let alone a girl who thinks she can make a living studying history. The two of you are ridiculous."

"Mr. Townsend." Cagney put her plate on the floor and shot out of her seat. "How dare you talk to your son like that." What was wrong with this man? Had he no fatherly compassion?

"Brad is one of the outstanding students in the geology department"—she emphasized the word geology—"and he's on track to graduate with a doctorate soon. How dare you suggest he throw away his time—"

Matthew Townsend glared at her. "Young lady, this is none of your business. And I'm not suggesting anything. I'm giving my son a direct order. He has got to get his nose out of those rocks and go to law school."

Brad stuttered something, but Cagney wasn't sure what it was.

"Mr. Townsend, you can't order an adult around like he was a puppet. Brad is not you. He's not his mother." She pointed at Claire Margaret Townsend. "He's Bradley Townsend and he deserves to live his own life."

She took a deep breath. "Neither of you love your son. If you did you wouldn't push him into a slot like he was some homing pigeon. He's an individual with his own thoughts, desires, and dreams." She threw up her hands. "And you know what, you don't deserve him. If you knew him, you'd know he was a loving, kind, compassionate human being. You would know that his favorite rock is a quartz, that he hopes to help to combat erosion and contribute to bettering the climate through his PhD. And you probably don't even care that through geology and astronomy he feels like he belongs in the world."

She didn't mean to blurt the last part out, but now, it all fell into place for her. "Because obviously, you never made him feel as if he were worthy of your love, a place in your household,"—she waved a hand—"because you can hardly call this a family. You never tried to understand anything about him."

She took in a deep breath.

"That's enough, young lady." Now Claire Margaret Townsend stood. "You don't know a thing about our family."

Cagney pivoted to face the woman. "I know enough that you only seem to love your children if they're obedient." She crossed her arms.

"I think you should leave my home. I'll not have

you talk to my husband and me that way."

"I'm going upstairs and calling a ride. I can't stand the hypocrisy in this house."

She rushed out of the room, headed for the guest room.

****

Brad

"You sure know how to pick them, Brad." His mother stared at him. He still hadn't digested everything Cagney had said in his defense. Things he should have said to his parents a long time. He patted his pocket. Damn, he forgot he had given it to Cagney. But that was all right. Because she had just made him believe that even if he didn't fit in his own family, he knew he fit in the universe.

"She's a brazen one, isn't she?"

That was it. He should have seen the writing on the wall a long time ago. But how could he have? Cagney just gave him the strength to do it.

"Stop. It. Now. Mother." He leapt out of the chair. Fists balled at his side, he took in a deep breath. "No, Mother, she's not brazen. She's truthful. You're the brazen one, stringing your children along, withholding your love if we don't live the lives you believe we should.

"You only love Missy and me when we follow your orders like good little soldiers. All you ever wanted from us was to be clones of you and Father. You never thought to ask us what we wanted to do with our lives. You were too damned busy molding us to fit your desires and dreams."

"Son, you will not swear in my house. I forbid it." Brad's father took a step toward him. "I will not have you talk to your mother like that. I can take this chance of law school away from you like that." He snapped his fingers. "I can't tell you how many strings I pulled to get you admitted into the finest—"

"So I wasn't even going to get into law school on my own? You already had me enrolled? I'm sure at your alma mater."

"It's a great school. And the only reason they're accepting you at your age is because of me."

"Don't you get it? I don't want to go to law school. And I clearly don't want to go to a law school that you had to pull strings to get me into. I'm in graduate school doing what I love. You can shove your law school"— Oh, God was he really going to say this?—"where the sun doesn't shine. I'm out of here. Cagney and I are going back to UNO as quickly as possible."

He took several steps across the room. Keenly aware that his entire family, including Uncle Jon, had just listened to his every word, and were now watching him like a hawk, he prayed he didn't do anything stupid like trip. He knew he would survive, even if his parents never talked to him again. And at the moment, he felt he had severed the ties permanently.

"Bradley Lincoln Townsend." His mother's shrill voice sent goosebumps down his arms. He froze. "If you leave now, you're never returning. You're cut out of our inheritance, and we'll never speak to you again."

"Wow." He pivoted. "You've just proved to me that everything Cagney said about you is right. You're willing to disown me because I stood up to you. That's unconditional love. Not.

"If you two never talk to me again, that's fine. It only shows me you never loved me to begin with. The only thing I regret is all those years I spent as a kid trying to get your approval. I can't believe I was naïve enough at one time to think you cared about me and my future."

He turned on a heel and walked out.

****

Cagney

Cagney threw herself on the bed and the tears flowed. *I did it now. Brad's never going to talk to me. He'll throw me out of his apartment, and I'll have to get a room at the Crimson Canopy.*

A knock at the door startled her. She pushed herself up. "I'm sorry, Brad. I mucked up. I'll leave quietly." She chuckled at how that came out.

"I'm not Brad; I'm Missy. Can I come in?"

She let her arms go and plopped back down. "Do you have to? I know I've screwed things up. I don't need a lecture."

Surprisingly, Brad's sister laughed. "I'm not here to lecture you. I'm here to congratulate you."

She pushed herself off the bed and hurried to the door. She pulled it open. "What?"

"If you let me in, I'll tell you."

She walked in and gave Cagney a bear hug. "I love you because you love Brad," she whispered in her eye. She let go. "Let's sit on the bed."

"Obviously, my parents gave up on me a long time ago," Missy said. "I'm not attacked every time I come home like Brad is."

"Gave up on you?" Cagney cocked her head. She was so shocked about the phrase "gave up on me" that she couldn't correct the woman about loving Brad.

"Yeah, they tried to mold me into the woman they

thought I should be, but I have too much of my grandmother in me. They knew that." She paused, her lips turned up slightly. "Besides, I'm a girl. So I'm not a direct heir to the Townsend name. It's okay if I do my woo-woo self. If I have children, they won't have their name. They don't have to claim them."

It took a while for that to sink it. Could parents deny their own grandchildren? What kind of…

"But they want Brad to be just like them so badly. They don't want to be embarrassed. Our dad looks up to Uncle Jon. It's a thing of family pride, I guess." She sighed. "Brad doesn't fit the mold."

Cagney picked up her legs and sat cross-legged. "I thought everyone would hate me for what I said. It just came out. I couldn't take them talking to Brad like that."

"Summer loved it. She's planning your wedding. You're part of the family as far as she's concerned."

"Oh, no. No, I'm not—" She almost said she's not even Brad's girlfriend, but now was not the time to blurt that out.

"I know. Summer told me. You guys are fake dating. To avoid blind dates."

"Yes, but I still don't think—"

"So when did the relationship become real?" Missy took her hand. "Because what I saw in that rec room was someone who's passionate about defending her friend. Love isn't a noun. The words you spouted sounded like love in action to me." She gazed into Cagney's eyes. "Summer thinks so too. But you already know that."

Before Cagney had a chance to answer someone knocked at the door. Her eyes widened. "Do you think it's your mom? Am I not leaving fast enough?"

"I heard that, Cagney. No, it's me, Brad. Can I come in?"

Was she ready to face him? She had no choice.

"Of course, please."

She jumped off the bed as the door opened and rushed to it.

"I'm so sorry. I didn't." She stood close to him. Probably too close. She stared at his chest and recalled the first time she found him in the kitchen without a shirt. His cologne tickled her nose. She whimpered.

"Are you okay?" He placed his hands on her shoulders. He barely touched them, but they felt protective. "I'm sorry about my parents."

"No, I'm sorry, Brad. I'm sorry I couldn't keep my mouth shut. Your relationship with your parents is none of my business. I should never have spoken out like that. I'm just your fake girlfriend. I had no right to inject my opinions in that conversation."

"No, you said everything I should have told them a long time ago. And I said that when you left. We're both leaving. I hope you haven't called a cab or anything yet."

He looked beyond her. "Missy, tell Summer I'll call her. And maybe the three of us can meet sometime soon that's not here. That is if you two still want to associate with me."

The words made Cagney's heart ache.

"Now more than ever, little brother. You're my hero. Well, you and Cagney."

Missy stood between them, with a smile that could light up the entire city. "I'm so glad you two found each other. I've decided you two really don't know what you mean to each other." She looked from Brad to Cagney. "And it's sweet. Summer is right. And one day you'll discover it yourself, too."

She grabbed them in a big bear hug. "Mother and Father have no idea what they're missing."

Chapter 48

Cagney

"I feel like I should apologize again for the fiasco." Cagney stared out the windshield of the truck, the sun slowly setting, casting a golden glow over the rural landscape.

"Nope, you don't need to. Actually, I need to thank you." Brad took his eyes off the road for just a minute to glance at her. That curl behind his ear trembled ever so slightly. He smiled. A genuine smile that crinkled his eyes.

"I'm in a great mood. I'm free from the subtle and not-so-subtle condemnation of my parents. I hated going there anyway. I only visited my parents for the holidays and their birthdays. And well, Missy and Summer's birthdays too."

"You're just saying that to make me feel better." The rock she had in the pit of her stomach at his parents hadn't disappeared yet.

"I can't believe I single handedly ruined my fake boyfriend's relationship with his parents." She chuckled weakly. "In front of all of his aunts, uncles, and cousins."

"I'm telling you I love my newfound freedom." His right reached over to her and found her hand. "Thank you. A thousand times, thank you."

"You do seem okay with it." He just grinned.

They rode in silence a few moments when his cell phone pinged. He touched the phone hanging from the top of the dashboard. "Yes, Missy, what's up?"

He glanced at Cagney, winked, and mouthed: she's worried about us.

"I was just making sure you two were okay. Summer and I are in her bedroom talking about you—"

"And smoking, no doubt," Brad added.

Cagney giggled.

"Of course. The party broke up after you guys left."

Brad laughed. "I'm sure there was a lot of griping about what an ungrateful son I am."

"Not as much as you think. Summer here put Uncle Jon in his place."

"We just wanted you to know, Brad"—that was Summer's voice—"that we love you both. Always will. Missy and I will come up and visit you soon."

"Love you, Summer and Missy," Brad said.

"Love you both too." Cagney didn't lie. In Summer, Missy, and Brad, she had found the family she hadn't had in a long, long time.

Brad clicked off the phone, negotiated a curve, and then leaned back in his seat. Without taking his eyes off the two-lane road, he asked, "Do you know Missy is responsible for my studying geology?"

"No, I thought it was your high school teacher." Whether his statement was true or not, Cagney knew she wanted to hear the story behind this.

"I wandered into her room one day. I must have been nine or ten. Which would have made her fourteen or fifteen. Just the age a big sister doesn't want a little brother nosing around her room."

"You went in without her permission?"

He grinned and nodded. "You sound horrified." Then his smile slowly faded. "You were an only child, right?"

"Yes, I didn't have any other rooms to wander into other than my own."

"Sorry."

"No, go ahead with the story. I want to know how this incident got you hooked on rocks."

"She had a set of crystals in her room. She was woo-woo even back then. She believed they would help her get a date with the quarterback of the football team."

"Did they?" Cagney had heard of the reputed healing power of crystals, but she never knew they could help with your love life.

"No, she never did date him."

"Oh." She let out a sigh.

"Disappointed?"

"Immensely." She giggled.

"I picked one up, fascinated by the way it gleamed. It was without a doubt the coolest thing I had even seen. But I didn't see them like she did. I saw them as rocks. She caught me, of course. And yelled at me. And Mother yelled at me. And I spent the rest of the day in my bedroom with no supper. I needed to learn a lesson, Father said."

Before Cagney could think too much about a punishment she had never received, he continued.

"But do you know what Missy did?"

Cagney shook her head. "No, what?"

"She snuck into my room after supper and gave me the crystal I was looking at. And she told me that if I went to the library, I'd find lots of books on rocks."

He stopped the truck for a red light. And gave his full attention to Cagney. "She knew I wasn't into it for any reasons but its looks and what it was made of. But because of her, I learned everything I could about rocks. All types of rocks. I had a rock collection of my own."

A car horn beeped behind them. "Oops." The traffic light had turned green. Cagney wasn't sure how long it had been since it turned. But she loved that the kindness of a big sister transformed into a lifetime of learning for Brad.

"By the time the high school teacher told me about the elements, I already had loved geology, but he helped me secure my place in the world."

He paused, negotiated a right turn, and sighed. "I think his words were the only thing that kept me going when my parents got on my case."

Cagney nodded as she tried to imagine living with parents who didn't approve of any of your choices.

Chapter 49

Cagney

"Cagney, I'm so glad I found you here." Alex slid herself into the bench seat across from her.

She had literally sat down three seconds ago. Okay, she didn't know the accuracy of that, but it sure felt like it. She had just put her tray with a cup of Manhattan Project Clam Chowder and a half of Time Warp Chicken Wrap on the table. She didn't need Alex's prying questions.

"I can't wait to hear about your weekend at Brad's parents. How did it go? Do they love you?"

"19K." Alvin's voice came over the public address system.

Alex bounded out of her seat. "That's me. I got the Fission Chips. I'll be right back. I want to hear all about your romantic weekend."

Cagney didn't want to talk about the weekend to anyone—but especially to Alex. She knew, though, Alex wouldn't relent until she had learned exactly what happened. In all its gory detail.

Maybe that was good, she thought. Maybe the titanic debacle of the weekend—she smiled as she recalled Brad's reference to an historical event—would show her that they weren't the romantic couple she envisioned them to be. Hell, she was barely a decent fake girlfriend.

Yeah, once she heard this story, she'd give up and go back to her fictional world, where the happily-ever-afters flowed like a river.

"I'm back." Alex tucked herself into the bench seat with an agility Cagney could only hope for.

Alex picked up a fry, wagged it at her, and said, "I'm ready. I can't wait. Just how wonderful was it?"

Cagney sighed. She looked at her food. She hadn't even touched it yet. She dreaded reciting the heartbreaking events of the weekend, even if the end result would be Alex abandoned her notion of her and Brad dating for real.

"It wasn't wonderful at all. It was a nightmare." Cagney picked up her spoon and stirred the clam chowder.

"No, I'm sure it wasn't. How could it have been?"

"For starters, his parents couldn't get my name right." She told Alex how they insisted on calling her Casey.

"How cute. It's like when there's typo in a book. You become a typo. It happens all the time in publishing. In our first round of editing, I found myself calling Blake Jake. Well, the editor was overworked and confused us for a couple in another romance she was working on. Welcome to my world."

Cagney doubted it happened all the time, but she refused to push the issue. She took a bite of her chicken wrap, hoping Alex's ebullience would subside some.

"Then there was the issue of me telling his parents off. Quite forcefully."

Alex gagged. Cagney thought she would choke on her fish. She waited for the fictional character to take a drink of her proton shake before detailing the event.

"That's so romantic." Alex put down her fish. It looked as if her eyes had glazed over.

"It was in no way romantic." What was wrong with this person? "It was, in fact, the worst moment of my life. And it was right out of a horror book, if you ask me."

She closed her eyes as she fought back tears. "Don't you realize that I, Cagney Adler, fake girlfriend of Brad Townsend, ruined his real-life relationship with his parents? How awful am I?"

"You're not awful. You stood up for the man you love." Alex let out a long sigh. Cagney wondered if she were busy writing the chapter in her mind.

"I definitely did not stand up for the man I love. I stood up for a friend. I do not love Brad." She flailed her hands. "I wish everyone would stop telling me I love Brad. Just stop telling me what I'm feeling. Because you and his sister and his grandmother can't tell me how I feel about him. You don't know how I feel about him."

She covered her eyes with her hands. "Can't everyone just leave me alone?"

She scooted toward the edge of the seat and struggled to get out. Her body shook. She didn't know if her legs would hold her. But she knew she needed to get to the bathroom, run into a stall, and slam it shut and stay there until Alex left. Cagney hoped she would finally realize her relationship with Brad would never be real and go back to her own world, where life's mistakes and wrong turns could be remedied with edits.

She stood. Yeah, she decided she probably could make it and jogged toward the restroom. She bumped into Simon. "Sorry, I didn't see you." But otherwise made it to her sanctuary without incident. She found an empty stall, entered, and slammed the door. Tears flooded her eyes and rolled down her cheeks.

It shouldn't have been this complicated. Fake dating. *Just sitting at the same table with the man working on our dissertations. That's how we planned it. Where did it go wrong?*

****

Alex

Alex sat motionless as Cagney ran off. Why would she do that? Then she remembered something her psychology professor said about individuals denying their feelings. Cagney really did love Brad. She was just afraid to admit it to herself.

"That's it," she said to absolutely no one and ran to catch up with her. She knew where Cagney was headed. She ran past the counter area where she almost collided with Simon. "Sorry, I'm in a hurry."

"Yeah, there's a lot of that going around these days."

Now what did he mean by that?

She pushed the door to the women's restroom open and screamed, "Cagney Adler, get out here this minute. I can't let you do this."

Two stall doors opened. Women emerged, tiptoed around her, hastily washed their hands, then left. "Cagney, I can hear you crying. You're going to come out here and talk to me." She paused. "I can outwait you any day of the week."

In a moment, a stall door opened, and she saw Cagney peek her head out.

"Can't you just let it ride for once?" Cagney stepped into the open area.

"Let what ride?" Alex seriously had no idea what the woman was talking about. Okay, she did, but she couldn't let on she did.

"Since you entered my world, you've talked nonstop about my relationship—my fake relationship—with Brad. And frankly, it gets old."

"I'm sure it does," Alex said as she watched Cagney walk over to the sink and turn on the water. "But what if Brad Townsend is your soulmate? What if he is your one and only love? And you've tossed this relationship, which looks damn real from where I'm standing, away. And what if, that's it? I don't want you to spend the rest of your life regretting walking away from Brad."

She stared at Cagney's back. Because that's all she could see as the woman was throwing water on her face. "Are you even listening to me?"

Cagney turned off the water and pivoted. "Yes, I've heard every word you said." She grabbed for a paper towel, then dried her face. "I've heard every word you've said since you unceremoniously dropped yourself on my doorstep, so to speak."

"Well, you don't act like you do. Can't you see—"

"Can't you see I'm scared to death? After last weekend, I think I may very well be in love with Bradley Townsend. But I'm not right for him."

"What do you mean 'you're not right for him'? You're perfect for him. You two were meant to be together." What was wrong with this woman?

"Brad needs someone who can share his love of rocks with him. Someone who appreciates his love of the earth. Not someone who hunts down a century-old conspiracy theory."

Alex was about to rebut her, when Cagney continued. "Even if I do love him, we still have nothing in common. Nothing to build a relationship on. It would never last."

"What a complete jerk you are." Alex threw her hands up in frustration. "You've just broken up with a man you're not even dating yet. You don't know that."

"I've seen too many of my friends' parents get divorced. I'm not sure how my parents stayed married for so long."

Alex sighed. The women's restroom at the Physics Café was no place to have this conversation, but she didn't have much choice. "Your parents' marriage worked because they worked at it. And your relationship to Brad can become very real and very forever, if you decide that's what you want and you work at it."

Chapter 50

Cagney

Cagney's heart pounded at the sound of the smoke alarm. She jumped out of her chair and rushed to the door of her bedroom and opened it. Dark smoke billowed out of the kitchen. And it smelled like…no it couldn't. He couldn't.

Brad rushed out of the kitchen flailing a towel. "It's okay." He yelled to be heard over the alarm. "I just burnt something."

Cagney waved her arms in a vain attempt to dissipate the smoke. Realizing what a stupid move that was, she rushed to the door to the balcony and opened that. Hopefully, that would let some of the smoke out. After a few moments, the alarm stopped.

"I'm sorry. I didn't mean to disrupt your studies." He smiled and that damn curl moved ever so slightly. "At least, not this way or so rudely."

"What were you doing? Wait, do you mean you were intending to disrupt my studies?" She crossed her arms. If Brad doing anything in the kitchen that caused the smoke alarm to go off didn't pique her interest, his insinuation that he intended to interrupt her studying did.

"I was…" He looked down at his shoes. "I wanted to thank you for how you stood up for me to my parents—"

"And you do that by burning down this apartment? You do know my track record with apartments and disasters?"

"I was making you that delicious popcorn you always make me, and I had a movie ready for us to watch." Evidently, he chose to ignore her remark.

Wow. She didn't expect that one. She smiled. "How sweet." She walked past him into the kitchen. "I'll make the popcorn. You queue up the movie."

He rushed in after her. She was already at the stove, staring at the blackened balls of what probably was popcorn at one time.

"Here." Brad stood next to her, their arms grazing. "Let me empty this." He reached over and retrieved the large pot. "I can't believe I did this."

She couldn't believe the spark of electricity that shot through her at his touch. She shivered and tried her best to overlook it. *Purely my imagination.*

He opened the door under the sink and threw out the ruined snack in the trash.

"I hope we can salvage the pot." He showed her the black bottom, smudged with, well, who knows what.

"We'll probably have to soak it. For a while." Cagney stared at it as he put it in the sink.

"We may have to make a sacrifice this one time and watch without eating."

They went back into the living room and took their usual seats on the couch that gave them just enough space between them without it getting weird. Brad picked up the remote, but hesitated. Instead, he turned to her.

"You made me realize something I never wanted to face: my parents don't love me."

Cagney's heart shattered. "No," she said and shifted her weight to face him. "They do love you. I should never have said that. I've done a lot of thinking about this since we got home…well, back. It really has been on my mind all week." That fiasco of a trip was only a week ago?

"They love you in the only way they know how. They had successful lives. And they want that for you. I don't understand it, but I have to believe they love you and your sister Missy. They're just not very good at showing it."

Brad laughed weakly. "That's the understatement of the year."

"But I'm sure your confrontation with them hurt them as much as it hurt you."

"I never said—"

Cagney touched his hand. Another shot of electricity. Her instincts told her to pull her hand away, but she resisted. "You don't have to say it. I saw it in your face right after. When you came up to my bedroom. It's okay to be upset and hurt."

Brad nodded. "I was hurt. I mean, when they told me if I left, they'd disown me…wow."

Cagney fought back tears. What she would give to have her parents around. Brad deserved to have a mom and dad who saw him as the great person he was.

"But it's also liberating." He raised his eyebrows. "I didn't realize how many times I did something and wondered what my dad would think—or my mom. I guess I always hoped they'd give me some credit for something. I suppose I always wanted to hear them say, 'We're proud of you, Brad.' " He leaned against the back of the couch. "I was only fooling myself."

"It's not your fault. You know that, right?"

"I do now, thanks to you. I spent my life believing they'd eventually come around. I couldn't go into law like my dad. I just couldn't. I almost applied for law school…"

She saw the pain in his eyes. "Had you done that, you wouldn't have been true to yourself. And you would never have been happy. You seem to love studying geology." She shrugged. "I don't get it, but then—"

"You study dead people." He laughed. "I'm not sure which of our obsessions is worse."

"You've got a good point there."

The sat in silence for a moment—a comfortable quietness that arose naturally between good friends. And Brad Townsend, fake boyfriend, rock nerd, was also her good friend.

And those zings of electricity? Was that the Universe answering her doubts about loving him? She tried to put that thought out of her mind.

****

Brad

"Let's watch the movie." Brad needed to break the silence. If it had continued any longer, he thought he may have blurted out things to Cagney he'd regret. No, he wouldn't regret the words. He'd regret the outcome. He and Cagney were actually friends. Who'd have suspected that all the way back on their blind date? Surely, not he.

And who would have thought, now a couple months later, he had thoughts of having something more than a friendship with her? When they were in the kitchen, he swore he felt some type of tingling when their arms accidentally touched.

Instead of dwelling on it anymore, he clicked the remote control on. He had already queued the movie up.

"Wait." Cagney jumped off the couch. "Do we...I mean you...still have that bagged microwave popcorn?"

"Yeah." He tilted his head. "But someone said that was garbage, if I recall correctly."

"Oh, Mr. Townsend, you do recall correctly. But any port in a storm, as they say."

He rose. "I'll go make it."

"No. Don't move. You've already burnt one batch of popcorn beyond recognition and set off the smoke alarm. I'll make it."

"I'll follow you so I can learn how not to burn popcorn." He didn't want her to leave the room. How silly was that?

She had already started the short walk to the kitchen. She pivoted. "That's probably not a bad idea. This place still has that lingering smell."

She opened the cabinet and pulled out a pack. He watched her every mood. He realized he felt something for her that went beyond friendship.

"Are you even listening to me?"

"Uhm, I'm sorry, I don't know what I was thinking." He knew exactly what he was thinking. He was thinking what a beautiful, loving woman she was. And how she didn't realize her own beauty. Oh, he knew he'd said that before and thought it often, but it was so very true.

"Well, the important part of the popping is still to come." She put the bag in the microwave and set the timer and continued to detail the proper steps.

He smiled at her, and she caught him. "What's so funny?"

You are, he wanted to tell her. You are too beautiful for words. Instead, he asked, "How do you know so much about making garbage popcorn. I thought you only made the real deal?"

"Two years in the dorm." She flashed a smile at him. "Two solid years of eating garbage popcorn."

The timer dinged and she took the bag out. "Now, we're ready for that movie."

"Yes, we are." And maybe ready for something more?

Chapter 51

Alex

"Alex, remember Mariah? She's in my art history class."

Blake's hair bounced a bit. The man introduced her as if she hadn't been on her hit list for the last several weeks. Of course, she remembered Mariah. Even if she had been calling her Mary Jean. She always knew her real name.

How dare he do this to me? Why? She had so many things to tell that woman. Instead, she took a deep breath and said, "We've met. Remember, you introduced me at the start of the class. And then I re-introduced myself at the bookstore several weeks ago."

"Oh, I didn't know. Or did I?" His hair bounced faster.

"I needed to get a good look at her. I hope you don't mind. I don't think she suspected a thing." Mariah smiled at him.

Oh, lady, I do suspect a thing. Or two. Maybe three. Cagney must have felt her blood boiling because she had grasped Alex's hand across the table.

"May we sit?" Blake looked like a little boy.

"Suit yourself." She scooted over on the bench seat. Cagney did the same to make room for Mariah.

"I have a confession to make, Alex." His chocolate-brown eyes bore into her. This was it. He was leaving her. So much for JJ not writing a sequel. How dare she do that to me?

"I've been working with Mariah on a project. I didn't want you to know about it."

"What?" She put some space between him. "What type of project and why couldn't you tell me? I thought we told each other everything."

"We do." She watched as his hair trembled. Good, she thought, he ought to be scared.

"But we don't when we have a surprise for the other." Blake took her hand, but she pulled it away.

"Alex, give the man a chance."

Easy for Cagney to say, she's still fake dating Brad. It's not a real relationship yet. Come to think of it, this is all her fault. She and Blake could be home with Mr. Whiskers, her cat, if Cagney would only admit to herself that she loved Brad. A soft pang of homesickness hit her stomach.

"Okay, but there had better be a darn good reason for all of this." She waved her hand. A weariness overcame her.

"I wanted to get you something special, because you're the most special part of my life. You're all I think about all day."

Right, she thought, when Mariah isn't playing with his hair and whispering sweet nothings into his ear.

"In addition to being my classmate, Mariah"—he nodded her way—"is also an accomplished artist. She's practicing in the impressionist style."

Alex nodded, but Cagney seemed enthusiastic.

"I love the impressionists. How long have you been painting?" Cagney turned toward Mariah and didn't see the dirty look Alex shot her.

"I've been painting in some form most of my life. It's only been a couple of years I've tried my hand at impressionism."

"And what does this mean for me?" The words came out more sharply than she had intended.

"I'll show you." Mariah leapt from her seat. "If you feel you're ready, Blake."

"Yes, now's the perfect time. I don't think Alex can wait another minute."

No, I can't, she thought. She cast a glance at Cagney, who seemed to be enjoying her discomfort.

"I'll go to my car and get it."

Blake rose. "Do you need any help?"

"No, I can carry it. You stay here with Alex and Cagney."

Strained silence filled her absence.

Finally, Cagney spoke. "How long have you been planning this surprise for Alex?"

"Ever since I first met Mariah. I knew she was the one to paint my dreams into reality." He nodded, his hair bouncing enthusiastically.

Just then Mariah reentered the café with the help of Alvin opening the door for her. She carried a rectangular object that was three-quarters her height and more than three times her width. A white sheet covered it.

She awkwardly made her way to the table, followed by Alvin, Simon, and Ted. The last two had miraculously appeared from the kitchen. Chills flew up Alex's spine. What in the world did he do? What is that thing?

She glanced at Cagney who smiled and said, "I told you to give Blake a chance. This looks interesting."

Did she know what this monstrosity of a thing was?

Blake jumped up when Mariah approached and stood next to her. Yeah, good for her. Alex folded her arms and huffed.

"Alex, I want to thank you for being so patient while I spent time with your boyfriend." Mariah looked into her eyes. Her tone sounded conciliating.

"I know you were frustrated, and Blake was nervous you would leave him. My project is over now. Blake, would you do the honors?"

Blake nodded, his hair bouncing more than usual. "I'd love to, Mariah."

He took a step toward the item and pulled the sheet off.

Alex's mouth hung open. She knew it did. Tears streamed down her cheeks.

"Alex, it looks just like you." Cagney reached over and grabbed her hands and shook them. "It's beautiful."

And it was beautiful. It was the most beautiful thing she had ever seen. It was a painting of her and Blake, arms wrapped around each other. In the living room in her home in her own story.

"And look," she said, tears streaming down her cheeks, "Mr. Whiskers is in the corner."

"Couldn't not include him." Blake shrugged.

"But why? It's not my birthday and it's not our anniversary." She smiled. "Or wait. Did you think it was?"

Blake took several steps toward her and wrapped her in his arms. His strong, tender arms.

"You're right, love. It's neither your birthday nor our anniversary. It struck me how lucky a bloke I was to have you in my life, to have you love me so fiercely." She felt the strum of his sigh against her chest. "And I wanted to let you know how much I love you. I'm not an easy man to put up with."

Everyone burst into laughter. Blake looked up. He shrugged. "I'm not."

"I'm so sorry." She tightened her grip on him. "I'm so, so sorry."

"For what, love?" His grasp tightened in response.

"For thinking you were cheating on me. How dumb could I be?"

"And, Mariah, if you only knew the names I called you in private. How can either of you ever forgive me?"

"If I had been you,"—that was Mariah's voice—"I would have felt the same way. No need to apologize."

Alex released Blake and ran up to Mariah, who had passed the portrait off to Alvin. She hugged her. "Thank you. You're so very talented. Thank you. I'll name my first daughter after you."

"Daughter." Blake pivoted. "First daughter?" he stuttered. "When? When are we having this daughter?" His hair quivered. "Will there be more than one? How many?"

Chapter 52

Cagney

"My landlord just called." Cagney walked out on the balcony. She had come to discover Brad spent a lot of his spare time out here. He sat in one of the chairs. She took the other.

"My apartment is ready." She smiled. "I can move back in any time."

"That's great."

Neither one of them spoke for a long moment.

"I guess maybe I'll move back this weekend. That is, if you can help me." She looked up at the evening sky. It wasn't yet quite dark enough for all the stars to be out. But a few blinked.

"Of course. Maybe Blake and Logan can help too. That'll make it go faster."

"Yeah, I'm sure they will. It'll lighten the load on you." She nodded.

She found the silence uncomfortable, as if there was something between them left unsaid.

"I guess, that's it then. We'll move you Saturday morning? Unless you want to start Friday night." He rubbed his beard. She watched as the one curl shifted ever so slightly.

"No, Saturday's fine." Why was this difficult? She knew this arrangement was temporary. She thought back to how horrified she was when Brad suggested it.

But over the months, it had become easier. What was happening?

"I'm glad for you, Cag, I really am." He rose. "I've got some research to do. I'll see you in the morning."

Cagney sat alone on the balcony. Brad hadn't reacted like a man who was eager to have his apartment back. And she didn't act like a person excited to return to her own place. She shook her head. Alex had been right all along. *And I'm too afraid to admit the truth.*

What happens to me if I allow this moment to slip through my fingers? What if there was such a thing as "the one" as Alex insists? What happens if I don't tell Brad how I feel?

She shook her head and rose. "I'd regret it for the rest of my life."

****

Brad

Brad closed the door to his bedroom and flung himself on the bed. He had forgotten Cagney's stay in his apartment was temporary. Who was he kidding? He knew this day would come. And he dreaded it.

They were still in an official fake relationship. Nothing more. He sighed. Why did his chest hurt then? Why did a sadness invade every muscle of his body?

The buzzing of his cellphone startled him. His first thought was to ignore it. No, that wasn't right. His first thought was to throw it across the room. He pulled it out of back jeans pocket, checked the caller ID, then rolled over on his back. Summer. Perfect timing. Not.

But he couldn't ignore her. "Hi, Summer. What's up?"

"Brad, what's wrong? You sound sad."

"Nothing, Summer. Nothing at all." He sighed.

"Is it Cagney? Are you still seeing her? Wait, pretend seeing her?"

"Yes, and yes." Why he felt comfortable confessing this to his seventy-something grandmother, he had no clue. But he knew she would understand. God, she suspected it when they stayed the weekend several weeks ago.

"Her landlord called. Her apartment is fixed. She can move back in any time."

"I'm so sorry. You do like her."

"Summer, I think I love her. When you talked about it when we were there, I thought you were nuts. But I keep thinking about what you said." He paused. "Do you think she might love me too?" The moment he asked he knew the answer. "Of course not. I'm sure not."

"Bradley Townsend, why would you say that? Of course, she does. A woman doesn't stand up in the middle of a party like she did passionately defending you and not love you."

"Summer, can I confess something to you?"

"Of course, dear."

"I don't want her to move out."

Chapter 53

Cagney

Cagney put the key in the lock and opened the door to her own apartment. She walked through the kitchen and into the living room. The last time she had seen this room a thick layer of dust had covered everything.

She studied the ceiling and smiled. The cracks she had counted since she first moved in had disappeared. She assessed the new ceiling with textured plastering. It gave off an incredibly stylish look. "Well done, Mr. Jackson."

She felt Brad's presence next to her. "Looks like he did a decent job."

"Thank you for that." She turned to him. "You did a great job."

"Me? I didn't repair the hole and plaster it. Hell, I can barely drive a nail into a board without hitting my thumb."

"No, you didn't do the repairs, but you created that wonderful story about my brother who was part of some legal committee looking into…you know whatever you told him."

"I remember that now." Brad laughed. "I also remember the look on his face. Priceless."

She sighed. "I guess this is it. I suppose I can move back in anytime."

"Whenever you want to move your stuff back in,

Cag, I'm there." He paused. "I'm sure you want to get your privacy back."

"And I'm sure you're tired of sharing your bathroom with me." She laughed weakly. "And you can go back to eating in your bare chest." She still regretted he had begun to wear a shirt when he ate breakfast.

"I don't mind sharing the bathroom with you."

"Good to know. We were just lucky…"

Tears welled up. She vividly remembered how her heart nearly stopped when she saw his bare chest in the kitchen. She recalled the first time he entered the bathroom when she was showering. The first time it was awkward, but then she had come to enjoy his time in front of the mirror while she showered. They'd make small talk. And it excited her in a way she couldn't describe nor understand.

"What's wrong?"

His voice, full of concern, interrupted her memories. It was now or never.

"Brad, do you remember asking me to tell you when our relationship was developed enough for a kiss on the lips?"

Cagney's legs shook. She didn't know how much longer she could stand. But she knew this was it. This was the moment. She could let Brad walk out of her apartment without telling him. But that would be oh, so, wrong. She would regret it for the rest of her life.

"Sure, I'm clueless about those things. Why?"

Her heart pounded. What if he rejected her? What if his end of the relationship was still fake?

"Because I don't want to live here alone." She waved her hand around the room. "I want to continue to live with you and I feel our relationship has matured to a kiss-on-the-lips level. We've leveled up."

Her legs trembled more.

Brad stared at her. Those blue eyes unblinking. The little curl around his ear motionless. What was he thinking? Did she blow it? Now he'd turn around and look for another fake girlfriend because this one became real—too real?

"I-I thought…" He rubbed his beard.

This didn't look like a man who liked the words he just heard.

"Are you s-saying you think—"

She couldn't stand the tension one minute longer.

"I'm saying that I'm in love with you. That fake relationship I was so against at the start, well, it's not fake anymore. I love you, Bradley Townsend. I don't know exactly when it happened. But it did."

She took a breath. "And if you don't feel the same way I totally understand. Our agreement was to fake date. To pretend to be a couple. Not to wind up actually being a real—"

He took two long strides over to her.

"Are you sure our relationship is at the kiss-on-the-lips level?" He looked down at her, his blue eyes gleaming, that little curl shaking ever so slightly.

"I've never been more sure of anything."

"Good. Because I've been waiting for this level for so long."

His large, warm hands gently took hold of her shoulders. His grasp slight, as if he were afraid of breaking her. He drew her close. He lowered his head and his warm lips met hers. They were soft and warm, and excited her.

He pulled away too quickly. Did he have second

thoughts?

"Cagney, my grandmother was right. When we went to my parents' house for the birthday party, I knew I already loved you."

He led her to her couch. Her new couch by the way, replaced by her landlord. They sat, his arm around her.

"I have a confession. I think I loved you from the moment I saw you on our blind date. But I didn't think a woman as beautiful and smart and funny as you could possibly love me."

Were those tears in his eyes? She wrapped her arm around him and pulled herself into him. Finally. She had wanted this for so long.

"Your grandmother is a wise woman." She glanced up at him. "Are you okay?"

"I've never been better." He wrapped his arm around her more tightly. "I'm never going to let you go."

She sighed. "So I don't have to move back in here?"

He laughed. "No. I want to take you home right now. We'll figure out what to do with everything that belongs to you later."

"Sounds perfect." She rose.

"You don't know the half of it," he said as he stood behind her and wrapped his arms around her. Cagney placed her hands over his.

He bent low and whispered, "I'd like to fulfill one of my fantasies of you."

Her body tingled. "And what is that?" She barely got the words out. Excitement and trepidation filled her.

"It involves you and me and the shower. You killed

me when you'd stick your head out to talk to me. Would you be interested?"

Cagney laughed. "That sounds like one my fantasies about you."

"One? What are the other ones?"

"I'll tell you once we get out of the shower. No, better yet, I'll show you."

"We best be on our way, then."

Chapter 54

Cagney

"Something's different about you, Cagney." Alex cocked her head and gazed at her over the booth at the Physics Café. To be truthful, it felt more like a stare.

"Yeah, Alex, now that you mention it, I think you're right." Dr. St. Clair mimicked Alex's actions. Great, now she had two people staring at her.

It couldn't be that obvious. *They couldn't know just by looking at me that I finally told Brad I was crazy in love with him.* Or could they?

"I don't know what you're talking about." She tried to act innocent.

"I mean you're not acting like the normal Cagney Adler we're used to." Alex's explanation lacked, well, detail?

"You are, love." Blake put a finger to his lips. "Firstly, you're smiling more today than I've ever seen you." He paused. "No offense."

"That's right. You are." Alex's enthusiasm ramped up. "Those little lines you get on your forehead when you're thinking or upset? Gone. Poof. Not there any—"

"I get the concept. Thank you." She patted her forehead in several places. "Do I really get those lines, Dr. St. Clair, when I concentrate?"

"Afraid you do." She patted her arm. "We all do, though. Don't worry about it."

"There. I see them now." Alex pointed at her.

"Stop it, all of you." Cagney rubbed the scruff of her neck.

"JJ, if I didn't know better," Alex placed her full attention on her creator, "I would say that our friend, Cagney, is acting like she's in love."

"Do you think?" Dr. St. Clair studied her even more carefully than before.

Her cheeks warmed instantly. When did this meeting with her advisor to look at her primary sources morph into a what's-different-about-Cagney convention?

"No, you're all crazy." She drew in a breath. "I learned my apartment has been repaired." Not a lie.

Alex shook her head. "Not buying it. Not even for a moment."

She closed her eyes and braced herself. Oh, hell, they'd find out soon enough. Can't keep it a secret forever. A secret? It hit her. She didn't want to hide her relationship, her for-real relationship. She chuckled lightly. She'd survived whatever slings of "I told you so" Alex would throw at her. She not only found herself crazy in love with Brad, she found a family in Summer and Missy. That deserved shouting it to anyone who would listen. Tears streamed down her cheeks.

"Cagney, are you okay? We're sorry." At the sound of Dr. St. Clair's voice, she opened her eyes.

"No, I'm sorry. I was just thinking."

"We didn't mean to make you uncomfortable. I know I've probably been a pest." Alex's lower lip jutted out slightly. Even sulking the woman radiated beauty.

"As your advisor, I shouldn't be acting like that. I

know better."

"Bloody hell, both of you." Blake's frustration showed in the sway of his hair. "I still want to know. And I'll just ask her." His British accent grew noticeably thicker.

"Cagney Adler, you're acting like a woman in love. Rest assured, you're sitting with three experts at romance. Two fictional characters who live it every day. And our wonderful creator, who conjures the magic for us." He waved a hand in her direction.

"I'm asking you directly, are you in love?"

With three pairs of eyes trained on her, she knew the moment had arrived. It's a shame, she thought. Brad should be here when I tell them. We should be telling them.

She nodded slightly. "Yes, I am." Her words came out as a whisper, but they prompted a boisterous response. She thought Dr. St. Clair cheered the loudest.

Alex leaned into the booth to give her a hug.

"Damn, this isn't working. Blake, let me out. I need to give Cagney a real hug." She nudged him. No, she pushed him until he moved.

She stood in front of the booth. "Wait. This won't work unless JJ lets you out too." She placed her hands on her hips and gave the professor a hard stare. "Professor, please?"

Relief flooded Cagney when Alex didn't resort to pulling JJ out of the booth. At that moment, she believed the fictional woman would do anything.

Dr. St. Clair moved, and Cagney found herself the recipient of a bear hug that didn't seem to end.

Alex whispered in her ear. "I want to tell you 'I told you so,' but I'm just thrilled you've found love."

Alex released her. Cagney said, "I have. I never would have believed it. But it happened."

"Sit down, you two. You're making a scene."

Cagney scanned the café. Sure enough, people were staring at them.

"Only if Cagney promises to tell us the details," Alex demanded.

Cagney's cheeks burned. Everybody returned to their seats.

"Not those details," Dr. St. Clair immediately countered.

"Oh, no. I want to know how you finally realized Brad is The One." Alex raised an eyebrow.

"The conversation we had in the ladies' restroom, Alex, made me—"

"I wondered what went on in there." Blake shrugged. "Is there some secret women's organization for global domination? I always thought that. In fact, did you know in India, the matriarch Khasi tribe—"

"Focus, Blake." Alex raised her arms and held them about six inches apart, palms facing forward. "Focus, please. We're talking about Cagney's love life, not world domination."

"Right, righto. Sorry, Cagney. Go on."

Cagney stifled her laughter. Dr. St. Clair had created the perfect couple, as bizarre as they were at times.

"I searched my heart—as dramatic as that sounds—after your talk. And I discovered I had feelings for Brad that keep bubbling up and I kept pushing them down. If I didn't acknowledge them, I just might be walking away from my one true love. What if I never found another man like him?"

Alex nodded and she took it as encouragement to continue.

"Then I got the call the repairs on my apartment were complete." She felt the tears well up. "Instead of being happy, this strange sadness enveloped me. Returning to my apartment meant not seeing him every day. It meant no more movie-and-popcorn nights. No more banter in the…well, no more banter."

"Now I want to know where the banter took place." Blake leaned forward, brows raised.

Alex slapped his arm lightly. "Stop it. The woman is baring her soul as it is."

"Anyway, when we visited my apartment, it hit me. And well, we decided to sublet it."

Alex sighed dramatically. Well, of course, she did. The romantic in her ate the story up.

"I confess I'm scared. I've been in relationships before that didn't work. I don't want to get hurt again. And frankly, I'm not sure I won't get hurt this time."

"Do you know why love is such an amazing experience?" Blake asked.

Cagney knew she didn't need to answer. Blake would tell her regardless.

"It's because of all the pain you've experienced in the past. When a relationship doesn't work out, you feel as if the world is crumbling. You wonder what you did wrong." He raised an eyebrow.

"But more than that, you wonder what is fundamentally wrong with you. You think that you're unlovable."

"How sad." Alex sniffed. "Everyone was made to be loved."

Blake seemingly ignored her. "When you do find

love—like you and Brad—the experience is magnified because of that. You discover you can be loved. You were made to be loved. You're made whole. Every single person comes to a relationship scarred. Even if it's only the girl in second grade who wouldn't let you in a game of cricket on the playground."

"Oh, Blake, I never knew. I'm so sorry." Alex flung her arms around him and sobbed.

Cagney looked at Dr. St. Clair. She had tears in her eyes. Who knew Blake had that in him?

"That was moving." Alex kissed him on the cheek.

"That was beautiful," Dr. St. Clair agreed. "As much as I would like to continue to talk about love, I would be remiss in my duties if I didn't at least try to talk history with my student."

Cagney stifled a laugh. She had forgotten the original reason for the meeting. Not every grad student was lucky enough to have two fictional characters attend. *Yeah, I guess I finally believe they are fictional. No hoax. No hallucination.*

She pulled her laptop out of her backpack and booted it up. After waiting a bit, the screen brightened, and she navigated her cursor to call up the documents she had found in DC.

"Look at this, Dr. St. Clair." She moved the laptop closer to her advisor so she could get a full view of a copy of a newspaper article published shortly after Harding's death. "Right here, it brings up the theory his wife poisoned him. I didn't know how early those rumors started."

Dr. St. Clair studied the screen. "That's fascinating. You're really on to something. Good work. Your dissertation will be fantastic."

"Wait, the best is yet to come." Cagney showed her a few more documents. Cagney's excitement grew as Dr. St. Clair thought the research to be as important as she suspected.

"I think you should start writing anytime, now. It should flow for you."

"Thank you. I can't wait to start. I know what chapter one will look like."

Dr. St. Clair glanced at her watch. "I can't believe it's this late. I've got to get back to the office."

Cagney shut the laptop down, then closed it. When she looked around, the seats across from her were empty. "Where did Alex and Blake go? I didn't hear them leave."

"We were in the zone for a while. They probably got bored. I'm sure they're close by—like begging Ted to use the de-particlizer."

She scanned the café. They were nowhere to be found.

"I'll give Alex a call. Tell her we're done." Dr. St. Clair pulled her phone from her pocket and hit speed dial.

"We're sorry this number is no longer in service. If you believe you reached this number in error, please try again."

"That's odd. It says the number isn't in service."

"That's ridiculous. She just texted me this morning."

Dr. St. Clair leaned back, her eyes widened, and she grinned. "Of course. I get it."

"You get what?"

"What did Alex keep telling you about her visit?" Her advisor couldn't stop grinning.

Cagney knitted her brows. "I don't… oh, no…I get it now too. She said once I was in a relationship with Brad, their work would be done and they'd go back to their own world."

She shook her head. "Back to Mr. Whiskers." She fought back tears. "Thank you, Alex. Thank you, Blake. Wherever you are."

Epilogue

One Year Later

Cagney

"Those colors!" Summer wrapped Brad in her arms. "Your gown is lime green."

They stood just outside UNO's stadium, fresh from the graduation ceremony with more than a hundred other graduates and their families. Cagney beamed as Brad and his grandmother embraced. Not only had she earned her doctorate before she turned thirty, she had found love and a new family, too.

Summer released her grip and moved on to hug Cagney. "And you in that purple."

"Those are your school colors?"

Cagney nodded. She was overwhelmed by the attention, but she loved it. Ever since his grandmother discovered that she and Brad had "confessed" their love, as she put it, she had included Cagney in her life. After she got off the phone with Brad, Summer would call her. And they would talk about everything.

"All right, Summer, give me a chance to congratulate them too."

Missy, standing several feet behind her grandmother, strode toward them. She embraced Brad. "I'm so proud of you, little brother." She scrutinized him for a long moment. "By the way, I agree with

Summer. That color is hideous. Who in the God's green earth would choose those colors?"

She crossed over to Cagney and hugged her. "I'm proud of you too, sis. Not only for your doctorate, but for loving my brother."

Summer's gaze flitted from her and to Brad. "Summer, what's wrong? I mean I know—"

"Nothing. I just realized how I know those colors."

She had everyone's attention.

"You know I attended UNO about"—she scratched her head—"my goodness, has it been fifty years already?"

"Yeah, you did." Brad eyed her.

Cagney burst into laughter. "Are you telling me your class chose these colors? We have you to blame for this atrocity?"

Brad eyes widened. "Really, Summer?"

"If I recall properly"—her cheeks turned crimson—"I had just got off an acid trip." She paused. "Which I no way endorse, by the way." She shook a finger at them. "Scary. Just scary. I didn't get any type of spiritual insight, either."

She shifted her weight. "Yeah, those colors were the only cool thing about my trip." Summer sighed and let out a weak laugh. "I hadn't thought about that in decades."

"Let's go," Missy said, "I'm hungry."

"My advisor and her boyfriend are waiting for us at the Physics Café."

Dr. St. Clair had conferred her degree on her with the hooding ceremony but left to meet Dr. Cooper at the Physics Café.

"Yeah, even though we made reservations," Brad

said. "We were worried Alvin would give them away. He and his partners are brilliant physicists, and normally great businessmen, but sometimes a touch absent-minded."

They were crossing the parking lot, when Brad stopped in his tracks. "What's wrong?" Then, Cagney saw it—actually them. Matthew and Claire Margaret Townsend. His alleged parents.

Her body tensed. The nerve of those two to ruin Brad's graduation. She grabbed his hand and squeezed. Summer appeared on the other side of Brad. And Missy stepped up next to her grandmother. At least he had those he loved surrounding him.

****

Brad

"What are you two doing here?" Brad heard the anger in his voice. He couldn't believe it. "Did you come to tell me you can get me into law school, Father?"

"I came to watch you graduate."

"What? I didn't get tickets for you."

"We called UNO's president. He had two he could spare."

Brad shook his head. "Father, what's the real reason you're here? To tell me my diploma isn't worth the paper it's written on?"

"Son"—his mother took a tentative step forward—"Brad, we came because we're proud of you and—"

He let go of Cagney's hand and waved it at them. "You expect me to believe that?" He studied his parents. The swagger they usually carried didn't seem to be there. His father's tone sounded sad, or perhaps, resigned, would be a better description.

326

"We wanted to give you and Cagney something for your achievements. Neither of us ever earned a doctorate." His mother's eyes glistened. "I do mean you both earned your degrees. You worked hard for them."

His parents had never told him they were proud of him.

Brad glanced at Summer and saw a slight nod. Then he looked at Cagney. She nodded too. He pursed his lips, unsure if he could trust his parents. Cagney pulled him lower and whispered in his ear, "It's obviously your decision, but I think they're trying."

He straightened himself and took a deep breath. He may live to regret this. But the chance to start over, make amends…

"Thank you, that's kind of you."

His mother stepped forward and handed him and Cagney each an envelope. Should he open it now?

"Go ahead, son—Brad," his dad said. "Open it now. You too, Cagney."

Hey, he got her name right.

He opened the envelope and found a check, a generous check. "Are you trying to buy me?"

"No, no. I understand you both acquired very good positions with universities in the DC area. I thought that could help toward moving costs and getting started."

"I can't accept this, Mr. Townsend," Cagney said. "This is far too much money." She showed it to Brad.

"Please do. Summer not-so-gently reminded Claire and me how difficult it was for us when we first started out. If it wasn't for Summer's financial help, I would never have started my law firm and Claire never would be the businesswoman she is today."

His father took a deep breath. "And as I recall

when we first started out, your grandmother never put any strings on her gifts." He blinked several times. "I'm sorry for how I treated you all these years."

"Me, too, Brad," his mom said. "And I want nothing more than to start over in our relationship and get to know you again and what you love. And I surely want to get to know Cagney." She glanced at Cagney. Brad squeezed her hand.

"I-I think I'd like that." And he meant it. In the year he hadn't had contact with his parents, he missed them. Sure, they were dogmatic, but they were still his mom and dad.

His mom took several steps and embraced him, something she hadn't done since his childhood. It took a moment, but he returned the embrace. Tears ran down his cheeks. The two released their hold.

"Cagney, please forgive me for the way we treated you. I hope to get to know you better. After all, my son loves you. I want to love you too," Claire said.

She extended her arms. Cagney nodded, and they hugged.

Tears cascaded down his girlfriend's perfect cheeks. His mother hiccupped, then blubbered as salty tears dribbled from her chin. He grinned.

There was nothing fake about this.

A word about the author…

I'm the author of *Rewrites of the Heart*, the N. N. Light Book Paranormal Romance of the Year and *Heartquake*, a 2023 Rone finalist and the novella, *The Wizard of her Heart*.

Two things you should know about me: I have an offbeat sense of humor and characters are constantly talking to me, trying to get me to tell their stories. Other than that, I'm a normal person.

I've spent most of my adult life writing in some fashion, from small-town reporter, to editor-in-chief and ghostwriter for a national natural health publishing firm. The last decade and a half I've worked as a freelance writer, penning ebooks that range from starting a doula services business to Native American herbs.

All my novels are set in fictional towns in northeast Ohio, where I grew up, and I write about things I love—like coffee.

I live in North Lima, Ohio, a real town in northeast Ohio with all my characters. Yes, it does get crowded at times.

http://terrynewmanauthor.com

Thank you for purchasing
this publication of The Wild Rose Press, Inc.

For questions or more information
contact us at
info@thewildrosepress.com.

The Wild Rose Press, Inc.
www.thewildrosepress.com